Love, Alabama

Love, Alabama

A novel

Susan Sands

TULE

Dear Reader,

This book is for my parents, Linda and Ray Noel. I have been the luckiest person alive to have had such love and support from birth that has continued until this moment. They have suffered many devastating losses over the years, but remain steadfast in their dedication to me. I only hope I can live up to that unwavering standard of parenting with my own children. The world would be a far better place with more parents like them.

As always, many thanks to my agent, David Forrer, for standing solidly in my corner and working so hard on my behalf. Thanks to super editor, Sinclair Sawhney, who makes everything she touches shinier. Great appreciation goes out to my author friends who continue to support and give a hand up with promotion and advice. Karen White and Eloisa James, I continue to learn so much from you. Christy Hayes, Tracy Solheim, Kimberly Brock, and Laura Alford; you all are my handhold in this ever-shifting industry.

I have to give a shout-out to my home town of Negreet/Many, Louisiana. It's so tiny I have to include two names. No small-town girl ever had it so good, y'all. The love and support I've received from my Footloose town couldn't ever be matched by a city a hundred times its size. Love you all!

Thanks to my readers who've supported me through the insane process of the release and promotion of my debut novel, *Again, Alabama*. Thanks for your support and patience as I screamed from proverbial mountain tops on social media and likely drove you all crazy. You're the best!!

I appreciate my husband, Doug Sands, dentist golfer extraordinaire's willingness to take over and accept my deadline crazies with good humor. And for Kevin, Cameron and Reagan, whose love of their mother and Chik fil-A relieves my stress on a regular basis.

Thanks also to Meghan, Lindsey, and Danielle, the amazing women at Tule Publishing and Lee Hyat, cover designer, for their dedication and willingness to help me achieve my dreams and work with me toward a shared vision.

Love to all!

Susan

Chapter One

"CAN SOMEONE GET this hairy mutt off the set?" The director sneezed again and cast an irritated glance toward the large Golden Retriever. He didn't bother to make eye contact with Emma.

Emma stiffened at the unflattering reference to Big Al, who currently hugged her side in an effort to gain refuge from the angry vibes cast his way. Big Al's fur was cut close, so he hardly shed at all. Besides nabbing a poorly placed donut from the edge of the snack table, he'd been a perfect gentleman thus far today.

As soon as the filming segment ended, Emma couldn't help asking, "Are you sure you're allergic to the dog? Lots of folks react strongly to the flora around here when they come down from up *North*." The word north might've slid off her tongue just a little distastefully, as Emma smiled sweetly at Mr. Matthew Pope from Manhattan. Not that she had anything against the North. Just some products of it—like rude, impatient men and very cold weather.

"I can't do my job if there's hair and dander flying around and I'm sneezing my head off. Animals have no business on the set of a cooking show, anyway. Get rid of it." He made an offhanded, sweeping motion from his elevated position in the director's chair, as if he manned the bridge of a star ship on Star Trek. *Make it so...*

He'd referred to her baby as "it." Emma would keep her mouth shut, as this wasn't her gig, but why the network had sent someone down from New York with such an obviously pissy attitude to produce her sister, Cammie's, new smash cooking show baffled Emma.

She couldn't argue that he was slickly handsome and extremely male, despite his rafter-rattling sneezes, if one liked that sort of thing. Emma could appreciate those pleasing attributes from a detached and cerebral place. No emotional stuff for her, and no physical stuff either. She was different like that—had been for almost a decade.

Matthew Pope was simply a gorgeous pain in the ass, to her thinking. He sneezed again. Somebody oughta get him a pack of Claritin and call it a day.

As Emma led Big Al into the next room, her sister, Cammie, caught up with her after Mr. Producer/Director yelled cut again. "Hey, everything okay?"

"Yeah. Mr. Hotshot doesn't want Big Al on set," Emma said.

Cammie nodded and rolled her eyes. "I heard him complaining."

"Why would they send such a stinkpot? I don't think he's cracked a smile since he got here." Emma gathered the honey-blonde hair that had fallen forward and smoothed it back so it hung between her shoulder blades. She should have put it up, but hadn't taken the time before she left home this morning.

"I haven't seen one if he has, but I guess we're stuck with him until he goes into anaphylactic shock or gets fed up and quits."

Emma shrugged. For now, she was helping her sister out on the set. This wasn't her real job, so he wasn't going to be her problem going forward anyway.

Just then, the call rang out for Cammie to get back on set. "Gotta go. Thanks for all your help today."

"Sure. No problem. I'm teaching all afternoon, but I can come back in the morning, if you need me."

Cammie gave her a quick hug. "That would be a lifesaver, if you don't mind. I still can't seem to find anyone to do makeup and hair that doesn't make me look like Jessica Green's love child." Cammie grimaced as she said the words.

"Girl, we can't have that." Jessica Green was Cammie's former boss, and how she'd gotten her start in the television cooking world. But things had gone badly between them due to Jessica's jealousy of Cammie's rapid rise in viewer popularity. Jessica was Southern as sweet tea and wore *all* the makeup that Bobbi Brown put out—pretty much at the same time.

"Okay. See you tomorrow," Cammie said, just as Matthew Pope bellowed, but was cut short by a sneeze.

That made Emma smile. Kind of hard to be effective as a star ship commander with seasonal allergies kicking your ass.

"Bless you!" She singsonged toward the overbearing jerk, and then whispered under her breath, "And bless your heart." She thought she might have heard mumbled thanks through his tissue.

Just as she and Big Al were about to exit the barn where Grey had recreated the large farmhouse kitchen inside, Emma pulled a doggie treat from her pocket. "Who's a good boy? Who's a good boy?" She crooned.

In answer, he launched himself toward the treat, taking her right off her stilettos and dumping her in a pile with her appreciative pup. She managed to sit up just as Big Al licked her right on the mouth.

She couldn't help it; she laughed, "I was rewarding you for being such a fine gentleman this morning and you go and do this." Recognizing her unladylike position, Emma hoped nobody had just witnessed her takedown.

No luck.

"Do you know what dogs eat besides their food whenever possible?"

The deep voice lacked humor. She hadn't heard him approach, or never in a million years would she have allowed this man to catch her roughhousing with Big Al in the middle of the floor. Commissioning as much dignity as possible, Emma Jean rose from her position, temporarily ignoring her best retriever buddy.

She wished she could sic Big Al to knock Matthew Pope on his ass and give *him* a big ole sloppy kiss. But a Southern lady hid her crazy with fine manners—always.

Instead of using her manicure as a deadly weapon, Emma said, "Well, I'd rather eat my dog's shit thirdhand than spend another minute being insulted."

She nailed him with her best beauty pageant, dazzler smile and made a slow, deliberate runway pivot, whistled to Big Al, and exited the room; head high, her five-inch heels clicking across the tiles.

Emma would love to have gotten a photo of his comical expression at her response to his rudeness, but a leave-taking like that prevented looking back to enjoy the moment. It was an epic exit.

HOLY MOTHER OF God. The realization smacked him upside the head. The corn-fed, six-foot-tall blonde who'd just sashayed out the door with a Southern queen's bearing—her infectious mutt in tow—was none other than former Miss Alabama, Emma Laroux. He shook his head to clear it. Then, he smiled. Emma Laroux. *Well, shit.*

Their time together hadn't been romantic. It had been brief, chaotic, and quite frankly, more intensely confusing than either of them had been prepared to cope with on a college football Iron Bowl weekend.

For Emma, he realized that weekend must have had serious implications not of his doing. He'd tried once to contact her—after. But he hadn't heard a word. So, against his better judgment, he'd let it go. It hadn't been the last time he'd thought of her though. He hadn't even been certain what all had happened, only that Emma, who'd been Miss Alabama up until that time, had stepped down and became former Miss Alabama after that weekend.

Today, he'd not recognized her at first. Maybe because he was in the throes of a wretched allergy attack, or because now she was less a fresh young beauty queen and more an incredibly sexy woman, fully grown. Not mature in any sort of matronly way either. No, more a vibrant, fit, and completely overwhelming sexy female kind of way. Back then, she was young, model-thin, platinum blonde—gorgeous, yes, but without the depth of experience life and years tended to layer on. To Matthew, all the things that made women the most interesting and appealing.

If you'd asked him ten years ago, he'd have sworn Emma Laroux was perfect, with no room for improvement, especially after he'd seen the woman behind the perfection. She'd been vulnerable at that time, made so by circumstances that likely had shaped her into the woman who'd just marched cleanly away and left him dazed.

Ten years ago, he'd been a heavy-set football player, not the lean, fit man he was today. No wonder she hadn't a clue who he was. He'd even changed his name—not that she'd even known his name back then. But she'd also been out of it the evening they'd met. Her memory was more than likely fuzzy from whatever had gone down—whether it had been of her making, or not.

When Matthew had later reflected on that night, he realized someone had surely drugged her earlier in the evening, and that must have been why she was wandering, in her underwear, around the fraternity house where he'd been a visitor. The thought had brought up such intensely angry emotions within him later, but it was after the fact, and it was truly none of his business. Plus, she'd not returned his call when he'd tried to contact her.

The local news reported she'd given up her crown and stepped down from the Miss Alabama title for "personal reasons." He hadn't seen any sensational news reports aside from that. He never really knew exactly what had caused the shit storm, but he knew she'd been in trouble that weekend, because he'd done his best to help her out of it.

Maybe she was married with kids. No one had mentioned anything about her current personal situation within his hearing, but he hesitated to approach her again after today's rather disastrous encounter. She obviously hadn't recognized him. He'd like to think those changes were for the better. It was sort of a relief she didn't know who he was now. That would have been truly awkward because of how they'd met again.

Since he'd gotten back here—here being Alabama—things hadn't gone well. The idea of a downward move, career-wise, made him want to roar in frustration. The squirrelly network executive responsible had been threatened by Matthew's presence at the New York office. Or maybe by the fact that Dave had found out about Matthew's past dating relationship with his current girlfriend, Brandi.

Dave *was* pretty short, or maybe it was because of his receding hairline. Perhaps both contributed to his insecurity. The exec made far more money than Matthew, and Brandi had seemed far more impressed by the size of a paycheck than the man. So, surely sending Matthew down here was overkill. And it was an asshole thing to do.

Not that this was a bad assignment; *Cammie Laroux at Home* was a hot, new show for the network in a sweet primetime slot. It just happened to shoot in Ministry, Alabama. Might as well call it *Mayberry, RFD*.

But things just got a bit more interesting in Mayberry. He was well aware that he'd been an insufferable grouch—angry and frustrated with his situation thus far. Time to address these allergies, and maybe a tall blonde.

✦≫≫≪≪✦

EMMA KICKED OFF her high heels and poured herself a glass of chardonnay. She'd put in a full afternoon and evening at her studio. Students began filing in at 2:30 every weekday for various classes and tutoring sessions. She taught group classes, but others were private lessons. Her specialty was pageant preparation; she was a pageant coach. She taught runway, deportment, grace, grooming, and other preparatory skills that went along with it. She didn't offer dance or voice lessons, personally, but rented space to those who taught them. Some pageants hosted talent competitions as a part of the programs, and some didn't.

After growing up in the pageant community, and being crowned Miss Alabama during college, she offered the community the wealth of her experience and advisement. And they paid for it. There was a demand and she supplied. But she drew the line at toddlers. Those were some crazy mommas with a capital C.

False eyelashes on a two-year-old bordered on abuse in Emma's book. Her competitor on the other side of town supplied the toddler training and more power to her. Emma took on girls once they were well into elementary school, but preferably later, when they truly understood what she was trying to teach them. Good manners, grace, and carriage of self were valuable traits for any young lady, whether they entered pageants, or not.

When the deafening strains of Gone With the Wind sounded, Emma nearly spilled her wine. She'd turned up her cell ringtone to the loudest setting so she could hear it above the students. "Hello?"

"Hey there, honey. Heard you left the set in a huff this afternoon. Everything okay?" It was her mother.

"Hey, Mom. I'm fine. The producer they sent to work with Cammie was acting like a butthole and didn't like Big Al. The guy was sneezing and griping about his allergies."

"Uh-oh. Cammie said he was a bit of a grump. Did you offer him some Claritin or Benadryl or something? Maybe you could leave Big Al at my house tomorrow while you go to Cammie's, if that'll help."

Emma smiled. "Good idea. Thanks for offering. I'll drop him off in the morning. Wouldn't want to cause my sister problems because of my sweet Al."

"He is a big sweetie, but some people don't feel the same about animals as we do, dear."

"I know, Mom," she agreed, then asked, "Hey, how's Howard?" she asked about her soon-to-be stepfather, and the newly-discovered biological father of her oldest sibling, Maeve. It was all very complicated and confusing, especially for Maeve. But Howard had been her mother's first love what must have been a hundred years ago, and he really seemed to adore her. Dad had died tragically twelve years ago, and now that Mom wasn't alone, she seemed to have a whole new lease on life.

"He's wonderful, thanks for asking." Her mother sighed.

She sounded like a teenager in love. They were planning an intimate wedding to be held in a few weeks.

"Please tell him I said hi. I'll see you in the morning with your grand dog."

Mom was quiet for a moment, and then said, "I wish

you'd seriously consider dating again, Emma. I could stand to have another grand baby running around here, you know."

Crap. She'd set herself up for that one, hadn't she? "I'm fine, Mom. You've got plenty of grandchildren. I'm sure Cammie and Grey will get right on that for you. Don't worry about me."

"You know I worry. It's been ten years since you and Tad broke up, honey. Don't you think it's time to give someone else a chance?" Her mother's voice was sweet and soothing, and Emma felt an indescribable urge to run to her childhood home two miles away and curl up in Mom's lap like a little girl again.

"I'll think about it. And you know I've tried dating from time to time, but haven't really connected with anyone. But I'm really happy. I've got wonderful clients, a successful business, and a nice home. I feel very lucky." This was her mantra, and it usually worked to soothe her own occasional restlessness.

"Okay, honey. I'll stop for now. See you in the morning."

"Night, Mom." Emma hung up and turned down the ringer.

A tiny familiar emptiness crept up before she could shove it back down. Being alone had its advantages, but right now it was hard to name them. What would her life have been like had her ex, Tad, not turned out to be such a big turd and she'd met someone nice to spend her life with? She really couldn't go there, because that place was an angry, dangerous one filled with ugly emotion and foggy frustration. Emma was all about control.

Sipping her wine, she flipped through the mail, the television muted in the background. Big Al nosed his stuffed squeaky squirrel at her feet. She really did have lots to be thankful for. She hardly thought about dating, or any of the other stuff these days.

Chapter Two

O N HIS WAY out the next morning, Matthew stopped at the tiny quick mart and picked up a package of antihistamines. Determined to begin today as he meant to continue, improving his physical symptoms were tantamount to getting off to a better start mentally. No matter how annoyed he was with this assignment, he couldn't compromise the quality product of his work.

Plus, the people around would believe him a whiny jerk—probably already did. He was nothing if not a consummate professional. A little prickly at times, yes, but his exacting personality bore technically excellent shows. He had a reputation to maintain. And yesterday's performance hadn't been up to standard.

After the convenience store stop, he swung by the local diner for coffee and a quick breakfast. "Well, aren't you a fancy pants? What can I get you, baby?" The hundred-year-old waitperson, Thelma, if her nametag was to be believed, asked with a cackle. *Great*. This morning was beginning with a bang.

"I'll just have black coffee, two scrambled egg whites on a whole wheat English muffin and well-done turkey bacon." Thelma's near-toothless smile slipped.

Her smoker's mouth puckered into a million wrinkles as if sucking on a dill pickle while smelling something vile.

"We call that a 'stick up your ass' breakfast," Thelma informed him.

"Do you serve those here?" Matthew raised a brow and asked, mildly amused by her judgment of his dining choices.

She continued to eyeball him with disdain. "We do, but we don't like it." She spun on her old, scuffed orthopedic shoe and shuffled toward the pick-up window.

"Oh, Thelma—" He called after her.

She turned and cut him off, "Yeah, yeah, you're in a big ole hurry, too, aren't you, slick? The 'stick up your ass' comes with a rush. Nobody who orders it takes the time to sit and enjoy their food. Goes with the territory. It's a 'type,' you know?"

Before he could respond to her rudeness, the bell on the door jingled, distracting him.

Emma Laroux appeared, fresh as spring rain on a daisy. Her long, blonde hair was pulled up in some sort of floppy bun construction with wisps trailing on either side of her face, a contrast to her startlingly clear hazel eyes and inky, arched eyebrows. She was wearing well-fitting jeans and a white cotton sweater with an equally flattering neckline, which made him swallow his very hot coffee a little too quickly. That made him cough and sputter. She quite literally took his breath away.

He was halfway hidden behind his newspaper, but she spotted him immediately, perhaps due to the noises he was making. Judging from the small furrowing of her brows and pout on those lovely wide lips, she still held a grudge from yesterday.

As she approached, old Thelma brought his breakfast to the table, dropping it from about a foot above the surface. It clattered deafeningly. "One stick-up-your-ass, hold the butter, hold the jelly, and hold all the possibility of the joys of living."

"Hi, Miss Thelma." Emma giggled.

Thelma turned at Emma's approach. "Oh, hey, baby. What can I get you? The usual?"

"That would be great. Thanks." Emma grinned at the old bag, who pinched her cheek and crowed, showing all five of her teeth.

Emma turned and looked down toward him, eyeing his rather dry breakfast. "I see you're making friends with the locals."

He lifted a brow, a little surprised she hadn't slung the nearest mug at his head. He took a chance and motioned with a hand for her to join him across the booth.

SHE WOULDN'T HAVE considered joining him after yesterday's dramatic exit, if not for the need to keep peace for Cammie's sake. So, against her instincts, she sat.

The moment she did, Thelma swooped back in. "Emma, dear, do you know this young man?" Nothing like everyone in town looking out for you.

"It's fine, Thelma. Mr. Pope is the producer working on Cammie's show. We have some things to discuss." This answer seemed to satisfy the older woman enough so that she shuffled away after giving them both a speculative glance.

"Is she your grandmother or something? Why the security measures?" Matthew asked.

"It's a small town." She shrugged, as if that was all he needed as explanation.

He reached toward the inside of the booth and snagged a container of sugar-free fruit spread. Emma cringed as she watched him smear it on the dry English muffin.

He noticed her reaction. "You have something against bread?"

Before she could answer, Thelma approached with two, large blueberry cake donuts and a steaming cup of hot chocolate piled high with whipped cream. Emma smiled her thanks.

"No, I love bread. I just hate cardboard with no sugar." She sank her teeth into the heavenly indulgence. Thank God for her fast metabolism and good genetics. Plus, she was in constant motion, running her own business—not to mention the yoga and Pilates workouts. For a small town, Ministry had a kick-butt workout studio.

She licked her finger, eyes closed. This was the only way to start the day. When she opened her eyes, Matthew was staring at her with an odd expression.

He cleared his throat. "Well, some of us have a care for our health."

Better to just jump right into this. "Have you had a visit from the mayor yet?"

"No. Is there a reason why I should?" He asked.

"He, uh, has a way of wiggling himself into anything happening here in Ministry. He'll be be a pain in your butt soon enough. But don't tell him I warned you. But I'm warning you."

She noticed his jaw clench. "Problem?" She asked.

"No. I just don't like people getting in my way while I'm working."

"Well, just smile and grit your teeth. He's not worth making an enemy of."

"Good to know. Anything else?"

"Nope."

"Hmph." He apparently wasn't sold.

Thelma showed up, checking on her customers. "Everything okay here?"

"Yes, ma'am," Matthew answered.

"At least he's got some manners," Thelma said to Emma. "Haven't seen you sit with a young man at one of my tables in here besides your brother in quite awhile. Surprised me."

Emma realized that no one in town ever expected to see her with anyone male. It was kind of a thing.

Emma glanced over to see Matthew studying her intently. She fought back a near-overwhelming urge to stick her tongue out at him. But part of being a Southern beauty queen was leading by example. What if one of her girls or their parents was to happen by? So she smiled with *all* her teeth and said, "You'll have to excuse me. I've got to get going. See you at the set."

"I'm headed there now." She just noticed his lack of allergic activity. "You aren't sneezing today."

He pulled out the small packet of Benadryl from his pocket.

So she added, "I left Big Al at home."

A tenuous truce had been declared. For now.

She sailed out the front door, not waiting for him to pay his check. She'd already handed Thelma a ten for her food.

⇶⇷

THE WOMAN WAS a force of nature. She'd breezed in and out, and left him reeling. Something in her warning about the mayor gave him pause. She'd gotten fidgety as she'd warned him. Was he some old handsy geezer? Or some corrupt politician?

Matthew couldn't help but wonder why she'd gone out of her way to bring up the mayor in conversation unless he played a really big role in things in town, or in Emma's life.

As Matthew drove past the ice cream shop, Scoops, with it's red and white striped awning and tables and umbrellas out front, he had a faint memory of stopping here with his grandmother as a kid. They'd passed through Ministry on their way to Birmingham before the interstate was built. After that, he couldn't say he'd ever been here again.

It was a nice, old town, small and neat with lots of green space. The main street was well maintained. From a producer's point-of-view, it would make a terrific movie set. There was little new construction in the downtown historic district, and most of the buildings had been restored to some degree. Even though he'd escaped the South with the ferocity of a bat from hell, he could appreciate a visually appealing setting.

The social aspect of it, not so much. Nosy neighbors, backward, narrow-thinking and extra syllables added to words raised his blood pressure and made him nearly break out in hives. His breathing became heavier, his heart rate increased, and he began to sweat. The physical symptoms he'd believed a part of his distant past suddenly threatened to choke him. Matthew rolled down his window, trying to get some fresh air. He pulled over at the nearest parking space.

Trying to tamp down the rising sensations of impending doom and certain death, he breathed hard and heavy. "You're not dying, dumbass. Relax." Not exactly a positive affirmation. But he did as he'd been taught. He breathed deeply, trying to slow down his hammering heart before it actually beat out of his chest.

"Hey, mister, are you okay?" A young boy of about ten years old stopped beside Matthew's window on his bicycle. He had carrot-red hair and freckles.

Matthew focused on the kid in front of him for a second and thought, *Oh good, Opie's here.* Then he shook his head to clear it. "Yeah. I'm okay. Thanks for asking."

"You don't look too good. My mom tells me to drink some water when I don't feel good. Maybe you should try it. Bye." He pedaled off just as quickly as he'd shown up.

Matthew gave the retreating kid a weak smile, and pulled out a water bottle to affirm that his mother was a smart woman.

He was fine now. The distraction was all it took to snap him out of it. He couldn't remember if he'd registered a truck backfire, some other loud noise, or if he'd simply talked himself into mentally unraveling in the middle of town.

Pulling out of the parking space, Matthew again let out a ragged breath. He was sapped of energy and considered for a split-second returning to the cozy little house he'd rented for the next couple months, and flinging himself in the oversized chair that resided on his back screened-in porch. Whether or not he enjoyed living back in the South, he really liked that porch, and the chair.

But he had a down-home Southern cooking show to

produce. Thankfully, today it would be minus one big, furry dog on the set. With his heart rate and breathing returning to normal, Matthew could move forward with his day. Those who knew him would likely laugh their asses off if they'd witnessed his panic attack. Unless they'd ever experienced the sensations themselves. Matthew could only imagine how that must appear to anyone unfamiliar with one.

He'd seen a counselor after his second trip to the emergency room, where the doctors had assured him once again he'd live to see another day, in fact, many more years if his vitals were to be believed, barring any unforeseen accidents. They'd suggested he reduce his stress levels and that he see "someone" to determine the source of his panic trigger.

He knew the trigger. Fear wasn't manly, and Matthew was pretty manly, at least he considered himself so. But he'd gone ahead with the counseling, realizing he'd needed to get control of this thing. Nothing good could come from paralyzing fear of death at a given moment when one lived and worked in New York City. It certainly wasn't good for his reputation as an up-and-coming producer and current director at the network, not to mention his man card.

The idea that this could happen in the wilds of rural Alabama was simply not acceptable. He'd have to figure out what the trigger was besides the horror of coming back here that had set him off. For now, he felt nearly normal and was eager to get his mind on something else. Work. He was in control at work. He could kick work's ass.

✦✦✦✦✦

EMMA HAD LEFT Matthew at the diner and driven straight to Cammie and Grey's farmhouse fifteen minutes outside of town. Where before, Matthew had appeared rested, sharp, and neatly groomed, he now had an edgy, restless look about him. Besides just his generally untidy exterior, he seemed unsettled somehow.

He even moved differently now, with less confidence and control.

People and food camera operators, techs working the color-accurate monitors, and assistants to the talent—everyone was in place and waiting for direction. This seemed to annoy Matthew instead of pleasing him, like he'd come in shame-faced late to a party and he was the host.

"What's everyone staring at?" He snapped as soon as he entered the large, equipment, lighting, and people-cluttered room. Everyone looked away, busying themselves with sound checks and whatever else they could.

Cammie thus far had held her tongue at his rudeness, but this was her show, and Emma was wondering when she would step up and act like she had some say in how things went along. It took every bit of Emma's self-restraint to keep a hand slapped across her own mouth when he'd barked at them all.

Emma was highlighting Cammie's cheekbones when her sister's face tightened, and her jaw became rigid. *Uh oh.* Cammie was a peace lover by nature, and she couldn't stand for anyone to get a raw deal. She'd had enough of that in her past, and Emma saw the shit about to hit the fan around here.

Emma had been working off to the side on Cammie's makeup in front of the lighted mirror area they'd set up for that purpose. They were inside a section of the barn that had been renovated into a replica of a farmhouse kitchen. Grey was a historical architect who did renovation work, and that had worked out perfectly. The barn's high ceilings allowed for easy transporting of large camera and lighting equipment without breaking any personal belongings.

Cammie stood and pulled off the cape that covered her clothing. "Excuse me, Mr. Pope. Could I have a word with you in private?" Cammie's tone brooked no argument, and, even if no one else recognized it, Emma was quite familiar with it, having lived in the same household together growing up. Cammie was a few years younger, but when she stood up for herself, she suddenly became everyone's elder.

Matthew's head swiveled in her sister's direction. His eyes narrowed as if he deliberated taking Cammie's head off with a verbal tirade, but he took a visible breath and obviously reconsidered.

"Of course." He stood and followed Cammie into her home office, leaving behind an uncomfortable silence among the assembled professionals.

Emma hadn't yet finished Cammie's makeup, so she took a seat and waited. What had changed between the diner and his arrival here? It was like a Jekyll and Hyde thing with him.

Emma tapped her long nails on the arm of the high folding chair vacated by her sister and waited, and waited. Apparently, those two were having quite a come-to-terms behind closed doors, because it was another ten minutes before they emerged. Cammie's expression bore no visible signs of upset and neither did Matthew's. They appeared as if they'd had some sort of unemotional contract agreement, by the look of them.

When Cammie made her way back over to the makeup chair, Emma was dying to know what had transpired.

She hissed under her breath, "Well, what the hell happened in there?"

Cammie turned and furrowed her brows. "We've come to an understanding."

"That's it? That's all you're going to tell me?" She glanced over where Matthew was peering through a camera lens to check a shot before they began filming.

Cammie shrugged. "We have a business relationship, and what's said behind closed doors stays put."

Emma knew when to push and when to let up. "Well, fine. Close your eyes. You need more shimmer." Emma responded, highlighting her lovely sister's brow bones.

At least the storm in Matthew's presence had passed, thanks to Cammie. Still, she wondered what had happened to get him so worked up.

Emma sat back and watched as the filming began, still amazed that her little sister was such a rock star. It wasn't that she was famous, because she was; it was that she totally rocked it. The girl cooked during filming like she was born to do it. Despite the unfortunate hair fire incident with Jessica Green last year, which had likely worked to her advantage in the end, Cammie charmed the audience while whipping up a lovely crawfish etouffee and bread pudding with bourbon sauce.

The kitchen area smelled divine, despite the fancy up-draft, and Emma hoped she could score some of the dish to take with her for lunch at her own studio. She had a couple private lessons early in the afternoon today. The older gals, Sadie Beaumont and Judith Dozier Fremont, the Mrs. Alabama contestants from the area, had approached her requesting a little tune-up practice. Both were thirtyish, each had a child, and were still reliving their pageant queen glory days. Emma wasn't foolish enough to turn down the business and she certainly wasn't foolish enough to refuse Tad Beaumont's wife, Sadie. Emma knew better.

Sadie was great friends with the Dozier-Fremont twins. They were local old-moneyed sisters who'd married more moneyed brothers from over in Greenville. Judith and Sadie had lessons, but Jamie always came with to offer her snide remarks.

It was the Doublemint twins meets the Sugarbakers. Too bad Emma couldn't slam a quick shot of strong bourbon before they arrived to settle her nerves. Those two mixed with Sadie Beaumont were enough to weaken the strongest resolve not to run screaming naked out into the street after about ten minutes.

When one thought of mean girls in small towns who never realized there was a global community beyond their own first world problems of hair, nails, and popularity, these were the poster children. Sadie was a puzzle to Emma. She'd appeared to have promise as a compassionate and caring person when Emma remembered her from school, though obviously materially spoiled by her parents.

Soon after Tad had dropped Emma at the lowest moment in her life, he'd turned to the lovely and wealthy Sadie. She was everything his family would have desired in his future spouse. She demonstrated the grace and elegance her kind of upbringing naturally produced. She'd never had a chance to develop into the down-to-earth rich girl she might have had she spent time around a less affluent crowd. This was only Emma's opinion, of course.

Sadie never mentioned Emma's past relationship with her husband, to her credit. Unfortunately, Jamie and Judith weren't so discreet with their tongues.

"I'd like to apologize for before." Matthew had moved beside Emma, snapping her out of her wormhole. She was still sitting in the tall, folding director's chair where she'd applied Cammie's makeup. "You thinking about what I said, or are you about to take me down? Because you look like I kicked your dog."

"Huh?" Emma shook her head to clear it. "No. Sorry, I was distracted." She took a deep breath and tried to smile as if things were peachy. "So, you wanted to apologize?"

His gaze was slightly puzzled at her weirdness. "That's where I was headed. Would you be willing to have dinner with me this evening? As my apology?"

Dinner. As in, a date? She didn't often date. But he wouldn't understand how things were. "Um, I don't think—"

He stopped her by holding up a hand. "It's not a date, Emma. I'm just tired of eating alone. Since I've been in town, I've hit the Mexican place, the Cajun place, the barbeque joint—"

She laughed, discontinuing his litany of food establishments in town. "Okay, fine. I'll go, but we have to go where I say." It wasn't a date.

It was acquaintances having a meal together. They had no romantic connection, so why not? But still, it would be putting herself out there in town to be talked about. Every time she'd done it, it hadn't ended well.

"I'm at your mercy." He raised his hands in surrender.

"Fine. Meet me at my studio around eight after my last class. Is that too late?" She asked.

"Nope. I've got plenty to keep me busy after shooting wraps up today." He smiled at her. It was—bone-deep sexy, and *that* wasn't something Emma was prepared for. "Thanks for taking pity on me."

Tamping down the sudden crazy galloping of her pulse rate, and working to control the flush she was certain had just stained her cheeks, neck, and every other exposed area of skin, Emma tried to sound normal. "Sure. Give me your number and I'll text you the address. The restaurant is casual."

He nodded. "See you at eight."

And just like that, Emma Laroux had a dinner date. Even though it wasn't officially a date, people around here would think it was. And that would get around. Rumors of their short breakfast likely already had.

Chapter Three

❦

"WELL, *I* WOULDN'T have worn it so early in the season, if at all, that's for sure." Judith Dozier-Fremont stated with a finality that bore no argument from her sister, Jamie, or Sadie Beaumont. Emma gritted her teeth and swore she'd get through this for about the fifth time since they'd shown up fifteen minutes late discussing last night's Junior League planning dinner.

"I thought it was a little tacky, but the color wasn't bad," Sadie inserted.

It was her way of agreeing with Judith while showing a little support for the fellow member whose fashion choices were being maligned.

"Have you had your eyes checked lately, Sadie? It was lime green *linen,* for Pete's sake."

Sadie's lovely lips pursed. "I like green in all shades. What do you think, Jamie?"

Jamie, instead of taking the side of her sister, appreciated the opportunity to needle her whenever the opportunity arose. "Sister, I do believe I saw a similar ensemble hanging with the tags still attached in your closet. Could it be that somebody made a debut in an outfit you recently purchased but haven't had the chance to wear?" It was obviously a fine moment for Jamie, a rare opportunity she'd decided to enjoy to the fullest.

Judith's face reddened and her hands fisted at her sides.

Just as she took the first charging step toward her sister, Emma cut in. "Ladies, let's take a few moments to work on our mental relaxation techniques."

"Oh, let's do that," Sadie agreed a little to loudly and grabbed Judith by the arm, spinning her toward Emma.

Judith shot Jamie a glare that promised retribution after class ended, then turned her attention toward Emma.

"Imagine that you're on stage where all the attention is focused on you. The interviewer asks a question and your mind goes completely blank with anxiety and fear."

"I would never wimp out like that." Judith laughed.

"I might," Sadie said. "What would I do if it happened?" She asked Emma.

Emma couldn't help but feel compassion for Sadie and barely controlled the urge to strike Judith.

So, she smiled at Sadie. "First, don't worry. Always smile and say, 'That's a great question'."

Emma went through some breathing and relaxation techniques with the women, and was just finishing up when Tad Beaumont strolled in without a how-do-you-do. He wore his uniform of business casual with cowboy boots. All charm without the warmth to melt butter in his mouth.

"Oh, hey, honey, what a surprise." Sadie appeared taken aback.

"Just thought I'd take my best girl out to dinner since it's getting late," Tad said, slipping an arm around her shoulders.

"I left dinner for you and Sarah Jane warming in the oven before I left." Sadie reminded him.

"She's fed and all tucked in for the night. Gerta is with her until we get back."

Gerta was their house-keeper/nanny who lived in the small groundskeeper's cottage on the property of their pre-Civil War antebellum mansion. Emma also had grown up in a similar home that her family ran as an event-planning business.

Historical homes here in Ministry were the norm rather than the exception, some were far larger and grander than others, but one would be hard-pressed to find new construction within the city limits, or even nearby.

Judith and Jamie were heading toward the door, with Tad and Sadie following when—something made Emma look up. She'd almost forgotten about her dinner with Matthew. *Oh, crap.* The last thing she needed was a run-in between the two men.

For whatever reason, Tad had acted strangely on the rare occasions when she'd had a date. And, on those rare occasions, he'd managed to always be nearby.

Emma hurried over to the front entrance to see Matthew holding a small nosegay of wildflowers. "Well, hello there." This was from Judith, who'd never met a handsome stranger.

Matthew quirked up the side of his enigmatic lip in a half-smile of greeting. "Hello."

"Hey, Matthew. Let me get my purse and I'll meet you outside."

Unfortunately, that was enough for Tad to take notice and stick his mayoral hand out in introduction. "Hello, I'm Tad Beaumont, mayor of our fair city. You must be new in town. I don't think we've been introduced."

Matthew's eyes narrowed for a fraction of a second; and likely only Emma caught it, thankfully. Her stomach twist-ed.

"I'm Matthew Pope, producer of Cammie Laroux's cooking show." The two men shook hands a little too firmly in Emma's estimation.

"Well, no wonder we haven't met. I've been meaning to make it out there to lay eyes on things. Is our Emma here showing you around town?" The gleam in Tad's eye made her even more nervous than before.

"She's shown mercy and agreed to have dinner with me tonight. Apparently she knows the best places for someone who eats out regularly." Matthew wasn't showing his cards, thank goodness. His smile was forced, Emma could tell, and there was a dark current between the two men that seemed oddly intense.

"Oh, wow. How unusual. Emma doesn't date much," he said.

She wanted to rip his ears off and feed them to the pigs in Farmer Jensen's pen. He was taunting her.

Tad slapped Matthew on the back then said in a smug tone, "You two kids have fun." He shot her a look, but while his mouth still smiled. Was that a warning in his eyes?

Her gaze must have communicated some of what was in her mind.

"Hey, you okay? What gives with mayor Ken doll?"

Emma just shook her head and remained silent. If she actually said the words, Matthew would question a possible need for antipsychotic medication.

➤➤➤❮❮❮

ONCE THEY WERE seated at Marvin's Garden, a local soul food establishment and one of Cammie's favorite restaurants, Matthew asked, "So, you going to tell me what that was about between you and the mayor?"

"I'd prefer not to discuss Tad, if that's alright," she said.

"He seemed ticked in some weird way."

She sighed. "I guess saying that I don't want to talk about him isn't going to work." Emma put down her menu. "We dated a long time ago."

"How long ago?" After meeting Tad, it explained why she'd given him the heads up.

Emma rolled her eyes. "Almost ten years now."

Back when Matthew had encountered Emma that night in the frat house wandering around. "And he acts weird when you're out with someone else? And he's *married?*"

"I don't date much, so it probably surprised him."

"Why don't you date?" He tried to keep his tone neutral.

She held up her hand to warn him. "This isn't a line of questioning I want to continue. I might as well be having dinner with my mother. She and I do this all the time."

He knew it wasn't his business, but he really wanted to know. "So, you rarely date, and when you do, you get the evil eye from your ex, who's the mayor of the town? And you haven't put him in his place?"

"Calling Tad out is easier said than done, plus, it's really never worked out with anyone," she admitted.

"Is he some sort of homicidal maniac and killing them off?"

She laughed. "No, of course not. I just haven't found anyone I like enough to put a stop to his childishness, I guess. And Tad's annoyance doesn't bother me. In fact, I'm glad it bothers him in a way after how badly he treated me when we broke up. I've decided that it's not worth the end result."

Matthew didn't know what to say. He just stared for a second, trying to think of something.

"I know that sounds strange, but people around here are used to it. No one even asks me out anymore. I've got a good business and a wonderful family. My life is very satisfying."

"Don't you want more?" He asked.

"I have nieces and nephews, and I have Big Al. It's all good." But the sadness that touched her eyes belied her words.

He sensed she would lump him with all the others who'd not made it past the first date and then run the other way, if he confessed how they'd met ten years ago. He would tell her soon, but tonight didn't feel right.

Tad Beaumont might have been her boyfriend at the time Matthew met Emma after the football game that night. He'd keep that in mind.

The pretty waiter came over to take their orders. Matthew began by asking about carb and fat content.

Emma shushed him and ordered for them. "You really can't go around town doing that. This is natural and healthy whole food. It won't kill you—unless you start picking apart every item on the menu. Then, someone will likely do something really nasty to your food in the kitchen. That would be worse than maxing your daily intake of carbs, I promise."

He made a face at her that spoke his thoughts. "You just ordered fried pickles."

She waved that away with her hand, like she was swatting a fly. It was a graceful gesture. "So, Matthew, where are you from originally?" Emma asked, clearly using the break to change the subject from her dating or lack of.

Oh, boy. To lie or not to lie? He wasn't a fan of untruths, and had made a stand in the past on honesty and integrity.

This was truly his character put to the test. "I was born in Texas. We moved around a lot when I was a kid." Truth. He'd lived in Texas for exactly one month of his life, then moved around for a few years until they'd settled in Alabama when he was seven. So, true enough, he supposed.

"What about college?"

His heartbeat accelerated, breathing became shallow and rapid. He began to sweat. The roar in his ears was near deafening.

"Are you alright? You don't look so good." Beyond his overwhelming physical symptoms, he registered her concerned tone.

"Just—just need some air." He bounded out of his chair toward the exit, feeling as if the past were a giant wave gaining on him, threatening to engulf him and his almost lies.

⇛⇚

EMMA WONDERED IF all men had some major malfunction. Matthew was the first one who'd even asked her to dinner in a coon's age, and he'd gone thrashing out of the restaurant in a full-blown panic attack, poor guy. She figured she'd better get their orders to go, which would give him a minute to get himself under control. Hopefully, she wouldn't have to call 9-1-1. The dispatchers were the worst of the gossips; then there were the old biddies with their police scanners manned twenty-four-seven who stayed up to speed on everything as it went down.

So, going through official channels was really a last resort. She hoped his panic attack was not the hospital kind. Lord knew she'd had enough experience with them over the years, being in the pageant business and with some of the other—stuff. Fortunately, they weren't her personal drama. She'd managed all that without ever actually experiencing one, but several of her loved ones hadn't been so lucky.

By the time she'd paid the check and walked out the restaurant with a large to-go bag, Matthew was sitting on a bench reserved for overflow customers when there was a wait at busy times. Thankfully, this wasn't one of those times, and he was outside alone, leaned forward with his elbows on his knees and head in his hands. Poor guy.

"Do you need a paper bag? Or are you finished with the hyperventilating part?" She asked, handing him a paper lunch sack.

He took it and glanced at her with an incredulous expression. Clearly he'd gotten control of himself.

"How about we head over to my house and not let this delicious food go to waste?"

The lights from the overhang illuminated his face. His expression was guarded, embarrassed, even ashamed. She'd seen it all before.

"I think I'll just head home. Sorry about that inside." He

vaguely motioned toward the restaurant.

She set the bags of food down on the end of the bench and plopped down beside him. It was full dark out here and the crickets were chirping happily, unaware of the tense situation nearby. "Look, I don't know what set you off, but I'm way too familiar with a garden variety panic attack to freak out, not that a panic attack is anything to sneeze at, mind you. But I can't tell you how relieved I am that you don't need to be carted off to the hospital, because the whole town would know about it by midnight if you did."

"You don't think I'm a nut case?" His expression was stupefied, as if he'd just realized the world wasn't flat.

"Nah. Just somebody else who's had something rotten happen to them that they haven't dealt with all the way. Look, my dad drowned in the lake right in front of us kids when we were teenagers." She covered his hand with hers.

"How horrible." He looked at her with a softness that caused strange feelings she'd thought had taken off to greener pastures years ago.

She nodded to acknowledge his sympathy, but that wasn't why she'd revealed her tragedy. She wanted him to understand he wasn't alone, so she continued, "We were too far offshore to help. You can only imagine the nightmares and issues we've carried around. A couple of us had mild panic attacks, and we've all wondered if there was something we could have done differently since we were kids. Every now and then there's a recurrence. Sometimes it comes out of nowhere."

He nodded. "Survivor's guilt." He looked down. "So this is no big deal to you?"

"Nope. It's a big deal when it happens to you, though. But I do know the best counselor in three counties, if you want her card. She moved here awhile back and has worked miracles for a friend. That's if you believe in that sort of thing. Aren't most New Yorkers in counseling for one thing or another?" She smiled at him and gave him a little sisterly pat on the back.

"I'll try not to take offense at that insinuation, but I will take her name and number. Thanks." Then, he turned to her and said, "I'm still hungry if you are."

Emma grinned. "I'm starving. I was hoping this little episode wasn't going to cost me dinner."

They'd taken separate cars from her studio, so he followed her the mile-and-a-half to her house. It occurred to Emma she'd never brought a man here besides a worker to fix something, or her brother, certainly never a date. Because of that rarely ever dating thing.

As she unlocked the front door, she sincerely hoped there wasn't an errant pair of panties on the floor, dropped while transporting laundry or some such comedy. It wasn't something she'd ever given a thought to before.

Thankfully, after a quick glance inside she saw that her little two-bedroom, two-bath cottage was nice and tidy, exactly how she liked it. It was a refurbished historical home tucked neatly between two massive oaks. She'd adored this house since she'd been a child, and when the opportunity to buy it became available once her business was doing well enough, she'd jumped at the opportunity. It was her dream home and Emma cherished it.

As he approached the front door, he said, "Wow, what a great house. It's like something from a movie." As soon as the words left him, Emma saw him grimace.

She smiled. "I get that a lot, but I'll take it as a high compliment since it came from a bona fide director/producer in the business."

"Pretty cliché, huh?" He looked around as they entered and he said, "The interior is even better than the outside. Very comfortable. Your work?"

She led him through the vaulted family room that was well appointed with a few great antique pieces, a soft muted rug with a geometric pattern and a large, comfortable sofa and two chairs. The fireplace was the focal point of the room, with its rough-hewn barn beam mantle, covered with photos of her family throughout the decades. She'd loved making this space beautiful and comfortable.

"Yes. When you don't date or have kids, it leaves time for such things."

"Where's your dog?"

"He's at my mom's house. It's his second home. She has a huge, fenced backyard where he spends his time chasing the hundreds of squirrels who conspire to drive him nuts."

He laughed, a deep-throated chuckle that again stirred her inner-workings. What the hell was wrong with her tonight? Men didn't usually get under her skin like this.

She flipped on the kitchen lights, then dimmed the ones that hung over the bar area. "Can I get you something to drink? She asked.

"Water would be great."

"I also have beer and white wine, if you're interested." He shot her a look that she recognized as interested, but not in beer or wine. She cleared her throat. "Water it is."

➤❰❰❰➤

"EMMA, I WANT to thank you for understanding about the panic attack, and for bringing me back here for dinner. I know it's late, and you didn't have to. I haven't exactly been the nicest guy since I've been in town." He needed to make amends for his brutish behavior thus far.

"You and I haven't gotten off to a great start for a friend-ship, I admit, but I don't think you're a bad person. You just seem a little out of your comfort zone here. Let's face it, it ain't New York City." She took silverware out of the drawer and laid it next to two plates.

"Isn't that the truth?" He snorted.

They opened the containers, and without any discussion began serving food family style from both containers on the plates Emma had taken out of the cupboard.

"Something about you seems familiar to me," she said,

tilting her head sideways.

"Really?" Slow down, breathe.

If he told her now, she would wonder why he hadn't told her as soon as he'd recognized her. Should he pretend he hadn't recognized her before now? No, that would be too far-fetched. She hadn't changed enough to be unrecognizable. But apparently, he had, or at least he hoped so. Because if he didn't speak up now and she figured this out later, he was screwed.

"I think these are the best collard greens and black-eyed peas I've ever eaten."

"You're from New York and you've had black-eyed peas and collards?" Her gorgeous green eyes narrowed, as if catching him in some kind of fiendish whopper of a lie.

"Why does that surprise you? Just because I'm not a resident, doesn't mean I haven't had the opportunity and the pleasure of sampling Southern food."

"Okay. It's just that collards and black-eyed peas aren't exactly your average Southern fare. But I'm glad to know you at least like the food here, even if you're allergic to our lovely flowers and greenery."

"You mean the pollen and ragweed. I'm fine with the flowers and most of the greenery. I should be fine in a few weeks. These are seasonal allergies. I've had them my whole life."

"Hmmm. So, it's not Big Al."

"Big Al doesn't help when I'm in the middle of an allergy

attack, but, no, he wasn't entirely to blame."

"So, if you're not from the South, how do you know you have seasonal allergies to ragweed and pollen?" She asked.

"Like I said, we moved around. The South isn't the only place that has pollen and ragweed, you know." He verbally tap-danced his way around that one. If and when she ever figured out who he was, he hoped she wouldn't come back to this conversation.

"How about those fried pickles?" She changed the subject.

"I can feel my arteries hardening with every bite. But they are delicious. I can't say I've ever eaten a fried pickle. I do believe they fry just about everything down here."

"Ever had a fried Twinkie?" Her green eyes sparkled.

He clutched his chest, feigning a heart attack.

"Now don't have another panic attack, you hear?"

"I'm good for now. I'd appreciate your not sharing that information with anyone, if you don't mind. It wouldn't be good for my career, or my manly reputation around town."

She smiled then made a face. "Don't worry about your career. Secret's safe with me. I can't guarantee your reputation is though. People will talk now that you've been seen in public with me, you know?"

"What exactly will they say? That I was spotted with the hottest woman in Ministry, Alabama?"

She snorted. "Ha. Maybe that you managed to take out the weird chick in town who's rarely seen with men. Someone off the street might stop you and ask how that happened. There are those who think I'm a lesbian in secret, or that I'm broken."

He'd almost have to agree with the broken thing now that he'd heard her short version, but never would he say that out loud. "*They* are a bunch of gossips who likely have nothing better to do than make up stories about you. By the way, are you a lesbian?"

She laughed. "No. Not a lesbian. But maybe broken just a little."

"We're all broken just a little." They laughed at that.

He was certainly broken in several ways. An image of his stepdad crept through his mind and he shoved it down. Yeah, he couldn't point fingers at anyone else for being broken.

She pushed back from her plate and heaved a sigh. "I'm stuffed and broken right now."

He smiled at her. "I'd better get going. It's been a long day, and tomorrow will be another." He placed his napkin on the bar, stood up, and began clearing the dishes. When he reached the sink, he turned back and asked, "Do you have plans this weekend?"

"Um, I'm not sure. I'm supposed to help my mom with an event at Evangeline House, and then do some wedding stuff. She's getting married in a few weeks."

"What's Evangeline House? And your mom's getting married?"

They talked for a few more minutes about Emma's family's event planning business and her mother's unexpected rediscovery of Howard, her first love. That was fascinating stuff.

She let him out the front door and promised to lock up behind him.

He walked out to his car, nearly dragging his feet. They'd had a great night. But his guilt was weighing him down. Why hadn't he just told her who he was and that he'd recognized her from before? She'd given him every opportunity, even though she hadn't known it.

He realized that things had gone so well between them and telling her might blow it all up in his face. He really liked Emma Laroux, and he respected everything she'd done to create a successful independent life after her public fall from grace. But there was a part of him that wondered what the hell had happened after that weekend a decade ago to cause her to lead such a solitary existence. Besides what he knew, which wasn't much, there had to be something else.

Maybe she hadn't given up men entirely, but obviously she'd almost done so. To forge ahead without children or a mate for ten years? That didn't happen for no good reason. After the weird interaction with Mayor Tad Beaumont earlier this evening, it didn't take a genius to figure out that he'd had something to do with it.

Chapter Four

❦

"I'M STILL HAVING a hard time wrapping my mind around the idea that Daddy wasn't my real father." Maeve's deep blue eyes shone with tears. They were her newfound father's eyes. Maeve was the eldest of her siblings, and had recently discovered that Howard, their mother's fiancé, was really her biological father.

Emma didn't blame her for her confusion and emotional upset. The whole ordeal was like a heap of soap opera drama, and they'd only just found out about it a few months ago. "Sweetie, you know there's no one to blame here. I realize it has shaken your foundation, but Daddy loved you, even though he knew you weren't his blood, he loved you like you were."

Maeve said, "He used to tell me I was his special girl. But he never told me why."

"You see? You never felt like there was anything different between you. Learning that Howard is your father and that he's never had another family is a blessing. He adores you and Lucy. Finding the two of you has been like an answer to a prayer for him. For you, it's like having a chance at another father."

"I guess you're right. I believe him when he says he never meant to leave or hurt Mom while she was pregnant." He'd left their mother, Maureen, at the altar, not realizing she'd been pregnant at the time with Maeve. His parents had hatched a plan to keep the lovers apart. Maureen had believed he'd gotten cold feet and changed his mind.

"So, you have to go to the wedding and give them your blessing, right? And let Lucy participate. It's the right thing to do. Mom deserves to be happy. She's been alone too long."

"Of course, we're going to the wedding and will participate. I'm just struggling within myself a little right now." Then, before Emma could blink, Maeve cleanly turned the tables on her. "Mom's not the only one who's been alone too long, you know?"

Emma was used to this.

Emma held up a hand to ward off the offensive. "Mom just gave me the business a couple days ago. I'll tell you as I did her. I'm fine. I live my life on my own terms."

"Really? On your own terms, huh?"

"What do you mean?" Emma wasn't at all sure she wanted to hear Maeve's opinion on the subject.

"You appear to have it all together, but somehow you've never gotten completely free of whatever it was that set you back when you stepped down from Miss Alabama. Something happened and it stunted you. You won't share with us and it's gone on too long."

Emma felt the blood drain out of her face.

"You've let what happened all those years ago control your future. Just because one man screwed you over doesn't mean it will happen again. People get hurt and then move on. You have to get over Tad Beaumont. Do you really think by hardly dating and not committing to anyone else, he'll someday leave Sadie and come back to you?" Her sister asked.

Emma couldn't believe how wrong her sister was. And how right. Thank God, Maeve didn't know. Maybe what happened back then left Emma mistrustful of men to some degree, but none of this was because she wanted Tad back. In fact, the idea of that asshole touching her again made her want to run to the nearest fire hose and blast the skin off her body.

She whooshed a sigh of relief. "I wouldn't take Tad back if he were truly the last man on earth. And I've dated some. It just hasn't worked out."

"If that's true, why won't you ever give anyone else a real chance?" Maeve asked, now distracted from her own drama.

Emma ignored that because she didn't want to dwell on the truth of it. "It's been easier to stay single. Simpler. It's true; I haven't wanted to get hurt again. Once was more than enough. And don't you think if I met the right person, I would know, or at least feel a lot more than mildly interested. I haven't dated anyone more than a little while because there hasn't been a spark, much less a flame. Maybe someday I'll try again."

"Better hurry up if you want to try to have children." Maeve suggested.

"I'll take that under advisement." Trying to maintain her composure, Emma smiled.

The having children part struck at the heart of Emma's greatest fear. She desperately wanted them. Her own large loving family only solidified her need to have one or two of her own. The thought of spending her life alone, without children of her own to love, either biological or adopted, made her want to curl up and wither.

Before she fell headlong into her pity party, her sister brought her back to the present. "I heard about your dinner with Cammie's producer. Was it really just a mercy dinner—because they say he's hot?"

"*They* should keep their opinions to themselves. And it was a friendly dinner. He wasn't feeling well, so we took the food to go and ate at my house."

Maeve raised her brows. "Well, I'll bet that gets around town. Good for you. I hope it causes your self-imposed dating moratorium to end once word spreads that you're back on the market. Look out though, there could be a stampede." Maeve smirked.

"That's ridiculous." But it really hadn't occurred to

Emma that being seen with a man after a long, dry spell might encourage others to give it another a try.

◆»»»◆◆◆◆

MATTHEW'S PALMS WEREN'T completely dry as the phone rang again. Surely the return of panic attacks didn't have anything to do with what had happened before. But then, he couldn't very well take a chance of it happening again with no warning. He'd almost made an ass of himself—who was he kidding? He'd made a total ass of himself in front of Emma. He'd been fortunate she hadn't run off believing him to be a nut job of the first order.

"Hello? This is Sabine, how can I help you?" A female voice answered, cool but friendly.

Matt snapped out of it. "Y-yes, hi, my name is Matthew. A friend referred me. I've just moved to the area and wondered if you had any openings for new patients?"

"Yes, I do have a few. The first appointment takes a couple of hours because of the mountain of required paperwork."

"No. That's not an issue. When could I come in?" He asked, using every ounce of willpower not to slam the phone down and not look back.

"Let me see, I just had a cancellation tomorrow morning at nine. Would that work?"

"You see patients on Saturday?" He was surprised. Normally, in a town this size, most medical offices were nine-to-five on weekdays and closed on weekends. The only ones opened were the hospital and the one urgent care facility that he knew of.

She laughed. "Most folks are happy about that. I try to accommodate nine-to-fivers as much as possible."

"Oh, I'm not complaining, just surprised. That actually works great for me, since I'd rather not take time off for this, if possible." He breathed a sigh of relief.

Maybe it was a sign he was supposed to seek counseling for his little issue before it got out of hand again.

"Great. I'll put you down on my schedule. Could I get your last name and phone number?"

Matthew gave her his info and hung up. She sounded very professional. Good. This was beyond embarrassing, especially since Emma Laroux had witnessed it. The idea of her seeing him as fragile made him groan. Panic attacks weren't manly; though he knew from prior experience and therapy they weren't supposed to be due to weakness. It didn't make him feel much better about things. At least he'd made the appointment.

Emma was so lovely. She was tough and compassionate. But she lived on an emotional island, it seemed. He'd enjoyed her company last night. They'd laughed and talked, so unlike when they'd first met.

Around the mayor, she'd been tense and nervous, as if she was about to jump out of her skin at any moment. Matthew had a distinct feeling he remembered Tad Beaumont from that weekend in the past, when he'd first met Emma, but couldn't quite nail it down.

Matthew had played football for Auburn, so he'd been at practice and playing in the big Iron Bowl game most of the time that weekend. He'd come back to the fraternity house—after. The same evening he'd found her like that. There had been a big party going on with lots of girls, guys, drinking, and all the other things that went on at fraternity houses during a celebratory weekend, because, unfortunately, they'd been on the UA campus, and Alabama had won the game that night. So, the revelry had been amped for the partygoers. He, on the other hand, was a guest of the frat from the rival school's team.

He'd not been as thrilled with the outcome of the game, kicking himself for missing a key tackle. But still, he'd been invited to the party, and was determined to at least try to enjoy the evening.

Shaking his head, Matthew glanced at his watch. He'd need to hurry if he was going to make it to the diner in time for breakfast before work. He preferred structure and a solid schedule. Those things were part of his life now. They'd helped him morph into the successful man he'd become. He was no longer the pudgy, country boy he'd once been, content to watch life pass him by.

EMMA BACKED DOWN her driveway, softly humming to

Miranda Lambert's latest empowering tune, Big Al lying beside her riding shotgun, when a horn blasted right behind her.

Cutting off a muffled oath, Emma turned to see who'd pulled in behind her. Spotting Tad, she suddenly wished she hadn't stopped, and instead floored the accelerator. As he got out of his car, she was sorely tempted.

"What the—" She felt the boiling rage redden her face as she shoved the gearshift in park.

Emma schooled her features into neutral and let out an annoyed breath as she hit the power window button to the down position. Big Al gave a low growl.

Tad grinned, making her want to punch him in his too-handsome face. "Oh, sorry about that. I just wanted to make sure you were all right. A little bird told me there was a strange car here last night and they'd seen a man come inside."

How dare he? Her heart thudded. "You saw who I was with at the studio—in fact, you met him. He's not a stranger to me, and, as you can see, I'm fine. Thanks for checking on me." She smiled sweetly, trying to get him to move along.

"You know, Emma, I do still worry about you." Big Al growled again, Emma could feel his tension.

"Why, Tad? I'm a big girl. Why on earth would you stop by and tell me this?"

"Everyone in this town is my responsibility. And I still feel guilty about the way things ended between us." Big Al lunged across Emma toward the open window at Tad, barking and baring his canines.

"Al!" Shocked, Emma grabbed his collar.

Tad lurched back, taking two steps away from her car window. He gave Al a less congenial smile then. "You might want to keep that mutt inside just in case animal services *finds* him roaming around. You know we have a kill shelter here for feral dogs. Gotta keep our citizens safe."

"Big Al would never hurt anyone." She said through gritted teeth, "As you can see, I'm just fine. Now, if you'll let me pass, I've got to help my sister this morning."

"Maybe I'll stop by and see how it's going over there."

"It's a closed set."

"Oh, I'm sure they'll make an exception for the mayor of the town."

He gave her a little salute and then sauntered off toward his car.

She revved her engine. Never had she wanted to physically harm another human being more—well, maybe there had been another time. But it *had* been the same person.

No sense hurting her perfectly lovely car by giving him the satisfaction. Backing the rest of the way, Emma continued envisioning all sorts of horrible ends Tad might meet that wouldn't and couldn't be blamed on her. It did cheer her up just a bit. She wished she could expose Tad for the ass face he really was. People in town saw him as the great white hope. But she knew he had a dark side. She'd caught him slyly watching her when he thought no one was looking several times at town events, but he'd only gone out of his way a few times to really be a pain. She'd felt his interest and his presence though she couldn't really put her finger on specifics. But Emma wondered why he'd suddenly renewed his direct contact with her. After all, he had a lovely wife and a daughter, and he was on top of the town like he'd always dreamed. Of course, back then, his plan was to have her at his side. Now, it was as if he were closing in on her in some weird, undefined way.

The less her family knew of the Pandora's box of the disaster ten years ago, the better. She'd been able to keep it mostly contained by stepping down as Miss Alabama and refusing to grant interviews or discuss the situation with anyone.

Her cell phone startled her out of her maudlin thoughts. She didn't recognize the number. "Hello?"

"Hello, Emma Jean, this is Roy Miers from college, remember me? Momma called me with your number. I think she got it from one of your sisters." Emma Jean was her childhood nickname.

Somewhat shocked, Emma recovered her wits. "Hi, Roy. It's been a long time. What can I do for you?"

"Hey, I was wondering if you'd like to go out to dinner this weekend? Momma said you were dating again, and I really had a thing for you back then, but you and Tad were always together, you know? What d'you say?"

Emma had to recover a moment. It had been a long time since she'd been truly asked out to dinner, besides by Matthew, of course. She had a fuzzy memory of Roy Miers. He'd always worn a cowboy hat and Wrangler jeans. Nice looking. "I appreciate your calling, Roy, but I'm not available this weekend."

He sighed. "Well, Emma Jean, I'd love to take you out when you get a free night. I work in Birmingham, but I'd be happy to drive out and take you someplace nice almost anytime if you'd let me know."

She smiled. "I've got your number now, Roy. If I get some time, I'll give you a call, okay? Tell your momma I said hi."

After she disconnected the call, Emma sighed. It was flattering to be asked out, but after what'd happened earlier with Tad, she'd have to shut down the rumors she supposed. Just then, her phone rang again. Another invitation.

By the time she arrived at the diner not two miles away, she'd received a third call. Standing at the counter, she stared at her phone thinking how to get around all this without hurting anyone's feelings.

"You look like the phone might hold all the answers to the important questions if you could just figure out how to use it." Her head popped up at his voice.

She hadn't seen Matthew approach. How could she not? His dark hair was thick and perfectly groomed, his shirt stretched and fit over his obviously muscled torso as if it had been laser measured and cut specifically for his body. There wasn't a hint of stubble on his clean-shaven jaw this morning, as opposed to last night. She wasn't sure which way he was more appealing. Either way, her fingers itched to touch perfection.

His eyes bore into hers, questioning maybe, to see if she thought less of him after what had happened.

She smiled. "You look ready for action this morning." She nearly groaned as soon as the words left her lips. "I meant like when you say, 'action,' on the set."

He smiled and it really reached his eyes, which really reached her knees, almost causing them to buckle. "I got it, and I'm fine. Sorry again that you had to witness it. I called the number you gave me. But I'd appreciate it if you didn't tell anyone about—any of it."

Emma made an "X" across her left breast, drawing his gaze to it. Geez, could she stop already? "Cross my heart." Her face must be bright red, because she could feel the heat in her cheeks.

He, God bless him, appeared to ignore it, and said, "I really appreciate it. Wouldn't look so good for my cred as a boss around here if they thought I was weak."

Emma immediately pulled him away from the counter, and even though they'd been speaking quietly where no one else could hear, she whispered angrily, "I get it, okay? It's not a weakness, so don't put yourself down because of your traumas."

"Thanks, Emma."

She grabbed her donuts off the counter and headed out the door as he paid his check. "See you in *action*." That made him smile, which made her breathe like she'd run rather than walked out to her car in the parking lot.

Chapter Five

≈

D R. SABINE O'CONNOR'S office was fortuitously located in a nearly invisible spot at the end of a narrow street behind several tall oak trees. It was a good place if one was hoping for a little privacy. And that was exactly what Matthew wanted in this instance. He'd arrived ten minutes early, likely the first appointment of the day, this being Saturday. Only a small, red convertible was parked in the tiny lot. He assumed it was the good doctor's.

The office was a converted tiny, old house, as many of the businesses here in Ministry seemed to be. He approached the front door and tried the handle. Locked. So, he rang the bell. There was a click, so he pushed and went right in. The aroma of freshly baked cookies or something equally tempting assaulted him the moment he stepped through the door.

Sniffing appreciatively, he looked around. "Hello. You must be Matthew. Should I call you Matt?"

"No. Matthew is fine." He nearly barked at one of the most gorgeous women he'd ever seen. She had the shiniest, black-as-midnight hair and clear blue eyes. Her skin was completely flawless.

She blinked but otherwise ignored his sharp tone. "I'm Sabine." She held out her hand.

"Sorry about that. I'm Matthew Pope. I haven't been Matt since college. It kind of brings some things back that I'd rather not think about."

"Well, that's kind of why you're here, isn't it? To talk about things you'd rather not?" She smiled, her straight, white teeth gleaming at him.

"I guess you've got a point." He cleared his throat. "You said something on the phone about a mountain of paperwork?"

"Now that I've got you in my clutches, I'd rather dive right in as long as you promise to fill it out before you leave. You're not suicidal, are you?"

"No."

"Okay, then I'm not concerned about liability just yet. Why don't we move into my office and you can tell me why you're here. I sense it wasn't easy to make the call."

They moved into a comfortable office set up in what appeared to be an old bedroom. There was a fireplace, complete with gas logs, in case patients got chilly. "No. It wasn't easy, but it isn't the first time I've been in therapy. I thought I was done though, with the panic attacks, I mean."

"What was the original trigger that set them off, if you don't mind my getting right to the point?" Her gaze was direct.

He appreciated a direct question. "A bomb."

She blinked, but to her credit it was the only show of surprise. "Well, I suppose that would do it. Was anyone harmed?"

"Everyone. I mean everyone around me. I was knocked down and had some pretty serious injuries, but I recovered. My unit—I was Army Special Forces on my first tour in Iraq—all the men in my unit were killed. We were clearing houses in what we thought was a deserted village. My buddy, John, stepped on a trip wire. It was supposed to be a clean area. No devices." He covered his eyes with his hands, the scene clear again in his mind's eye. He began to shake.

Sabine sighed. "I'm so sorry, Matthew. I'm certain your earlier therapist assured you that your surviving was a good thing, and you in no way should feel responsible or guilty for not dying with your friends and comrades."

He took a deep, trembling breath. "Sure. She said all those things a hundred times. I know that in my head, but once you've seen it, it's hard to leave it behind. Loud sounds are usually what used to bring it all back. But I'd dealt with it a long time ago. I'm not sure why it's happening again."

"How long since the tragedy?"

"Right out of college. Nine years now. Like I said, it was my first tour—and my last. I received a medical discharge, and after my body recovered, I became hell-bent on becoming a success and leaving everything else behind."

"How did that work?" She asked, her tone neutral.

"It worked great. I changed my diet, worked out every day. I became a more organized, scheduled person. I lost weight and set goals that I've managed to achieve. But, for some reason, since I've been back here, I mean, since I've come here, I've had two panic attacks in a few days, and I'm not sure why."

"Sounds like you've tried really hard to become a different person completely."

"Pretty much."

"Is there something about being here that bothers you? Anything that causes obvious anxiety?"

"You mean besides one syllable words being pronounced with three or four, allergies, every single person wanting to know details of your life, or the general slow pace that even grass grows at around here?"

"Uh-huh. I'm familiar with those things. It's certainly an acquired taste. I noticed you slipped and said *back* here. Is there a significance?"

"I really don't want to go there, if you don't mind." He couldn't, or maybe, he wouldn't.

"Okay. Hopefully just breaking the dam and getting some of the words out today will alleviate a bit of your pent-up frustration and stress. Unfortunately, it sounds like being *back* here might be at the heart of the reoccurrence of those pesky panic attacks."

"Pesky?" He opened his mouth, shocked she'd make

light of something that made him feel like he could die at any moment.

She nodded. "We both know they won't kill you, even if you think you're going to die."

He exhaled on a laugh, realizing how dead-on she was. "I know you're right—now. Remind me of that when I'm in the middle of one." Her methods disarmed him. When had he begun taking himself so seriously that he couldn't let up?

"The good news is you can call me if you have a need." She handed him a card with an emergency contact number. "Put the number in your cell phone."

"Let's hope I won't need it anytime soon."

"Mr. Pope, you owe me some paperwork. Now that might kill you."

And it nearly did. He completed his paperwork and made an appointment for the following Saturday morning. Apparently, her previous standing appointment at that slot had graduated to checking in from time-to-time. Good for them. Far better than the other possibility. He shuddered, considering the deep and dark places the human psyche managed to dive during the really bad times. He was *living* proof—thankfully.

⟫⟫⟫⟫⟫⟪⟪⟪⟪

"I DON'T NEED a date for the wedding," Emma said to another person, for about the hundredth time since the planning had begun. This time she directed the very clear comment to her sister, Jo Jo, who sat next to her, pretty mouth pinched tight.

They were at Evangeline House, otherwise known as the house they all grew up in, and the family event-planning business. Mom had asked them to congregate here for family dinner and some last minute detail coordination regarding her upcoming wedding to their new stepdad, Howard the Great.

"Did you suck on a lemon, Jo?" Ben asked as he entered the room.

Emma snorted.

"What?" Jo Jo demanded.

"Your mouth has that old lady pinchy look like you sucked on a lemon. Emma, what did you do now?" Ben turned to Emma as he eyeballed his two sisters.

"I didn't do anything," Emma said, and then shrugged, praying Jo Jo didn't start in about Emma's need for a hot date to their sweet momma's wedding. This whole new daddy thing was stressful enough; even though they were thrilled their mother had found love again at this stage in her life.

"I'm not buying it, ladies," Ben said, not letting them loose from his scrutiny. "I've come in right in the middle of something here. Let's have it."

Emma sighed. She'd rather give her side of it rather than have Jo Jo go on the offensive. "Jo says I need a date for the wedding. I say, that's absurd. I haven't brought a date to anything in a coon's age, so why should I all of a sudden start scratching around for one now?"

Ben raised his eyebrows at Jo Jo, as if to ask the question, *yes, why now?*

"Why not? Don't you think she's wandered around here long enough alone? Cammie tells me her new producer took Emma to dinner the other night. And he's pretty hawt, from what I heard down at Cut 'n Curl.

Ben snickered. "No doubt the hens at the Cut 'n Curl are nearly chomping at the bit with a new man in town under the age of eighty."

"Oh, really, Ben? Like you have any right to talk. You, with your 'two-date' rule." Emma inserted.

"The two-date rule was implemented out of pure necessity and you both know it," Ben defended, holding his hands up as if to ward off physical attack.

"I think it's a way to simplify your life and prevent getting to know someone special. Because, heaven forbid, you actually become emotionally attached." Jo Jo followed up Emma's comments.

"Whoa, sisters! I thought we were discussing Emma's lack of a love life, not my intelligent choice to manage my social calendar."

Both girls snorted.

"So, I see we disagree. That's alright. You couldn't possibly understand how hard I try to keep everyone happy. I really just don't want to hurt feelings. And I honestly don't have time to juggle dating right now." Ben tried to explain his decision, but Emma knew how hard it was to do without sounding like a real ass.

He was so popular with the women around here they fought mightily for his attention. But, so far, he either hadn't found anyone who'd caught his notice or hadn't allowed himself to become involved, at least, not in a really long time.

"We get it, little brother. But if you don't want us all in your business, you really shouldn't get all up in mine." Emma had him there, didn't she?

"Okay, I get it. But really, Emma, it has been a long time since Tad. He's moved on. We know you've dated a little here and there, but you really haven't given anyone else much of a chance. You know we all just want you to be happy." He slung an arm around her shoulders.

Jo Jo smiled at the two of them. "He said it. That's really all we want, you know."

"I know. And do y'all really think anyone worth a darn has come within fifty miles of Ministry that I might even consider as a serious boyfriend? Why don't you let me handle it, okay? I'll consider your input." She flashed them her best beauty pageant smile.

"Hello, my dears. Is everything alright in here?" Mom entered the kitchen with Howard trailing in her wake.

"Hey, Mom," They answered in unison.

"Where are Cammie and Maeve?" she asked.

They looked at one another and shrugged their shoulders.

"I guess Cammie got hung up with some business with the show. I don't know what could be keeping Maeve." A small frown furrowed Mom's brow.

She worried for Maeve, Emma knew. Maeve, being the only biological child of Howard, and having just found out this rather shocking info only a couple months earlier, still had days where she couldn't decide if having a new daddy was a good or bad thing.

Howard stepped toward Mom, sensing her distress. "It's alright, honey. Go on and give the girls a call and see what's keeping them. I know you'll feel better after you talk to 'em." He squeezed her shoulder gently.

Nobody in the family believed Howard had anything but the best intentions toward their mother. Finding them naked together in front of the fireplace when they'd all decided to surprise her at the lake house during her convalescence after her back surgery had been rather unexpected, especially since no one had even known of his existence.

The most impactful and somewhat painful part of this had been the revelation that Howard had been mom's first true love. They'd all adored their father, and hadn't known about his marrying Mom while she was pregnant with their oldest sister, Maeve. Maeve was struggling the most with all the sudden changes.

Mom had dialed her phone. "Hey, Maeve, honey, just

wanted to make sure you were on the way. Supper's all ready and your brother and sisters are here. Love you!" The frown deepened.

She dialed Cammie's number, but the ringing sounded inside the house as Cammie made her way into the kitchen. "I'm here; I'm here. Sorry I'm late! I got hung up figuring out next week's menu. I was thinking strawberry shortcake, but somehow banana pudding has been really calling my name as a pairing with the fried shrimp and fresh cocktail sauce and coleslaw. You know we're starting a 'seafood Fridays' series. It was Matthew's idea. That guy's a smart cookie."

Ben reached over and put a hand over his twin sister's mouth as she rattled on about her food plans. "Stop it. Mom, it smells heavenly in here; is dinner ready? Now, I'm starved."

It did smell divine. Maybe not fried shrimp and banana pudding divine, but the potato soup, salad, and French bread came in a close second. Emma was quite familiar with her mother's talents in the kitchen.

Mom still had that distracted expression on her face. "Yes. Sure. It's all there on the stove. Everything's warm. Bread's in the oven." She waved toward the far end of the massive kitchen. It was a catering kitchen that somehow still managed to maintain a cozy family feel, even with the large industrial stove, ovens, sinks, and refrigerator. Everything had been chosen so as not to offend the home's historical origins. The original kitchen had been about half the size, but the need for extensive food preparation made expansion of the room a necessity. Emma wasn't certain when the work had been completed, but she thought her parents had taken it on while she'd been in high school, or had it been in middle school? She couldn't remember.

As they served plates, her mother's cell phone rang. "Hello?" All heads turned toward the sound. As much as they tended to fuss and argue, when one of them had a problem, it was everyone's problem.

"Oh, hello dear. No, we're all here now. Is everything alright?" Mom breathed a sigh of obvious relief. "Oh. Okay, I understand. I'll have Ben send you a recap of everything we discuss. Give Lucy all our love. And tell her not to worry, she'll do just fine on her history project. I'll save y'all some chocolate pie. Tell Junior he only gets one piece." The worried frown was gone, but a slightly puzzled one now replaced it.

"Lucy have a sudden project?" Emma asked.

"Apparently she does," Mom answered.

"Something Junior couldn't help her with until Maeve got home?" Jo Jo asked.

"Would you want Junior to have any input in your project?" Cammie asked Jo Jo. Cammie and Junior, Maeve's husband, had been in a practical joke war for years.

"Guess not," Jo answered.

"Children, let's have our supper and discuss wedding details. I wish Maeve could've made it, but she can't. Ben, you'll take notes, won't you, dear?"

Ben nodded. "Sure, Mom." Ben was an attorney, which designated him the note-taker and detail guy for the family.

Emma could tell Mom was disappointed that Maeve was absent, but it was obvious that Howard was even more so. His shoulders slumped after they'd received the call that Maeve wasn't coming. Emma felt suddenly angry with Maeve for skipping out on such an important and exciting time for her mother—and her father now. Maeve would need to get past her hurt and realize they wouldn't always have these precious opportunities to be together.

The world and life had a way of changing plans. There wasn't always forever. Emma realized she might do well to think about that herself. She'd been in a holding pattern for a long time. Her mother's courage in starting over with a new man and a new chapter in her life, even though she realized it might upset those she loved and cause gossip in such a small town should give Emma courage. Mom was following her heart and trusting her family to do the right thing and stick by her.

Chapter Six

"BABY, I JUST need a few dollars to tide me over until pay day." Her raspy tone was as familiar and as unsettling as Matthew's panic attacks. His mother.

"Mom, what did you do with your check this month? I sent you money last month, and I don't mind helping out, but I want to make sure you're not getting in over your head." He tried really hard to keep the exasperation out of his tone, because nothing good would come from losing his cool with her.

"My expenses aren't your concern, young man." Her tone was hard.

This meant she'd gone to the casino in Biloxi and blown it. Again. But he couldn't let her starve, could he?

"Your *expenses* seem to be getting more and more expensive. Mom, I understand you enjoy the slots, but it's beginning to cause a problem if you can't pay the bills because of your gambling." He tried not to sound judgmental, he really did. Maybe he didn't try as hard as he could've, but, damn it, what was he going to do with her?

"Young man, you are not to judge me. You left here after I nursed you back to health and never looked back—or hardly ever. After all I did for you after you got yourself blown up, the least you could do is come down from New York City and visit your poor mother every now and then."

The derision in her tone was deserved, especially since he hadn't admitted to her that he was living barely two hours away working in Alabama. He was a shit and a bad son to boot. He ran a hand through his hair and sighed. "Look, Mom, this can't continue. Lately, you've been running out of money earlier and earlier. You need to set aside the amount you can afford to lose every month, and no more."

Her breath came out in a ragged sob. "I'm sorry. I don't mean to lose the money; it's just that I've been so sad and lonely since your dad left. When I go with my friend, Sarah, to the casino, we have fun, and for a little while, I can forget that I'm unhappy." Sarah was her best friend at the hardware store where his mom worked.

He wanted to feel bad for her, really he did. But after what Frank had put them all through, it made Matthew want to put his fist through the wall. "First of all, Mom, Frank isn't my father. You forced the adoption and I went along with it to make you happy and stop you from begging me to agree."

"That's not fair, he loved you and Lisa—"

"He wanted the money Dad left for our future, and he

got it. Look, I don't want to discuss Frank, if you don't mind. He took the money and left you high and dry, whether you want to face it or not."

He heard his mother sob again. "It wasn't like that. There were expenses."

"Okay, Mom. I'll send the money, but this has to stop. You're still a young enough woman with an education. There's no reason you can't pull yourself out of this mess. Please stop behaving like a victim." He wished his mother could see how pathetic she'd become. She smoked like a chimney, worked a cashier job that she was greatly overqualified for, and spent her spare time gambling.

"I feel like a victim, even though I believe Frank was a good man. He says you were the reason he left." Her tone was peevish.

Matthew couldn't speak, because if he did right now, the words would be harsh and angry, and damaging. He sat there, gnashing his teeth, wishing for a way to release his boiling anger besides breaking something or roaring at his mother.

His silence must have spoken for him, because she said, "Fine. Just send the money. I guess I'll see you at my funeral." Her tone lacked emotion now.

Realizing that nothing positive would come from furthering the conversation, he said, "Mom, I'll talk to you later." Hanging up, he felt a familiar churning in the pit of his gut. He felt this way every time they spoke. No wonder he'd blown out of there as soon as he'd graduated from college and rarely returned. The military had been the quickest way to get the farthest from Alabama.

His injuries and recovery lasted the better part of a year, and his mother had cared for him while he'd rehabbed. He'd suffered broken bones and lacerations from being hit by flying debris, but no real burns, thanks to the fact that he'd been outside the building checking in with his commanding officer when the blast occurred. Up 'til then, there'd been no activity in the village. They'd relaxed just enough.

Broadcasting and cinematography were his majors at Auburn. He'd been fascinated by TV and movies as a kid. Television had been his escape growing up in such a small community, and within his stepdad's household. Frank hadn't wanted him around, so Matthew had played any sport where he could ride his bike to practice and go to games either on a bus or with friends. His mom did her best to attend his activities, but Frank always seemed to figure out a way to control her time. He and his younger sister, Lisa, had retreated to the television to escape scrutiny by Frank. Frank was a big critic when it came to them.

Matthew was stuffing a personal check into an envelope when he heard a knock at his door. He frowned. He knew very few people here in Ministry, and had made even fewer friends. Surely, it must be somebody trying to sell something or get him to change to a new religion.

His hair was still damp from the shower. He'd pulled on

old jeans and a faded gray Auburn t-shirt and his feet were bare. So, he definitely wasn't dressed for company. Stubbing his toe, he cursed, then headed from his favorite spot on the sunroom porch through the living area toward the front door.

Coming from New York, he never opened the door before checking the peephole first, because, well, it was New York, and one never knew. His current front door was old and heavy, made of oiled wood, inset with leaded glass from top to bottom, so as he headed toward it, he could just make out the shape of a man, or a very manly women, he supposed.

Just before he turned the handle, Matthew found a clear place on the glass to peer through. That spot just happened to be at eyeball level with Mayor Tad Beaumont. "Well, hell," he muttered under his breath.

The mayor was smiling widely as Matthew opened the door. "Hello there. Matthew, right?" Beaumont stuck a hand for a too-firm handshake.

"Yeah. What can I do for you?" How did he know where Matthew lived?

"I thought I'd swing by and see how you were adjusting here in our fine little town. It must be quite a change from the big city." The smile never left his lips.

In fact, Matthew wasn't sure the man had even blinked or that a hair on his head had moved. He was like a perfect Ken doll.

"My adjustment has been fine. A few allergies, but I appreciate all the greenery, just the same." Matthew had the distinct impression the guy wasn't here to discuss his state of satisfaction or his allergies. There was a glint behind his eyes, and the carefree, relaxed posture was tenser than on first glance. This dude was sizing him up as an opponent, as competition. But, why?

Matthew held eye contact, causing Tad to break the weird challenging stare first. "Well, alright then, hopefully I'll be able to make it over to the set and check out the filming y'all have going on over at Cammie and Grey's house."

"Wish I could help you there. It's a closed set during live shooting. We can't have people distracting the talent or moving around while we work. But you can set up an after hours tour. Cammie has generously agreed to limited times where she allows small, accompanied groups to come in. My assistant can hook you up." Matthew reached over to the side table where his wallet lay and pulled out a business card. He handed it to Tad, whose toothpaste commercial smile had slipped into a confused frown, as if he didn't understand what Matthew meant.

"But, I'm the mayor of the town. Surely, *I* could sneak in and observe y'all in action." He said this in a convincing tone.

"We've already got quite a crew assembled on the set. All of them have a job to do. Sorry, Mayor Beaumont, we can't allow special treatment. It's a liability issue—network policy." He managed to pull off an apologetic face; at least he thought he might have managed it.

"I've never been denied entry to *anything* happening *in my town*. That's unheard of." Tad's expression darkened.

Matthew was so put off by this guy's puffed up sense of self-importance that he couldn't help twisting the knife. "No offense, Tad. Can I call you Tad? We just can't accommodate your request. But do call my assistant, and she'll set you up with a behind the scenes, after-hours tour." It was Matthew's turn to pull out a phony-baloney, dazzling smile.

Tad Beaumont's eyes narrowed as his glare dropped to the logo on Matthew's chest. "Auburn, huh? What year did you graduate?" He pointed to the shirt. "You look a little familiar. I was over at Alabama probably about the same time. Have we met before?"

Shit. He hadn't thought about the shirt. The last thing Matthew needed was someone in town getting personal about his past. "No, I don't think we've met. Not that I recall, anyway." He avoided the question about his graduation year.

Tad looked thoughtful.

Then, as if a switch flipped, the big ole mayor smile was back. "Well, it was great to see you, man. If there's anything I can do to make your stay in Ministry better, just let me know." He did the handshake again and disappeared out the front door in a flash.

Matthew shut the door quickly behind Tad on the off chance he changed his mind and decided to step back inside.

"What a loser," he whispered.

Matthew hated guys like Beaumont, and he knew plenty in their business. Egos were in abundance around the television industry. Both behind, and in front of the camera.

He shook it off and cursed himself once more for forgetting to deep-six the Auburn shirt. It had no place here, where someone might ask questions, just as Tad had. Since most people in town were anti-Auburn, University of Alabama Crimson Tide fans, it would serve as more a ribbing kind of conversation starter, then lead to a local asking if Matthew knew his cousin, so-and-so, who'd gone there. Everybody knew somebody who had attended or was enrolled currently at the rival college, and the two schools were only separated by a two hour and forty-five minute drive. Sometimes, siblings even split loyalties within the families. It was often tough during football season.

Even though Matthew had shed the football player body and image, he still loved the game. He was a rabid fan for his alma mater, and actively anticipated college football season every year. Wearing his old sweatshirt aptly compared to a toddler's woobie blanket, he had to admit. It represented something he loved that comforted him, so getting rid of the shirt during football season wasn't high on his list.

Today had been a bitch of a day. His head camera guy had been out with a stomach bug, and by lunchtime, half the crew had gone down like bowling pins. They'd had to call it a day, and wiped everything down with antibacterial cleaner. Cammie kept such a clean workspace that Matthew doubted the source of the illness was food-borne. It was more likely some nasty virus brought in by somebody whose kid had picked it up at school.

The conversation with his mom and the subsequent, strange visit from the town's narcissistic mayor just put the final lid on the coffin of his gnarly day.

He grabbed a beer from the fridge, the remote control, and clicked on ESPN. Mindless television usually helped. But for some reason he couldn't keep a long-legged blonde out of his head. He grabbed another beer and an unopened bag of pretzels. Maybe some junk food would change the direction of his thoughts.

It didn't help. In fact, he felt a bit queasy.

>>>><<<<

EMMA WAS UP at the crack of dawn, as usual. She'd just taken Big Al for his morning amble and sniff around the neighborhood and was preparing to head over to the diner when her cell rang. "Hello?"

"I'm dying." It was Cammie and she sounded awful.

"Oh, dear. What are you dying from?" Cammie wasn't typically a drama queen, so Emma wondered what was up.

"My insides coming out. Everybody from the set has some kind of virus or food poisoning."

"Oh, yuck. You do sound like total crap, honey. What I can I do for you? Is Grey there? What about Samantha?" Samantha, Grey's nine-year-old daughter with his first and worst wife, Deb, was now in the process of being adopted by Cammie.

"Samantha's at a friend's house, and Grey's in Atlanta at a meeting for a couple days. Can you bring me some Gatorade or something? I didn't want to worry mom."

"Sure thing, kiddo. Do you need some Pepto or saltines?"

"All of it. Anything you can think of. Ugh—gotta go—" The phone clattered to the floor and Emma heard sounds of heaving and retching.

Poor baby. Cammie rarely got sick. She normally had a stomach of iron. Probably from all the cooking she did. Cammie said everyone on the set was sick. Emma wondered if Matthew had gotten the bug or whatever it was as well.

It was a fair assumption Emma wouldn't be helping her sister with makeup since Cammie's face was in the toilet at present, and likely would be most of the day. God bless her.

Emma detested vomit. Really hated it. But one did what one must for those in need, especially family. She settled Al with a brand new, stuffed toy duck, ready to kill, with the squeaker still intact. It would take him at least an hour to tear all the stuffing out of the lifelike waterfowl, find the source of the sound, and liberate it. Then, he would bask in his success by napping for at least another hour, exhausted.

She grabbed Big Louie, her siblings' nickname for her Louis Vuitton purse, and headed out the door. It was a perk of being single and self-sufficient—buying the things she liked. Emma liked nice purses. And shoes. And designer jeans. She was a pageant coach; what would one expect? Maybe she was filling a hole. Who cared? It was her hole to fill.

She hadn't taken time to change out of her yoga clothes or shower, which was unusual for Emma. Putting her best foot forward was a habit borne out of pulling up her big girl panties and pasting on a pretty smile. *Fake it until you make it, right?* Every single day until it had become her normal. Today was an exception. Her sister was ill and required vomit supplies. If Emma raised a few eyebrows in town with no makeup and tennis shoes, so be it.

As she parked she recognized several cars of women she knew. Of course, all the vultures were at the market.

"Emma, is that you, sweetie?" A perfectly-coiffed blonde waved a well-manicured hand as she pushed her buggy toward Emma in the bottled water and sports drinks aisle. An assortment of organic foods was on display in her cart.

"Oh, hey, Bettie Jo."

"Why, Emma. I don't think I've ever seen you so— natural. Aren't you *sweet?*"

Emma pressed her lips together, barely keeping her smile in place. "It's always nice to see you, BJ." *Do you know what your initials stand for?*

And BJ had lived up to her initials quite spectacularly in high school as the blowjob queen behind the bleachers. Emma couldn't help but think nasty thoughts in defense to the unspoken, barely veiled insult.

"Sorry, BJ, I've gotta run. Cammie's got a stomach virus and needs Gatorade."

The woman's eyes bugged, and her lips pursed, eyes hard and angry. "No one calls me that anymore."

"See you later." Emma didn't bother to address her comment, but continued on toward the bright yellowish-green liquid that looked almost as awful as what it was supposed to help, leaving her former classmate posed, hands on hips, staring at Emma's back.

Emma rarely ruffled feathers in town on purpose. In fact, she typically made a rule of going out of her way to placate and please folks, even if they treated her with barely concealed malice. She took their occasional rudeness as her due; innately understanding the female insecurities and jealousies weren't her fault, but theirs. She simply refused to take it personally. She credited her mother for teaching her about mean girls early on—and how not to become one within the pageant scene. Emma saw it for what it was—putting another down to feel superior.

But she'd gone and done it now. BJ would go and tell everybody how rude she'd been and how much she'd resembled a pile of dog shit without makeup and her hair in a ponytail. Emma could hear it now.

"Emma is that you? It *is* you. How's your momma 'n them?" The crinkly face was deceptive, as Emma well knew, as she stood face-to-face with the biddy of all old biddies who ever lived. Mrs. Weed. Mrs. Weed had been the neighborhood babysitter for all the little ones in her area when they were kids. She'd maintained the romper room in her house with the stern discipline and lack of fun like the wicked witch of the west, minus the green skin coloring.

Emma tried to smile. She really did. "Hello, Mrs. Weed. Mom's doing well. She's getting married in a couple weeks, as I'm sure you've heard."

"Oh, yes. I've heard." The thin lips pressed into a white, disapproving line before she sniffed. "I can't imagine her abandoning her dignity and reputation at her age for a *man.*" Oh, and Mrs. Weed detested men.

Emma laughed. "Mrs. Weed, my mother is very happy, I assure you. Howard seems to be a lovely man, and I believe he will be a wonderful husband. We are so excited for them."

The thin white lip line was firmly back in place. "Well, I hope it doesn't hurt her business around town. When people get wind of how she's gone light-skirt, they might think twice about using her facility for their most important celebrations."

Emma really didn't have time for this kind of attack against her sweet mother. "Mrs. Weed, I've known you since I was a little girl, and I've never believed you to be hateful or nasty. Our mother has always spoken highly and with respect for you. I hope that you will do the same about her."

The old woman lowered her head, then looked back up into Emma's eyes. "Emma, I'm ashamed. Please forgive a bitter old woman. Your momma is a sweet soul and has a right to be happy. Not all of us had that chance in life. Please give her my best."

Before Emma could answer, the old woman shuffled away, leaving Emma stunned for a moment. She realized that she could end up like Mrs. Weed. What a sobering thought.

Gathering double the supplies, Emma nodded and waved at a couple other familiar residents, one whose eyebrows shot up when she passed Emma, which resulted in Emma smiling extra wide at her.

⤜⤜⤛⤛

CAMMIE WAS A mess and so was her house. Emma stocked her fridge with ginger ale, Gatorade in all flavors, and Jell-O. Then, she set up a small section on the countertop of chicken bouillon, saltines, and teabags for when her appetite came back. Having watched their mother attend to the five of them growing up, she remembered all the basics of the stomach bug.

Emma tidied up the kitchen and wiped everything down with the antibacterial wipes she found under the kitchen sink. She tiptoed into where Cammie was obviously resting in her bedroom. The sight of her vivacious sister, pale and weak, lying in a tangle of bedcovers softened her heart. "Poor sweetie." Emma had brought a tray in with saltines and a hospital-type plastic mug of ice and ginger ale.

"Let me die." Cammie moaned.

"I would, but your mother would kill me. Remember the bridesmaid dresses we have to wear in a couple weeks." Emma set the tray down and began straightening up her sister's bed. Their mother had always done that when they'd been sick. She said it made her feel better to lie in a neatly made bed.

"Have you stopped throwing up yet?" Emma asked.

"I think so. It's been an hour or so since the last time." Cammie smiled weakly. "Do you mind checking on Matthew? I don't know if he came down with this, but pretty much everyone else did. I know he doesn't have any family in town, and I'd hate it if he was home alone without anything or anyone to help him through this."

Emma had already had that thought. "I'll stop by his house and make sure he's alright. I bought extra supplies just in case."

"Thanks, Emma. You're the best. It's funny; I called you first. I figured everybody else would be busy with their kids and other stuff. I knew you would come take care of me."

"Of course, sweetie. You know good old Emma will come running." It made her sound like a kinder version of Mrs. Weed.

"You know I only meant—"

"You meant you knew I have less on my plate this time

of day, generally. I know it wasn't meant as an insult. You're not the insulting kind, Cammie-girl." But the insinuation that her life was so predictably empty still stung, just a tiny bit, even though it was dead-on accurate.

She tucked the sheets in on her sister's bed and made sure she had everything she needed, and then washed her hands really well.

"I have a couple hours until my clients start rolling in this afternoon, so I'll swing by and check on our Yankee friend. Hopefully, those germs were afraid of him."

Cammie grinned. "He is pretty intimidating at times, but I think he's got a soft spot for you."

Emma laughed. "We got off to a rough start, but I think we understand one another well enough now. But I'm not cleaning up any man's vomit, just to be clear."

No response. Emma looked down at her sleeping sister. Poor thing; she was worn slap out from her battle with the bug. Emma tiptoed out and headed to her car. Hopefully, Emma had disinfected things well enough that Grey and Samantha wouldn't come down with the same illness.

She glanced behind her at the remaining supplies in the back seat. Her Florence Nightingale instincts warred with minding her own business. Matthew hadn't asked for help. Maybe he was just fine. But he didn't have any friends in town that she knew of. Nor was he the type of guy who was likely to reach out even if he was sick and needed assistance—at least that was the impression she'd gotten so far.

Emma sighed. She couldn't very well leave him in the same condition as her sister without any saltines or electrolytes, now could she? She certainly couldn't and feel good about it. Emma just then realized she'd already been driving her car toward his house. She hadn't needed directions. Everyone in town knew where the new hot, single stranger in town had moved in. Emma was surprised he hadn't already been the recipient drive-bys of home-baked goods and casseroles tagged with names and phone numbers of female singles in the area.

Southern women understood the path to a lonely man's heart might well begin with his taste buds. A good casserole and pecan pie couldn't hurt as an introduction. Big hair and a sweet smile when they came to pick up momma's favorite platter worked as a fine follow-up.

Emma had seen the success of this maneuver many times. Men came around on business of one type or the other—mineral rights or what have you–and found themselves completely leg-shackled before they knew what hit them. Mommas around here taught their girls how to spot and hook a promising catch from the time they were in training bras and learned that more eyeliner and mascara was better than less.

Emma pulled up behind Matthew's car and frowned, noticing that his taillight was busted. She got out and pulled the bag of items from the back seat, not giving his car much more thought.

Knocking gently on the door, she figured she would leave the bag on the front step if he didn't answer. He might be sleeping. But what if he'd gotten light-headed, fallen, and hit his head on the bathtub and was knocked-out cold, lying in a pool of his own blood? The thought, while mildly ridiculous, gave her just enough pause to knock again, this time more loudly.

No answer.

She rang the bell.

No answer.

Now she was concerned. His car was in the drive. He was definitely home. Her heart began to beat in her ears.

She tried the door.

Locked. She looked through the leaded glass front door. No movement. Nice house.

She knocked again.

Emma still had the bag in her arm. So, she carried it with her around the back of the house to the screened in porch. The screen door was open, so she stepped up onto the pretty porch with the comfy furniture. It appeared that Matthew spent time out here. There were pillows, a rug, a throw, a couple books, and a lamp. Nice.

She knocked on the back door. No answer. She didn't see anyone inside.

She bit her lip and tried the door. It opened. "Hello? Matthew?"

No answer. She moved inside and let her gaze wander

around the room. It was cozy and well decorated for a guy's place. She noticed the kitchen to the right and headed in that direction. She put her bag on the kitchen counter then headed toward what she knew must be the master bedroom. This house was similar in style to hers.

She called out to him again. Emma was getting worried now. Why didn't he answer?

As she entered the bedroom, she noticed it the blinds were closed and it was rather dark, but she could see no one was in the bed. Then, she realized the shower was running. Against any kind of decent judgment, she moved toward the bathroom door. She couldn't help herself; she peeked inside. He wasn't standing in the shower; he was sitting on the floor. She panicked and rushed towards him before her brain informed her to actually speak his name.

She pulled open the door, certain he was dead before she shrieked, "Matthew, open your damned eyes!"

He did. Open his damned eyes. Opened them really wide. "Emma? Why are you in my shower stall?"

She really didn't have a great answer to that. "Oh, Lord. I thought you were dead." It was the best she could do.

He did look nearly dead. He smiled weakly. "I've been really sick, so I thought I'd sit here for a little while. But I'm not dead. So, um, could you hand me a towel? Unless, of course, you prefer a shower?"

Emma then became acutely aware of her position. And his. He was naked. *Oh, Lord, was he naked.* The most delicious naked she'd ever seen. And now she couldn't stop staring at his naked. And apparently his naked knew it now. Because it was staring straight up at her, too.

"Emma—a towel? Because I'm a little more inclined to invite you into my shower now."

She raised her eyes beyond his naked to his eyes, horrified. "Uh, a towel. Sure." Looking around, she grabbed the closest towel she could find, the one hanging on a hook beside the shower. "I thought you were dead," she said again, as an explanation.

She was a complete idiot. And now she wanted to jump his sick bones.

Just as quickly as she heard him turn the water off, he all but shoved her out of his way to get to the toilet and throw up. That was enough motivation for Emma to snap out of it and get the hell out of sick, naked Matthew's bathroom.

While he was getting his clothes on, she did the same things she'd done for Cammie. After everything had been sanitized, she brought in a tray with saltines and ginger ale. She found him lying weakly in his bed wishing for death to take him.

"I'm sorry I invaded your privacy. Cammie asked me to come check on you. She's sick and wondered if you'd come down with the virus, too. When you didn't answer, I thought maybe you'd had an accident."

He opened one eye. "That's a bit of a stretch, don't you think?"

She grinned. "Probably. But I'm known for my dramatic flair on occasion. I'm artistic, in case you haven't heard." She straightened his bed like she'd done for her sister.

"Are you mothering me?" he asked.

"My mother always said you feel better when your bed isn't a mess."

"She's right. Thanks. Sorry you had to—see that."

"That's okay. It's nothing I haven't seen before." She swished her hand as if waving his words away.

"Not that. I meant, the throwing up part. I don't think anyone has seen me bare-assed, hanging over a toilet before. It's not very manly."

"I have an aversion to vomit, so I excused myself from the room as soon as I knew what was happening. Don't worry, still manly." She envisioned the other manly part and kept her opinion of that to herself. Holy moly, every bit of him was manly. It was all burned into her brain permanently.

"I've brought saltines, Gatorade, chicken broth, and ginger ale. Call me if you need anything. If it's a twenty-four hour bug, you should be fine in the morning."

"Emma, thanks again. I appreciate your looking out for me."

"We really need to find you some friends in town." She smiled and left the room.

Her legs were shaky. She could never look at him the same way again—not without mentally undressing him, knowing what lay beneath. She drew another unsteady breath.

As she passed his car on the way to hers, she again noticed the broken taillight. It made her pause, enough that she stopped, bent down and looked more closely and saw a small pile of broken red clearish plastic—his remaining taillight pieces. There wasn't a dent on the really nice slick, black Mercedes that she could see. What an odd thing. She'd meant to ask him about it while she'd been inside, but had been a little—uh—distracted by other things a few moments ago.

Should she go back and say something about this? Did he know? It almost looked like vandalism to her untrained eye. Like someone had come up with a tool or hammer and just tapped hard enough to break the taillight and the little light bulb inside and nothing else. Weird. Pulling out her phone, she snapped a quick picture of both the rear of the car and the little pile of plastic on the ground.

Avoiding another possible encounter so soon with naked Matthew might be wise, because this time she might just jump his bones whether he puked on her or not. The thought was deeply humiliating, even to herself. *But he'd been so naked.*

Oh, my. She was a little hot and bothered.

Emma climbed inside her car, rolled down the window to get a little air, and made a mental note to call him tomorrow. She'd ask about his broken light then.

Chapter Seven

"REMEMBER, LADIES, NO one else knows how you feel or what you're thinking. They only know what they see. If the judges see confidence, fantastic posture, and relaxed, graceful movement, they are sold on you. If your movements are uncertain and you show that you're not comfortable in your own skin, then you might as well hightail it home." Emma's least favorite evening of the week was upon her. The blonde threesome was in the house.

"I don't think *I'll* have a problem with my confidence." Judith assured them with a toss of her blonde hair and a smirk.

The massive eye-roll her sister, Jamie, then performed behind her back surely stretched ligaments within her sockets that weren't meant to take that sort of strain without damage. Then again, Emma was certain both sisters' eyes were well exercised over the years of just such behavior.

Sadie laughed at Jamie's expression, which made Judith's head whip around toward her sister. That pulled Judith off her precarious balance in her five-inch, high heels on the studio's runway, which stood three feet above the regular floor. What happened next, Emma would look back on with a mixture of horror and regret that she hadn't had a video camera to capture every detail for the retelling of it.

Judith fell. She didn't just fall—she more cartwheeled as she lost her balance, twisted her ankle, and missed solid ground on the way down with a screech and a very loud crash. The others' expressions were a mixture of shocked surprise. No one moved for a split second.

"Oh, my Lord! Judith! Are you dead?" Jamie, for once, sounded genuinely concerned for her sister.

Emma made a dash over to where Judith was lying in a heap, not moving. She'd crashed into a chair on the way down. That chair was now upside down beside her. There was blood.

"Call 9-1-1." Emma barked at the other two women.

One of them pulled out a cell phone and Emma heard Jamie making the call.

"Judith. Can you hear me?" The woman's eyes fluttered and she moaned.

Thank God. She wasn't dead. But there was an oozing gash on her forehead that was swelling and turning bright purple.

"Get her some ice out of the freezer, Sadie. There's a plastic baggie in the drawer beside it." The other woman shuffled around, obviously following directions.

Emma thankfully had a refrigerator with a small freezer on top. She always kept ice on hand for any kind of injury. And baggies. Not every young lady was born with the grace of a gazelle. And, God bless 'em, Emma had coached her share. While trying to develop grace, some pretty klutzy things tended to occur.

Judith moaned again. Her eyes were opened now, but they weren't focused.

"Judith, help is on the way. Can you talk to me? Do you know where you are?"

She winced, then raised a hand toward the injury on her head.

Emma caught her hand gently. "You've got a little bump on your head. We're getting you some ice."

Just then, Judith moved her leg and let out a blood-curdling scream. Emma looked down, toward the injured woman's legs. And she nearly passed out. Judith's foot was turned outward in a completely unnatural angle.

Emma grabbed both of Judith's wrists then and pinned them down. She put her face right over Judith's and said very calmly—at least as calmly as she could manage, "Judith, be very still. Your ankle might be broken, so you don't want to move it."

Judith's face was turning very grey and her breathing had become shallow and fast. Emma knew beyond a doubt that Judith was going into shock.

Sadie came around the corner of the runway at that moment with the bag of ice.

She gasped. "Oh, no. Oh, my gosh. Her leg—" Sadie slid down beside Emma, clearly having a visceral reaction similar to her own.

"Sadie, we need to keep Jamie from seeing her like this. Go over to where she is and tell her to stay outside and watch for the ambulance. Then, look in the closet and bring me a blanket.

"She's still on the line with the 9-1-1 operator. I'll make sure she doesn't come back until they get here." Sadie's hand was shaking when she handed the bag of ice over to Emma.

"M-my leg." Judith croaked. Her eyes were wide, pupils dilated.

"You're in shock. But you're going to be okay. Stay with me, Judith. Jamie called the ambulance. Help is on the way."

Judith squeezed a tear out the corner of her eye. "I'm scared."

Emma wiped away a tear of her own. "I know. Me, too. But it's going to be okay. I promise. I'm so sorry you were hurt, Judith." She could never stand to see anyone in pain. When her siblings were hurt or sick as kids, Emma suffered too.

"Where's my sister?" Jamie wasn't having it, apparently. "I need to see Judith, right now."

Emma heard her before she saw her. "Jamie, she's okay, but I really don't think—"

Too late.

"Oh, my Lord, Judith, your leg's broken half in two!" Nothing like overstating the obvious and trying to keep the patient calm.

Judith began making keening noises. Emma tried to shush her.

"Jamie, we need to keep her calm," Emma said sternly, hitting her with a meaningful stink-eye.

Jamie appeared ready to go on a tirade when her body language changed completely, and she… smiled.

What on earth?

Matthew appeared from around the corner, eyes concerned. "Emma, are you alright?"

She nearly fainted with relief. No wonder Jamie smiled. A big, strong man had come rushing in.

"I'm fine. But Matthew, look at Judith's ankle," she whispered and pointed.

He did then, and frowned. He noticed Judith's glazed eyes and shocky look. "Go get her another blanket. We can't move her until the ambulance gets here."

He took over talking to Judith. "Hey there, beautiful lady…" He was obviously good in a crisis.

Jamie slid down and sat next to him. As Emma reached the closet, she heard the siren and saw the flashing lights. *Finally.*

>>>>><<<<<

AT THE HOSPITAL, chaos reigned. The husband brothers

arrived about the same time as the ambulance carrying the sister wives. Brothers marrying sisters still made Emma's head spin with confusion. Matthew had driven her and Sadie to the hospital, but Sadie had called Tad in to pick her up because she'd ridden over to Emma's studio with the Fremont sisters for pageant practice. Surprisingly, Tad waited out in the car for his wife instead of bursting in on the scene and trying to divert attention to himself. Curious. It was unlike him to pass on such a ripe opportunity.

They were all now in the surgical waiting area, well, all except Judith, who was in surgery having her ankle repaired with who-knew how many plates and pins. She'd likely set off metal detectors in the airport for the rest of her natural life.

"What the hell happened?" Judith's husband, Jefferson Fremont, asked Jamie and Emma, though he didn't deign to speak directly to Emma.

Jefferson had made a play for Emma back in high school, and when she'd quietly turned him down, he'd held it against her all these years. Jefferson had gone to a rival high school, thankfully, but it was a small community, and word had gotten around that she'd turned him down in favor of Terrific Tad. So, his male ego and pride being what it was, he'd just dismissed her as beneath him and moved forward, holding a grudge. Perhaps that was why Jamie and Judith both snickered behind her back as well.

Jamie was sitting between the two Fremont brothers and

answered before anyone else. "It was that runway thing at Emma's place. It's so narrow; I almost fell off the thing last week in my flats."

Hot color surged into Emma's cheeks. Now it was *her* fault? But the accident had happened at her business on her property. So, instead of allowing Jamie and company to see how her comment had gotten under her skin, she directed her comment to Jefferson. "I have insurance, Jefferson, but I'll need to go get the paperwork." Then she stood, and turned toward Jamie. "If the two of you hadn't been so busy swapping insults, as usual, Judith might not have lost her concentration and taken a swan dive off the runway."

Matthew stood then, "I'll drive you." He gently wrapped his big hand around her elbow and nudged her away from the Dozier-Fremonts.

Once they were outside the hospital and walking toward his car, it was all Emma could do not to shriek in frustration. "I know I shouldn't have given in and said that. But those women are the devil!"

Matthew chuckled. "I think it's not just the women. I'm beginning to suspect Tad Beaumont of some nastiness, too."

Emma's head whipped around. "What do you mean?"

"He stopped by my house a few days ago in his unofficial mayoral role to make sure I was settling in. He wanted to know if there was anything he could do to make my transition from the big city easier."

She narrowed her eyes. "Hmm. Sounds like he was up to

something."

Matthew nodded. "Later that evening I came down with the stomach bug, and I hadn't left the house until I was on my way to your studio tonight to thank you for bringing me the crackers and stuff."

She nodded, face flushing again at the memory of that ill-fated evening when she'd entered the bathroom and found him stark naked.

He cleared his throat. "Anyway, I was pulled over by one of Ministry's finest for a broken taillight on my way over to see you."

Then it hit her. "Oh, my goodness, I saw your broken taillight on your car in the driveway when I left that night. There was a little pile of red glass right under it. I thought it was weird that the glass was still there. If you hit something in a car, the glass doesn't follow you home. Wait, I took a picture."

She pulled out her cell phone and showed him the photos she'd taken. "I'm sorry I didn't think of it before now. I've been busy with my classes and family stuff." But she'd thought of him. Oh, boy, had she thought of the last time she'd seen him.

He took the cell phone from her hand and looked carefully at the photo, then nodded. "I'm sure he was trying to send me a message."

"To stay away from me," Emma said, fisting her hands until her nails dug in.

"I definitely got the good ole boy, 'We'll let you off with a warning this time, but you'd better watch your step around here, city boy.'" Matthew put on such an authentic Alabama accent, it freaked her out.

Then, he pretended to spit tobacco like a true hayseed redneck. Just like Boss Hogg on the *Dukes of Hazzard*.

She laughed. "That was really good. You should go into television or movies—oh, wait." He rolled his eyes at her. Then, she said, "Maybe we shouldn't be seen together."

His expression darkened. "Are you kidding? I'm not afraid of a pissant like Tad Beaumont." He didn't look afraid at all. In fact, he appeared more than ready to defend himself and her.

Emma bit her lip. "He has a lot of pull around here and can make life miserable if you cross him." Back to the reality of things.

"What's he going to do? Have his minions on the police force put me in jail?" He snorted. Then, their gazes connected, and they realized Tad had the power to do exactly that.

They headed inside her house to retrieve the insurance papers from the safe inside her bedroom. Having him there beside her wasn't so great for her peace of mind. He was so manly. She'd even seen him naked. And here he was, in her bedroom.

"The safe's back in my closet," she said over her shoulder as they walked into the bedroom.

HER BEDROOM, LIKE everything else about Emma Laroux, was beyond sexy. She sauntered inside the closet with a sway of hips that was as natural as breathing to every other mortal on the planet. She moved like no woman he'd ever met. Pure grace and style in every gesture and step. She'd never believe that kind of line if he tried it on her, but it was true.

The bed was a huge, four-poster with a fluffy white duvet covered in pillows. His jeans tightened just looking at it. Did the woman have no clue how she affected men? How she affected him? She behaved with no apparent guile whatsoever. But her appeal was pure Eve—totally organic and not derived from anything artificial.

He'd never experienced such a base level of attraction to anyone. Even when he'd met her the first time, nearly ten years ago on that fateful weekend, when she'd been in whatever kind of stupor, she'd been utterly gorgeous. But, at the time, he'd not allowed himself the indulgence of attraction. She'd been compromised, and he'd taken on the role of protector only. Men who took advantage of women in that state were the lowest form of scum, in his opinion. That tick of guilt crept in, and he again firmly pushed it back. He *would* tell her about meeting her before. But not today.

"Found them." He heard her say from her cavernous closet, which looked to be nearly as large as her master bedroom—which was quite generously-sized by any standard.

He'd approached the doorway to the closet, somewhat

blocking the way out. She made to squeeze by and he gently put his fingers around her wrist. "Tough day, huh?" This surge of attraction, coupled with an over whelming urge to protect her had him pulling her close.

Emma sighed raggedly, allowing it. His arms went around her shoulders, and she shivered as she stepped into his embrace. His body instantly responded to having her curvy one cuddled against his. He was sure she was aware of his—response. But instead of pushing away, she unexpectedly pressed closer, especially *that* part of him. With her arms around his waist, it was obvious. He kissed the top of her hair, which smelled like the honeysuckle that used to bloom along his grandmother's fence.

Then, she raised her face to his. He saw in her eyes a desire that matched his and somewhat of a challenge in her gaze. Matthew wasn't the sort to back down from such a delicious challenge.

He kissed her, softly at first, to see what she had in mind, but Emma didn't seem to want softness at the moment. This first kiss rapidly developed into a hungry, needful meeting of lips.

Were her legs really wrapped around his waist? *Holy God.* And look, her bed was right there.

A cell phone vibrated between them. Hers? His?

Emma's rational thought seemed to return just then. "Oh…oh—the papers." The envelope containing the insurance papers had fallen and scattered on the floor during their acrobatic embrace.

She pulled free, hair wild from one of his hands roaming free in it. The other hand, well, that hand had been having a bit more fun running bases.

"H-hello? Yes, I found the paperwork. I'm on the way," Emma said shakily into the phone. "Has there been any news?"

She hadn't met his eyes yet. He hoped Emma didn't have regrets. Certainly, there were none on his part. Best thing that'd happened since he'd set foot back in Alabama as far as he was concerned. Allergies, a panic attack, and stomach virus in the span of a couple weeks. Yep, definitely top of the list by a long shot.

"Okay. Thanks." She pressed disconnect on her phone, then looked him in the eye. Of course she looked him in the eye. She was Emma Laroux.

"Everything okay?" He asked, his meaning slightly double-edged.

"Jamie says Judith had to have a metal rod, plates, and pins put in, and will be incapacitated for awhile." She didn't acknowledge the double meaning, obviously choosing the easier path.

"Sounds painful. But after meeting those girls, I'm certain there's enough stubborn there to get her back on her feet soon enough."

Emma nodded. "No doubt." Then she narrowed her eyes at him. "You know, I wasn't going to sleep with you tonight."

So, she did want to engage. "I was giving you an encouraging little hug, and you nearly mauled me." He wiggled his brows at her. "I liked it."

She laughed. "Asshole." Then turned away and headed toward the door that led to her driveway. "This can't go anywhere, you know. I don't date."

"I didn't ask you to be my girlfriend." He smirked. His feelings might be a little hurt.

"Well, fine. Just so you know. It won't happen again." With a toss of her head, she led the way outside.

➤➤➤◄◄◄

TAD PULLED OUT the photographs and spread them on the table. This was his special time with Emma Jean. He loved looking at her like this. The way she used to be. The pictures showed a young, stunningly confident woman wearing a figure-hugging beaded evening gown. She was beaming, wearing her Miss Alabama crown. Had there been a more exciting night? He didn't think so. Emma had reached the top, and her success had been his. With her on his arm, he was a king no matter where they went in Alabama. She was the most beautiful woman in the state and wore the crown to prove it.

Until she'd gone and ruined everything for him. That fateful night, when things were supposed to be so perfect. He'd only wanted to enhance his and Emma's evening. But she'd gone and screwed it up for both of them by getting herself compromised. Tad shook his head. No, he shouldn't have left her alone, but who knew she would have her wits about her enough to get up and leave the damned room? It was supposed to be innocent fun.

He'd had to break off their relationship. She'd stepped down from her title as Miss Alabama, and wouldn't be involved in the Miss America Pageant. No, the first runner-up would have that opportunity. If Emma'd only stayed where he'd left her that night while he went to retrieve their companion. Oh, it would have been perfect. He got hard just looking at the photos of his Emma Jean and how she used to shine.

A sharp knock startled him. "Tad. Can you call the hospital and check on Judith? They won't give me any information at the desk, and I can't reach Jamie." It was his sweet Sadie. His second choice.

"I asked you not to disturb my work, Sadie," He tried not to sound as completely annoyed as he was.

"What are you doing in there, Tad?" She dared to ask.

"It's none of your concern. I'll be out in a minute."

Sadie knew her place better than to demand to know how he spent his time. Perhaps she was overwrought. Yes, that was the only thing that might explain her impertinence.

He was careful to lock the door when he spent time with his darling, Emma Jean. The idea of her spending her time with other men still made him physically ill. His sweet Sadie likely wouldn't understand what Emma Jean represented to him. The past that had to remain unsullied. The past Emma represented. He had to preserve her—not to have for himself, it was too late for that after what had happened, but he couldn't let another man touch her and ruin what had been near perfection. Plus, he had a wife and was the mayor. He wouldn't allow his own reputation to suffer by being an adulterer.

That Matthew Pope was the closest he'd ever come so far to having to take real action. Emma Jean had been so easy to keep in line until he'd come along. Maybe the warnings Tad had issued were too subtle. Surely, Emma Jean realized he'd keep his promise to ruin her family's reputation or worse. He didn't give two shits about them. They were white trash as far as he was concerned, along with most of this town.

The traffic stop obviously didn't leave an impression. Perhaps he'd have to ramp up his efforts, just to make certain the man didn't put his hands on her. He really couldn't have that.

He had a powerful family at his disposal, gobs of lovely money, political pull, and power all over the state, and control over all the city municipalities in Ministry. He could do all sorts of really awful things to dissuade Matthew Pope from living here. But he hoped it wouldn't come to that. He really did consider himself a good guy.

It was time to thoroughly research Matthew Pope and find out exactly who this guy was. He'd ask around about him to some of his Auburn friends who'd attended around the same time. It was a big school, but like the South, it wasn't so big that Tad couldn't find who he was looking for if he set his mind to it. Certainly not with his connections.

⊱⊱⊱≪≪

MATTHEW INSISTED ON following Emma home from the hospital after she'd provided all her insurance info to Judith's husband. Emma wouldn't have been the least bit surprised if they'd cut open an artery and taken her blood as well, considering the grilling she'd gotten, not only from Judith's parents, who had arrived while Emma was getting the paperwork, but from the police as well. One would think Emma had actually shoved Judith off the catwalk herself, the way she'd been treated by the near-mob at the hospital-sitting vigil. Emma understood their worry. She was concerned about Judith as well. The accident had been scary as hell for all of them.

Now that she was finally home, the last thing she needed was Matthew Pope tucking her in. So, the second she shifted into park, she wasted no time hopping out and heading back to where he was sitting inside his car.

"Thanks for everything tonight," she said from beside his open window.

"Do you want me to come in? You've had a pretty traumatic evening." His eyes were concerned.

She yawned and stretched for effect. "No. I think I'm

just going to go in and crash. I'm beat. But, I appreciate your coming to the rescue. You showed up just as things were getting hairy. I'm not sure what I would have done without you tonight." She smiled.

He reached out and gently encircled her wrist, pulling her toward him. "Are you sure you don't want me to hold your hand while you fall asleep." He wiggled his brows suggestively and inclined his head toward her house.

She disentangled her wrist slowly, fighting the urge to snatch it away like she'd been burned. "Um, no. That can't happen, as I told you earlier. I'm not in the market."

He shrugged and grinned. "Just wanted to make sure."

She wiggled her fingers in a playful wave. "See you on the set, Romeo." Then, she turned and resolutely walked into the house, not allowing herself to glance back.

Because he had no idea how much she wanted to drag him inside, fling him onto her down comforter, and do all the naughty things. He really did inspire new feelings within her. Deep down, carefully suppressed feelings she'd managed to keep control of for these past years. Why him? Why now?

It did not bode well. Emma was rather afraid her horny genie was out of the bottle. God help her.

She remembered then she'd silenced her phone at the hospital. The second she turned it back on it lit up like the Griswold's yard at Christmas. Texts, voice messages, missed calls and Facebook messages galore. All from her family, of course, wanting to know if everything was alright, if and how they could help, and did she need them to come stay with her? And many demands to call back or text immediately and let them know she was okay.

So, she dialed her mother first. "Mom? No, no. Everything's alright. Judith fell and broke her ankle and hit her head at the studio."

Her mother, a woman whose nerves were carved from pure granite when it came to stressful situations said, "Candy from the front desk over at the hospital called your sister, Jo Jo. Sounds like a real sad mess. Where's Judith now?" Her mother asked.

"She's out of surgery now, and the doctor says she should make a full recovery in a couple of months."

"Months? Lordy be. Was it that bad?" Her mother sounded concerned.

"Yes, unfortunately it was."

"Honey, how are you holding up? I know that must have been mighty upsetting for you."

"I'm okay. Matthew showed up right about the time things were headed South, but he helped keep it all from blowing up." Emma stretched out on her sofa; every muscle ached.

"Well, I imagine with all three of those girls in the midst, it could've turned into a real brouhaha."

"Mom, Judith was very badly hurt."

"I don't mean to be unkind, dear, I simply have known those girls their whole lives. You know I wish Judith well in her recovery." Mom wasn't a mean-spirited person, so Emma knew her comments weren't intended to be spiteful, only honest.

"I know you do; and yes, there was a ton of drama from Jamie, as you might expect, but nothing I couldn't handle. She was worried about her sister. Please tell everyone I'm okay and I'll talk to them tomorrow. Thanks, Mom. Love you." Emma was ready to hit her bed fully dressed at this point.

"Oh, and Emma?"

"Yes, Mom?"

"I hope you'll invite that young man to the wedding as your guest. Sounds like a good one to have around."

No strength left to argue, she said, "I'll think about it."

"Good night, darling—get some rest." Oh, her mother was a sly one, alright.

"'Night, Mom."

Chapter Eight

❦

THE NEXT WEEK flew by with pageant contestants doubling and tripling their private and semi-private lessons. Several festivals and big pageants were coming up, including the junior Miss Alabama and Miss Alabama pageants. So, the official "pageant season" began for Emma. Her busiest time of the year left her little time to do much more than maintain her studio and fall into bed exhausted each night. She did run over to Cammie's cooking show set early in the mornings on shooting days and do her sister's makeup and hair. Emma trained one of the girls Cammie had hired to do her touch-ups in between scenes.

The network had finally hired a clothing stylist/makeup artist/hair stylist from New York to take over the job next week, so it would lessen Emma's long hours a little once that happened. It seemed no one wanted to make their home in Ministry, Alabama. Hopefully, the girl would understand that in Ministry purple hair, multiple piercings, neck tattoos, and Lord knew what else might travel down from the big city in the name of style wouldn't quite fit in here. Emma had never heard of one person handling all those roles on a set before, but it seemed whomever they'd found fit the bill. Personally, Emma hoped so.

Not that she minded making her little sis shine; it was just getting hard to fit everything into her day. Plus, there was that not insignificant issue of fighting her ever-growing attraction to Matthew. The less she saw of him, the better. He seemed to make it his mission to put himself in her path every time they were in the same vicinity.

"I'm going to miss our mornings together," Cammie said, as Emma was putting the veil of finishing powder to make her camera-ready.

Emma grinned. "Me, too. It's been a fun few weeks. I hope they don't bring in a hippy freak to style you."

Cammie made a face. "I hadn't thought about that. Maybe I should ask Brent at the station who it is they are planning to send."

"I was just kidding. I'm certain that whomever they send, she will be perfectly capable. Or I'll have to whip her into shape."

"You'd be the one to do it, that's for sure."

The announcement came that Cammie was needed on set.

"Oh, gotta go. Thanks again."

"Sure, kiddo." Emma waved her toward the set.

"Hey there, can I walk you out?" She'd turned her back,

just for a second.

"How do you do that?" she asked.

"What?" He was pure innocence.

"Sneak up on me like that." She frowned.

It was better than climbing him, which was what she wanted to do.

"Have dinner with me."

"I can't." She began walking toward the foyer with him beside her. "I've got a late evening at the studio."

"After. I'll pick up food and meet you at your house. You've got to eat." She made the fatal mistake; she looked him in the eye. *Damn it.*

"Soul food?" she asked, almost in a whisper.

"You got it. See you around nine."

"Uh. Okay." *Crap.* Now what had she done?

Then he leaned down and whispered in her ear, "Oh, and this *is* a date."

His breath was hot and traveled down her neck. It made her shiver and it made her burn. How had that happened? Before she could protest, he was headed back toward the set, whistling.

She hadn't wanted this, had she? No. *Liar.* She wanted it all right. She wanted him with every tiny ounce of the stuff that made women want men. The long, long dry spell she'd forced on herself but blamed on Tad's underlying threats were the problem. She was responsible for her current situation. But what would this mean for her immediate future?

Without daring another glance backward, she made a very stealthy exit, trying her best not to make a sound or stir any attention toward herself that might garner notice. Her brain was entirely too full of thoughts to make small talk or big talk.

Emma put her car in gear and headed toward the rehab wing of the hospital where Judith had been moved. Emma picked up a small nosegay of yellow daisies to bring with her. The plan was to stop by and check on the injured woman and then swing by Mom's house and check on Big Al. Judith's surgery had gone better than the surgeon had predicted. She'd be wheeling around with the aid of a tiny leg scooter and a cast in a few days. The head injury, once cleaned, had required a couple stitches, but wasn't a concussion, according to the neurologist, thankfully.

Of course, Emma was nowhere near off the hook where Judith was concerned. Hopefully, there wouldn't be a lawsuit. If there was, Emma was well-insured, but in a town like this, Emma would have to tiptoe around, flatter, and for lack of a better term, do some serious ass-kissing to save her business' reputation and her own. Rumors and gossip were unavoidable, and Emma depended on Judith and her family's goodwill not to do a number on her. Emma understood owning a business had its risks—and serving clients like Judith was one of them. When somebody got hurt in your place, you were responsible... period.

"Hey there." Emma called as she knocked lightly on the partially opened door. She almost hid her tiny nosegay of daisies when she noticed the room was so filled with the kind of oversized, fresh flower arrangements Emma had only seen at weddings and funerals. She wanted to ask if someone had died, but bit her tongue just in time. That wouldn't help her case.

"Oh, hi, Emma." Judith's leg was elevated and was held in place by a complicated-looking contraption that was moving it every few seconds as it hummed. Judith did not appear pleased, if her pained expression was any indication.

"How are you feeling?" Emma asked gently.

"I'd be a lot better if the stupid doctor didn't insist on torturing me with this *thing* out of the dark ages. Can't they just put a cast on it and let me go home?"

"It does look like something from the dark ages. When did they say you'd be able to leave?" Emma asked.

She made a face. "Tomorrow, if I do what they say." Judith spotted the flowers behind Emma's back and her expression brightened. "Are those for me?"

"Oh, yes." Emma gestured around the room. "Looks like everybody in town's heard about your fall."

"Junior League." Judith rolled her eyes. "They know I'm in charge of membership and half of them want me to write sorority rec letters for their girls heading to college in the next few years. Suck-ups. I think they all wanted to see who could send the biggest arrangement."

Emma laughed behind her hand. "I almost asked who died, but didn't want to hurt your feelings."

Judith burst out laughing. "Maybe somebody died and I can donate these ass-kisser flowers to their funeral."

They both laughed. Then, Judith winced. "Ow."

"Oh, are you alright?" Emma moved closer, genuinely concerned.

"The pain meds have been so good that I forgot myself for a minute," Judith said. "Look, Emma, I know I can be a pain in the butt most of the time. Truth is, everyone expects it. But I'm not going to sue you, so you don't have to keep coming over to check on me. I fell off my high heels. It's not the first time, won't be the last. The attention's been nice. Most of the time, I have to be bitchy to get anyone to notice me."

Emma thought that was terribly sad. "Judith, I don't know what to say. I hate to see you in pain, and I really am concerned."

"Would you have bothered to visit me if this"—she motioned to her foot and then to the bandage on her head—"hadn't happened at your place?"

Emma wasn't a liar, which was what made her hesitate a split second before answering.

"That's what I mean. And I appreciate your honesty. Maybe I don't deserve real friends, only ones that compete with each other to stay in my good graces for what I can give them. Anyway, I don't blame you, and you won't be hearing from my attorneys, or my husband. So, rest easy." Judith gave her a sad smile.

Emma might sometimes exude a tough, confident exterior, but in so many ways, she felt exactly like Judith had just described herself. "Judith, I'd like for us to be friends, real friends. I know how you feel. My best friends are my sisters because I don't trust many other women's motives. What do you say?"

Judith eyed her suspiciously. "Do you want to be in Junior League or have a daughter that wants to be in a sorority?"

Emma crossed her heart. "Not me. I wouldn't be caught dead at a Junior League meeting—no offense. And, I might ask for a recommendation in about twenty years for my as yet unborn daughter. But that's looking less and less likely."

Judith smiled. "Alright, Emma Jean Laroux. We can be real friends. If you don't tell anyone my secret."

"What secret?" Emma asked.

"That I'm not really as big of a bitch wagon as I pretend, and that I work it for attention and to keep the phonies guessing."

"I'll take it to my grave," Emma said solemnly.

"If you have any deep, dark secrets you need to share, I'm a relative Fort Knox. I gossip with the best of them, but never reveal a confidence. I'll bet you've wondered why Sadie and I are such good friends. Well, it's because she knows the real me. She's a sweetie, by the way. My sister, too."

"I'm glad to know that. I like them both."

Judith stuck out her hand as if to shake on a blood oath. Emma took it.

Just then, as they were shaking hands, Judith's husband entered. His eyebrows went up, as if he what he witnessed shocked him to the bone.

"Oh, hey, Jefferson." Emma forced him to acknowledge her.

"Hi, Emma. What are you doing here?" His voice was cool and not especially welcoming.

"Jefferson! How rude. Emma and I have come to an understanding." She gave him a look. "From now on, Jefferson, you will be courteous to Emma. We are friends. I know she blew you off in high school. Get over it."

Emma's eyes went wide. Jefferson's face turned bright red and Emma wasn't sure what would happen next.

But he recovered nicely. "Well, Judith, you certainly know how to put a fine point on things, don't you, dear? Must be the fantastic pain meds." He turned to Emma, extending his hand in friendship. "Please forgive my rudeness, Emma. Judith has no issue letting me know when I'm behaving like a horse's ass."

She shook his hand. "No problem, Jefferson. Please let me know if there's anything I can do for Judith while she recovers."

Judith piped up. "Just stop by the house and have lunch with me. Being confined is going to drive me crazy, which will make me drive everybody else crazy."

Jefferson cleared his throat. "Yes, please do, Emma."

Emma smiled at both and made her way outside. Well, that went differently than expected, thank heavens.

⟫⟪

MAUREEN LAROUX WAS a practical woman. At least she'd always been one up until now. Now, she was planning her wedding to the man who'd fathered her oldest child. Not that he'd known it for the first thirty-five years of Maeve's life. But they'd gotten past that. He'd left Maureen at the altar all those years ago. It hadn't been his fault or hers. They'd gotten past that, too. Would they survive this wedding?

"Darlin,' I don't give a bald rat's behind what flavor our cake is, and you know it," Howard said.

She smiled at him sweetly. "Yes, but you deprived me of going through this the first time around. So, my love, you will try this cake and give your honest opinion. Please?"

He kissed her on the forehead and huffed. Typical man. But there wasn't anything typical about her Howard. Nope, not a thing. He took a bite and nearly choked. "It tastes like grass from the pasture." He managed to say after he'd spit it out in the trash. "What in God's name is that flavor, woman?"

"It has a hint of basil, I think." She sniffed it. "Oh, my. More than a hint, I'd say. I'll pass on trying it and take your word for it, dear."

"Hon, let's just get the white one. That's all we'll remember when it's over anyway."

She grinned. "White. Got it. You're dismissed from cake tasting for now. Have you spoken with Maeve this week?"

He looked down at his feet as if they could tell him the answer.

"You've got to reach out to her." She laid a hand on his arm. He was so dear.

"She scares the hell out of me," he admitted.

"I know. All of this has been especially hard on her. But I know she's not holding a grudge. I believe it's more about her feeling disloyal to the father who raised her."

"I've missed her whole life." His eyes were weary.

"Not her whole life, and not Lucy's."

"You're right and so wise, as usual. How did I live this many years without you?" He pulled her into his very strong arms.

"I don't know. But you don't have to live another day without me. Aren't you a lucky guy?" She teased.

"So incredibly lucky."

"I'll be even luckier when we don't have cakes and flowers to worry about anymore."

"Go. Out. I'll finish up here." She shooed him toward the door. "And please call Maeve."

"Yes'm."

Maureen thought about her children. About Cammie and Grey, now happily married after what seemed like a hopelessly miserable past filled with betrayal and lies. Her situation mirrored theirs in a way. Things had changed so much this year. Ben was still the most eligible bachelor in town, or more like the state of Alabama, to be truthful. But he would be okay. His own stubbornness kept him from finding the right girl.

JoJo was happily married with two adorable children. She was stable and always had been. Maeve was in crisis, but she had her lovely daughter, Lucy and her husband, Junior, to remind her of what was important. The rest of her siblings had circled around her the minute Howard had entered, or reentered, their lives. They had her back.

Right now, she fretted over Emma. Emma had flown under the radar these past several years. But suddenly Maureen was seeing some changes in her behavior. Changes could mean instability. Emma had always been a little high-strung, but completely reliable in every way. Well, except around the time she'd stepped down from her title as Miss Alabama. They'd all tried to figure out what had happened, but she'd never really given a good answer, only that she couldn't go through with it. Then, Tad had broken up with her. Maybe he'd broken up with her first and that had been why.

Maureen carried a mother's burden of guilt for not spending more time and care to get to the bottom of things, and for taking Emma at her word. Having Emma away at college had in some ways been easier after their father had passed. Maureen had struggled for such a long time after Justin's drowning and the children had as well.

As she sat staring out her kitchen window, sipping on a cup of coffee, she decided to get to the bottom of Emma's big mystery. Not because she was a nosy momma, but because she really believed Emma was stuck. She hadn't moved forward with her life. Not with the important stuff.

The back screen door banged. Maureen looked up to see her big, handsome son, Ben, come into her kitchen. It never failed to fill her with pride at these adults she raised. Their father would be so proud.

"Hi, honey. To what do I owe such a nice surprise?"

"I had to speak with a client about a goat and thought I'd stop by." She grinned, but he waved away the question in her eyes. "Really, don't ask."

"Well, I won't look a gift goat in the mouth—"

"Ugh. I had that coming." He gave her a hug and moved toward the coffeemaker.

"Help yourself. Coffee's fresh. And there's cake."

He grinned. "Looks like somebody's getting married."

It wasn't unusual for there to be mountains of wedding cake, birthday cake, and every other kind of cake lying about the kitchen since her house doubled as an event planning, hosting, and catering venue. The kids had grown up dashing through other people's occasions taking place within their own home. The house was a gigantic centuries-old planta-tion passed down from Maureen's mother's side of the family. It was known far and wide as The Evangeline House.

"That's the tasting cake for my wedding. Watch out for the basil-flavored one. Tastes like the pasture, according to Howard."

"Got it." He joined her at the oversized farmhouse kitchen table. "So, do you know what's going on with Emma and this director guy? I'm hearing rumors and getting a weird vibe. It's making me nervous."

Funny how her children were so intuitive to each other's energy.

⇛⇜

IT SEEMED LIKE every overprotective, shrieky momma in town graced her studio today. They were all stressed. It was time to outfit the darlings for all the events. There were garment bags everywhere. They all wanted her opinion. She appreciated that and could give good advice, but it got hairy sometimes.

Emma hated to be rude about what was her living, and the young ladies weren't the problem. It was truly their mothers. Either they'd never had the opportunities their daughters were being afforded and were living vicariously through them or reliving their own glory days in the pageant circuit. Young or old, today was the witching day. Perhaps there was a full moon?

Whatever it was, she couldn't remember witnessing so many meltdowns between mothers and daughters before and after class. Emma didn't allow the parents to have contact with the girls and one boy she coached during class. It was a hard and fast rule. No contact during class. If they needed to speak with their child, class was over for them that day. Distractions were trouble. Case in point was Judith, who remained homebound.

By the time she locked up at the studio, Emma was beyond frazzled. It was the worst time of the year. All the pageants happened within weeks of one another; some were scheduled on the same weekend. The entrants were all ages; so typically, it wasn't a problem, except for the one coaching all the girls at the same time.

Then it occurred to her—Matthew was coming over. How had she forgotten? Emma checked the time. She would have fifteen minutes tops by the time she got home to freshen up her bedraggled appearance. Had she shaved her legs recently? *Ooooh.*

⟫⟫⟪⟪

No woman had ever moved with the kind of lightning speed as Emma Jean Laroux from the time she hit the front door. Yes, her legs required attention from Lady Schick. Without a doubt, she required a shower and her teeth needed brushing. Matthew Pope wouldn't see her like this. She grabbed her toothbrush and toothpaste as she jumped into the shower. Nothing wrong with multi-tasking, was there? Thankfully, she'd had a recent pedicure and had washed her hair that morning. Twisting her hair into a clip, Emma managed a five minute scrub down and leg shave.

By the time she'd fluffed her hair, put on deodorant, dashed into her closet and grabbed a cute but simple sleeveless crepe shift in slate blue, and slid her feet into a pair of comfy leather flats, the doorbell rang.

She exhaled with relief. Right on time. She opened the front door. Matthew stood juggling two bags and a bouquet of lovely bright red tulips.

"You hungry?" he asked.

Emma didn't miss his appreciative sparkle in his eye. She caught a whiff of him. Maybe it was aftershave or shampoo, since his hair was still a little damp. Whatever it was, she resisted the urge to move closer. Then, she caught a whiff of what was inside the bag.

"Hi. Come on in. And bring those bags. I'm starving!"

He grinned, and she took the flowers.

"These are gorgeous. I adore tulips."

He followed her inside toward the kitchen. "I figured you for a tulip girl," he said.

Something about the way he said it, so easy, and so— *Southern* made her turn around and eye him speculatively.

"What?" He asked, innocence in his expression and body language. "Did I say something wrong?"

"Uh, no. You just sounded like somebody from around here the way you said that. Definitely not somebody from up North."

"Oh. I told you I moved around as a kid. I've been in New York for the past six years or so. It's definitely different from living in the South. I don't hate the South, if that's what you were thinking." He seemed to take a moment to choose his next words carefully. "It's just that I don't love everything about it."

She studied him for a moment. "I don't think I want to hear your analysis of those things you don't care for in my home."

"Maybe you don't. But you're not one of them." Then, he grinned again, with that deep dimple on the right side of his cleanly-shaved face becoming prominent and causing a rush of heat that went straight down to her—

She bit her lip and turned around quickly, absolutely certain the heat in her cheeks showed him exactly where the rest of her blood flow was diverted.

"I'm starving." she said again, still not facing him.

"Yeah. Me too," he murmured from behind her.

His silky tone made her think of hunger that had nothing to do with food. Suddenly, his warm breath was on the back of her neck. She shivered. He pulled her hair to one side and pressed the softest of kisses just behind her right ear. All thoughts of food fled.

Her next thought as they were wrapped around one another on the rug in middle of her kitchen floor was—*how did I get here?* Then—*oh, my God. Don't stop—ever.* She had been on hiatus from sex for a really long time, an embarrassingly long time.

So, the sounds coming from her lips might have been a little over the top. Was she a screamer? What a revelation.

She came the first time from his very skilled fingers touching her though her clothes. How embarrassing. He seemed to like it based on his continued interest.

From there he magically—and yes, she was convinced he was magic—had them both naked in her bed, condom on. She had to look at him. Because, well because, Holy mother of God, he was gorgeous. Not an ounce of fat on him.

"I won't make fun of your breakfast anymore."

He leaned back, his expression perplexed in the moonlight. "What did you say?"

"You—you are beautiful. All those egg white omelets and turkey bacon."

He threw his head back and laughed. But not for long. Because in the next moment, he was right back to the matter at hand, which seemed to be trying to make her scream with intense pleasure. She was going to die from it.

>>>>><<<<<

MATTHEW HAD EVERY intention of using all the manners he possessed by feeding her dinner at least before going caveman and flattening Emma on her kitchen floor. But his self-control fled when she'd bitten her lip and turned her back to him. He hadn't missed the flare of desire in her eyes. And that had done him in.

And, quite frankly, he'd never experienced such a powerful rush of instantaneous need as he had in that moment. He simply couldn't wait. Thankfully, her desire seemed to match his. She was incredibly responsive to his touch. And her body. Emma Laroux was luscious. Lucky him.

Frilly pillows were scattered in every direction about the room. Both were breathing heavy, and Matthew rolled onto his back, finally breaking contact. He was still reeling from what had just happened and stole a look at Emma. She was staring at him. They burst out laughing. It wasn't a nervous kind of thing, more a gut-busting kind of laughter that was both unexpected and freeing.

"Wow." It was all he could come up with as he wiped away the tears.

"Yeah, wow." She hiccupped.

"I'm starving." Matthew realized it as he said the words.

"Let's eat," Emma said.

"Oh, hell yeah." Matthew hadn't felt this light in years.

They finished every container, fried pickles and all.

Chapter Nine

M OM'S WEDDING WAS now two days away and prepa-
rations became the only other thing in Emma's life
besides work and thinking about Matthew Pope and their
night together. She'd been putting him off since then. Had
their amazing hot sex together been a huge mistake? It *had*
been hot and amazing. But she worried. And she was anxious
that Tad *knew*.

Matthew had shared with her that he'd been stopped by
the local police and mildly threatened after the taillight
incident. Of course, that was Tad's doing and his way of
showing them what he *could* do if he had a mind to. And
that was before Emma's night with Matthew. There were no
secrets around here. Somebody was sure to have seen Matthew's car here so late.

Tad could have even sent a patrol car by. Was she para-
noid, or based on her past experience with Tad and his
barely-concealed threats, was she completely realistic to
believe him capable of causing her real trouble? She knew it

would sound crazy to pretty much anyone she said the words out loud to.

She would sit tight for now, because he hadn't actually done anything for certain besides cause the broken taillight on Matthew's car and have him stopped by the police. Emma could connect the very distinct dots on that one. Plus, he'd stopped by Matthew's house that night. Proof positive in her mind. It might not hold up in court, but Emma knew, just like Tad wanted.

Shaking off the nasty Tad thoughts, Emma deliberately focused on the time she would spend with her family this evening.

She and her sisters and nieces had their final dress fittings for Mom and Howard's wedding. They were all going to be together at Evangeline House for dinner together. Cammie was cooking on set today, but at the same time, cooking for the family. It was kind of nice that her fantastic food was available to share. To be filmed, it had to be actually cooked. There was a food stylist on set who helped with the cooking, and made sure all the food on television appeared fresh and appetizing. So, there had to be a pretty good supply of fresh product on hand at all times to replace what sat for more than a few minutes and lost its beauty. That was the stuff they refrigerated for later.

Tonight, they would all come back to Evangeline House after their respective jobs and have a big try-on, then eat Cammie's jambalaya, one of Emma's favorite dishes. She did a pretty good job making it, too. Emma wasn't considered the cook in the family, but she'd learned a few tricks over the years. She did enjoy her food and wasn't too bad in the kitchen.

Emma had adjusted her schedule today so she finished early enough to make it to her mother's house in time for the dress fitting and dinner. She'd been squeezing her yoga and Pilates in early in the morning since she hadn't had to go to the set to help with Cammie's makeup. The new stylist/makeup artist had arrived from New York, though Emma hadn't yet met her. Nor had she heard anything about her from Cammie, or Matthew for that matter, which was odd. Emma had to admit, she hadn't taken time to ask either.

Matthew had called pretty much every night after work asking to see her. It had been almost a week since "the night of hot sex," and as much as she desperately wanted a repeat, she couldn't shake the idea that it was a really bad idea. She liked him, a lot, actually. But the warning bells were loud and insistent in her brain. She was a cautious woman these days due to lessons learned in her younger years. She'd trusted in a man, albeit a younger one. She'd believed him when he'd said forever. He'd broken her heart. And now he still refused to leave her be.

Disgusted with the ride on this train of thought to nowhere, Emma shook her head to clear it. Thankfully, the pageants started in force next weekend. Tonight was Friday. They would have all day tomorrow to get everything before the rehearsal tomorrow evening. The wedding was set for Sunday at six. It wasn't a usual time for a wedding, but there wasn't anything usual about any of this.

Emma stopped by the diner on her way to Evangeline House to pick up a couple of their locally famous lemon meringue pies—her contribution to dinner tonight. Cammie shouldn't have to do all the work. She noticed what looked like Matthew's car parked in the lot. Emma frowned.

The bell tinkled as she pushed open the glass door. Yep, there he was, still dressed in his bossy attire from the set—starchy, but a little less so than he generally looked in the mornings. He'd loosened the tie. Why in the world did he wear a tie?

He looked up as she approached. As soon as he recognized her, his whole demeanor changed. His shoulders relaxed and his gaze connected with hers, communicating his desire so blatantly her knees nearly buckled as she made her way toward his booth. She felt her cheeks flush.

"Hi there."

"H-hey. I didn't expect to see you here."

"Where else does a poor guy go to get a meal? It's not like I can convince you to eat with me." He looked so sad and lonely just then.

"Hi there, darlin.' You here to pick up your pies?" Thelma's stealthy approach startled Emma.

"Oh, hey, Thelma. Yes, please."

"Pies? What kind?" Matthew appeared interested.

"Lemon meringue. We're trying on our dresses for Mom's wedding tonight, then having dinner. You should join us—for dinner. Not to try on dresses."

Holy hell. Had she just invited him to dine with her family? They would eat him alive. Or, at least leave him writhing in discomfort from the all the shots they'd take at him with their unending questions.

"I'd love to. So, that's what all the jambalaya was about today. Usually, Cammie invites the crew to help themselves. But yesterday, she sent out a memo that suggested everyone bring their own lunch because she had plans for today's menu."

"Yep. She's feeding the brood. You sure you want to take part in a get-together with my family as a unit?"

"You recanting the invite?" He cocked his head and narrowed his eyes.

"Not me. Just want to make sure you know what a bunch of predators they are when new prey enter into their den."

"I've met most of them. They all seem perfectly harmless."

"Says the furry bunny with the wide, blinky eyes."

He laughed. "Don't worry, I can take care of myself."

"It's not that they're bad people, it's that they are incapable of holding in a single thing that pops into their minds. They'll grill you mercilessly until you beg for mercy."

"Worth it."

"Worth what?" She asked.

"Worth the time spent with you, even with your supposedly evil siblings. If that's the only way I get to see you, then I'll take it."

She blinked. "I didn't expect you to say that. What happened to the grumpy Northerner I met when you arrived in Ministry?"

"Your Southern charm has worked wonders, ma'am. And I'm now using the wonder drug, Flonase. Even your large, furry animal can't bother me."

"Ah, I see. Me and Flonase. Cool."

Thelma shuffled up, holding a couple boxes. "I threw in a cherry because I had an extra. Tell your momma I said hi."

Emma smiled warmly at the woman. "Thanks, Miss Thelma. You know how much I love the cherry pie."

"You taking this one with you or is he going to order?" Thelma nodded her head toward Matthew as if he wasn't there.

"I'll be heading out now. Thanks, Thelma. I'll see you in the morning."

Thelma harrumphed.

He opened the door and gestured for Emma to precede him. "I'm growing on her."

"Are you still ordering the same breakfast?" she asked.

"Last week I broke down and had real bacon," he admitted.

"You're going to hell. No wonder she's still stiff with

you. Miss Thelma loves people who enjoy their food. It makes her happy to serve happiness." Emma informed him.

"You should live to eat, not eat to live. I enjoy food, I just think it's important to have discipline."

"Were you obese as a child or something?" She laughed.

He didn't laugh. "Not obese, just heavy."

"Oh. Sorry. I had no idea."

"It's okay. I wasn't made fun of or anything; I just learned as I became an adult that if I eat lean, I stay lean. Of course, I exercise, too."

"You get stiff when you talk about your discipline. Your body language changes."

They were standing in the diner's parking lot next to her car. He opened her door.

"I'm sorry. I joined the military after college and it was— very highly disciplined. That was my take-away."

Her eyes were wide. "You were in the military? Did you see combat?"

His body seemed to tighten, and when he answered, the word was clipped and short. "Yes."

"Sorry. It's none of my business."

"I really don't like to discuss my tour of duty. It was— unpleasant. I got out right after." Still stiff.

"O-okay. I won't pry. If you want to talk, I'm a good listener." She smiled. "You can follow me and wait around with the guys and have a beer while we try on dresses or meet me at Evangeline House in about forty-five minutes."

"I'll stop by my house and change. I'd like to lose the tie."

"Good idea. I prefer you without one. You look a little severe when you wear a tie."

"I wouldn't want to seem severe."

"I'll send you the address. See you in a bit." She used her phone to airdrop the address to Evangeline House straight to his phone.

A tiny *blip* sounded and he looked down. "Got it. Thanks. See you there."

As Emma drove toward her mother's house, she thought about Matthew. The guy was way more complicated than she'd imagined. And obviously carried a ton of baggage. Baggage was the very last thing she needed to complicate her own life. She had enough of her own.

Hers wasn't the big, nasty kind some people carried. She didn't have a couple of ex-husbands and kids, or barely escaped an abusive situation. No, she'd all but sequestered herself at Tad's behest after he'd broken up with her following the whole Miss Alabama debacle. She'd seen her incredible father perish while trying to save the life of another as a teen. That had affected her deeply. But it hadn't broken her. Was she broken, really and truly broken?

Emma wondered why this was all surfacing now. Probably because she'd finally opened the floodgates and allowed Matthew past her dam of chastity. It wasn't like she'd been a virgin. No, but she'd been pretty damned close to it.

She'd approached sex with Matthew without a lot of thinking, allowing her body's overwhelming response to him to drive her actions. Never before had she behaved so wantonly or recklessly. She'd lost control with Matthew. But for some reason, it had felt safe to her. It wasn't as if he was a complete stranger. After all, they'd spent *some* time getting to know one another. She didn't know everything about him, that much was becoming more and more clear. But, Emma had an innate sense that he was a good man, even with the heavy baggage.

As much as she'd like to think she was a modern, adult woman who could maintain a friend with benefits, Emma had the sinking feeling it wasn't quite the way she was built. But Matthew wasn't necessarily here long-term. He was here to produce Cammie's show. He admitted that at anytime the network could call him to work on another project and send someone else in to take his place.

⟫⟫≪≪

MATTHEW TOOK A quick shower. He'd just tugged a shirt over his head when his phone rang. He checked the screen before answering.

He scrubbed a hand over his face and sent up a quick plea for patience before saying, "Hi, Mom."

"Hey there, son. I'm not calling for money."

"Is everything okay?"

"Well, not exactly. Your sister needs help."

This was a punch in the gut to Matthew. "What's wrong?"

"I really don't want to say over the phone."

"What do you mean, Mom? If Lisa has a problem, she knows I'll do what I can to help."

"Maybe you should just come home. Once you're here, she'll have to accept our help."

"What's the problem? I'm not coming home until you tell me what's going on."

"I can't believe you won't take my word that your sister needs your help."

He took deep breath, working to keep his cool with her. "Mom, I need to know you're not manipulating me to get me to come home."

"I can't believe you would think such a thing of me. Dub is cheating on Lisa."

He nearly punched the wall then, his anger rising so quickly it scared him. "That bastard! Are you sure? I need to call Lisa."

"No! You wait, now. She doesn't know about it."

"Wait. What? What do you mean she doesn't know?" He was angry and puzzled now.

"Well, somebody in town told me he was having an affair. I haven't told Lisa. She has no idea. I wanted to tell you first. We need to make sure before we tell her. I knew you would know what to do."

"Um, why don't you just tell her someone is spreading

rumors and let her handle her own business?" He asked. It made perfect sense. "Dub really doesn't seem like the cheating type. At least, not that I recall."

"Exactly; you don't know, do you? You've been gone for so long that you don't know much about any of our lives around here anymore. I want you to take a weekend and come down here to help get to the bottom of this. And if Dub is doing wrong, then I want you to help with the situation. It's the least you can do. You're her only big brother, in case you've forgotten."

His mother really knew how to twist the knife. "Fine. But you need to get as much good information together before I get there. I'll come next weekend."

"No, Dub will still be offshore then. Can you come the following week? I'd rather he was home, so we can talk to him about this. Lisa will need your support if the rumors are true."

"Fine. I'll see you in two weeks."

"It's about time you took an interest in your family. Let me know when your flight arrives and I'll plan to pick you up at the airport in Birmingham."

His guilt kicked up again. "Don't worry about it. I'll be driving."

"All the way from New York City?" His mother sounded shocked.

"No, Mom. I've just been assigned closer to home."

"Really? How close?"

There was no help for it. He couldn't outright lie to his own mother. "I'm over in Ministry producing Cammie Laroux's cooking show."

"I love that girl. So glad she's got a show of her own now!" There was a pause. "Wait; you've been less than two hours from home and didn't tell us? For how long now?"

"Just about a month now. It's been a busy time."

"We've spoken since then. You just decided to move back to Alabama and not say a word—to your own mother? I really don't have anything to say to you. I'll see you in two weeks, son."

Before Matthew could say goodbye, his mother hung up. He was a piece of shit. She was right. There was absolutely no excuse for the negligence toward his family. They certainly weren't perfect, but they were the only family he had. Just because his mother's recent behavior frustrated and embarrassed him wasn't a good enough reason to stay away. His past issues back home were complicated, but he was an adult and it was time to get a grip and face his past.

Good thing he'd established a dialogue with Sabine. She would be happy to address his issues surrounding his small-town Alabama personal history. He wasn't sure he was ready though.

He looked at his watch. "Shit!" He grabbed a bottle of wine as he headed out the door.

No way would he let his dysfunctional family keep him from the opportunity to spend time with Emma—even if it was with her entire family. She'd finally given him a chance to get closer, and he wouldn't squander it.

He'd knocked, then rang the bell. One of the sisters answered, a wide smile lighting her face at the sight of him, her dark blue eyes twinkling.

"Hi, I'm here as Emma's guest. I'm Matthew." He stuck out his hand.

She reached up and gave him a quick hug. "Oh, hey. Of course, you are. Come on in, honey. I'm Maeve; it's a pleasure." She had the most stunning eyes. So different from Emma's equally lovely light green ones.

When he stepped inside the the Laroux family home, he was struck by several beautiful women, all different shades of blonde who all resembled each other moving about, laughing, drinking wine barefoot in gorgeous satin dresses. The Laroux sisters. Wow. He'd briefly met each of them and, individually, they were all knock-outs, but collectively, just wow.

Emma was stunning, as usual, even more so tonight, as the fabric of the dress she wore hugged her curves in such a way that Matthew worked to control his physical response.

"I thought you might have changed your mind and gotten scared," she whispered into his ear.

"Are you kidding? You threw down a challenge I couldn't possibly pass up. So far, so good." He looked around the room, nodding at Cammie's husband, Grey, whom he'd gotten to know a little since working with

Cammie. Grey wasn't around much lately because he was in charge of substantial restoration projects of historical buildings throughout the South.

Right now, his main project was near Atlanta, so Grey was gone days at a time before coming home.

Emma officially introduced him to the rest of the clan.

Her brother, Ben, was Cammie's twin. Ben eyeballed him just a little longer than was comfortable. They shook hands.

"Good to meet you. I hope my little sister isn't driving you batty."

"Who, Cammie? No way. She's a real pro. I've never seen anybody keep their calm when something doesn't work out like she does."

"Well, she's had some practice. And I'm not referring to the stuff in her show. You've met my brother-in-law, Grey?" Grey had moved toward them and shook Matthew's extended hand.

"Yes, we've met," Matthew said to Ben and the others at the same time.

"Glad to see you somewhere besides the set," Grey said.

"Happy to be here and to meet everybody," Matthew said.

Jo Jo approached and said hello, her husband, Beau, in tow. Their daughter, Suzie, who couldn't be more than five, stood in a more childish version of a bridesmaid dress in matching fabric. The child was stunning with her big, hazel eyes. She smiled sweetly at Matthew and his heart nearly fell on the floor.

"Hi there."

"M'name's Suzy," she said shyly.

"I'm Matthew; it's very nice to meet you."

"Do you have a little girl, Mister Matthew?"

"No, but I have a niece about your age." The guilt hit him again at having been so absent from his own sister and her children. And of course, his mother.

A longneck was shoved, none-too-gently, in the grip of one hand by a somewhat burly man, who thrust out a beefy hand to shake the other one. "Name's Junior. Maeve over there's my wife."

Matthew's hands weren't small by any means, but the crushing grip put on him by Junior made him hide a wince.

"Junior, knock it off. I swear if you break his hand, I'm gonna break this bottle over your hard head. Apologize to our guest." Maeve stalked toward them, giving Junior such a communicative look that Junior's handshake immediately eased to human pressure.

"Uh, sorry, dude." But he smirked the second his sweet wife's back turned on him.

"Sure. No problem."

Junior grinned at Matthew and slapped him on the back like he'd passed some sort of pansy guy test. "You wanna come on out here on the porch and hang with the guys until dinner? The ladies are trying on dresses and shoes and stuff."

"Uh, okay." He cast a questioning glance toward Emma who laughed behind her hand, then winked at him.

"You'll be okay with Junior. I'll come out and check on you in a minute."

So, out on the "porch" he went. But this wasn't an ordinary porch. It was a veranda or fancy patio at the very least. There were trellises with flowering vines woven through surrounding the flagstone area. And it was huge. Big enough to set up tables to seat a hundred or so people. The grassy area that lay beyond was immaculate, and led to a small pond. Off to one side, Matthew noticed a well-kept garden area with an aging but very nice gazebo.

"I hope Junior didn't hurt you with those meat hooks he calls hands," Grey said.

Matthew flexed his own hand and held it out in front for inspection. "Nah, I'm good."

"My father lives through the back gate. Cammie and I grew up as back door neighbors." Grey had approached while Matthew was taking it all in.

"It all seems—extensive."

"They use the spaces for outdoor events. Most people don't have this kind of setup, even if they have a big house and yard. Everything around here is meant for events of some size or sort." Grey explained.

"Got it. That makes sense. It's nice."

"They do anything from family barbecues to formal evening weddings out here. You wouldn't believe how versatile it is."

Having worked in television, Matthew could see the infinite potential of this kind of setting for commercials and filming all sorts of promos. "I can see it," he said.

"So I hear you're a Tiger fan?" Grey asked. The question, while so innocent, held so many opportunities for him to trip himself up.

That damned sweat shirt was going to bury him. Maybe he'd worn it to the grocery store, or to buy gas? Or maybe Tad had said something to Ben. Were they friends? "Yep. You?"

"Roll Tide," Grey answered.

There was a short, awkward silence, then Ben said, "Sounds like you and Emma might have been in college at about the same time. Of course, she was at 'Bama. You probably at least know some of the same people."

Matthew rubbed away a trickle of sweat off the back of his neck. "I guess so." His heartbeat had nearly doubled, and so had his breathing rate. He worked to remain calm.

"You know she was Miss Alabama during that time. I'm surprised you wouldn't have known that."

Easy, man. He covered his discomfort by walking to the edge of the patio nonchalantly and pretending to survey the backyard. "I knew she looked familiar to me. But I was pretty deep in getting my degree during that time. I didn't pay much attention to pageants." All that was true. He hadn't known a thing about her before *that* night. Ben, obviously done with the grilling, became engaged with Junior about some animal Junior had just stuffed. Apparently, Junior was the town's taxidermist. And it was hunting season.

"You wouldn't believe the rack on that thing," Junior was saying.

Ben nodded, but didn't seem particularly impressed with the buck's number of points.

Junior's interruption gave Matthew the opportunity to get control of his anxiety. He had grabbed a napkin lying on the table and wiped the sweat that had beaded on his forehead. So far, Emma hadn't grilled him on his college days. If she did, he would tell her he'd attended Auburn. And if the truth came out, he'd have to deal with it then. For now, he would just marinate in all the guilt from his life choices.

There was a slight hubbub inside distracting Matthew from his own mire. Emma popped her head out the door and motioned for him to come inside.

"Hey there. How are you holding up?" She asked when he sidled up to her.

"So far, I haven't been eaten alive. They're just a little nosy." He smiled and tried to look casual.

She was so lovely. And he was a slug. No, he was lower than a slug. He was the trail of slime slugs leave behind for leading her to believe they'd never met. He'd been lying and it was killing him.

"Come and meet Howard. He's marrying my mom."

She led him across the room where a very vital older man was talking with a young girl who appeared to be around ten or eleven. She grinned at Emma when they approached.

"Hey there, Lucy. You look really pretty." Emma addressed the girl, whose dress matched the bridesmaids.

The child beamed. "Thanks, Aunt Emma. So do you. Are you going to wear your hair up or down for the wedding?"

Emma tapped her finger on her chin, looking thoughtful. "Hmm. Not sure, but I'll text you when I decide." Lucy grinned again, then she turned her gaze toward Matthew, as if she'd just noticed him standing there.

"Hi, I'm Lucy." She stuck out her small hand to shake his much larger one.

Matthew was charmed. "It's very nice to meet you, Lucy. I'm Matthew. Thank you for not crushing my hand."

Lucy giggled and rolled her eyes mischievously at Matthew. "Did my dad do his handshake thing where he tries to make you beg for mercy?"

"Yes, he did. But I made it out with all my fingers still working just fine." He wiggled his fingers.

Lucy shook her head and laughed. "He's so embarrassing."

Emma piped back up then. "Matthew, this is Howard, the groom."

Matthew nodded and shook Howard's hand. "Nice to meet you, sir."

"Likewise, son. So glad Emma invited you to dinner. I hear my son-in-law has quite a grip." He laughed.

Emma appeared slightly uncomfortable with his statement, but Lucy didn't seem to notice, because a young girl about her age, but very slender with very intense green eyes had approached. She was Grey's daughter and Cammie's new stepdaughter. She seemed a little skittish when they'd first met, but she appeared more at ease in this family situation.

"Hi, Samantha. I work with your mom on the show. We met before," He said.

She smiled tentatively. "Hi. I remember you." She turned to Lucy and asked her something about shoes. And they were off.

"They're both junior bridesmaids. Picking the shoes has been a hard thing for them. Converse high tops aren't an agreeable choice, and neither are flip-flops," Emma laughed.

"They're wonderful and perfect. If they want to wear high tops, their grandmother Maureen should let them. If I had a say, I would let them." Howard gazed at the girls' retreating backs with such a look of adoration, Matthew puzzled it.

"You might think I'm a sappy old man, Matthew, but I'm sure you heard that I recently found out I had a daughter and granddaughter. Now, I have four daughters, a son and two granddaughters, not to mention three sons-in-law. My heart is so full." Howard placed a hand on his chest, his eyes misty. "I have my Maureen back after all these years. It's more than I could ever have dreamed."

"Congratulations on your infinite good fortune, sir. That's like something from a movie. And I should know. I'm in the business." Matthew grinned, thrilled for this kind soul who'd found love and happiness after a lifetime of being alone.

Emma had filled him in on some of the details of her mother and Howard's love story. It was truly an amazing tale.

"Thank you, son. I wish you the same kind of love and happiness some day. Hopefully, you'll find it sooner than I did." He made an obvious nod toward Emma, who'd gotten momentarily pulled aside by her sister, Jo Jo.

Howard obviously thought he and Emma were an item. Were they an item? Matthew wasn't going to naysay it to Howard, but he also didn't want the older man to get the impression things were farther along than they were. "Thanks, Howard. I appreciate it."

"Now that I found my family, I've taken them all on. And I feel very protective of my girls. Keep that in mind, you hear?" His quick wink and nod was a silent and almost nerve-inducing communication.

Don't hurt my family or I'll hurt you. Matthew believed the older man. He was intimidating in that split-second. Had Emma mentioned that Howard had been in some kind of secret government ops all these years?

Matthew gave what he hoped was a reassuring nod.

After the ladies changed out of their bridesmaid finery, Ms. Maureen announced, "Okay, everyone, it's time to eat!" She called them into the very large kitchen to serve plates family-style. Like everything else at Evangeline House, the kitchen was built to create food for an army or two, but somehow still maintained a welcoming atmosphere without feeling too industrial. The island in the middle was a huge granite slab that currently held tonight's dinner. A massive pot rack hung high above it, and held many high-end cookware pieces of all sorts.

It was obvious where Cammie's love of cooking had been cultivated. It was a veritable playground for anyone who might have the slightest inclination to try their hand at baking or being creative with food of any kind.

"You are looking around like you've never seen a kitchen before," Emma said, startling him.

"This one is especially impressive."

She looked around. "I hardly notice it anymore. I grew up with everyone in a constant state of preparation for some event or another. There was either a wedding or a massive party of one kind or another all the time, but that was the family business, so we all strapped on an apron and helped out."

"Do you cook?" He asked.

"Of course. We all do. Cammie just went the official route and pursued it as a profession by going to culinary school. We've all been making pastries and following all sorts of recipes since we were kids. It's kind of second nature in this family. Ben is a fantastic cook, as well."

This surprised him a little. "I've never seen you do anything but take out." She blushed. He assumed she was remembering their last shared takeout experience at her house. He certainly was.

"Well, takeout has its benefits, you know." Then she spun on her heel with her full plate and headed toward the large kitchen table, which was teeming with her family.

This vein of conversation would wait until they had a bit more privacy. Smart girl.

Emma gave as good as she got as the family took shots at each other during the course of dinner. In fact, she even seemed to be more likely to jump in with both feet and mix it up with the guys than the other sisters. She was certainly feisty and not likely to back down. He liked that about her. But it didn't add up. Emma didn't seem like the type to run from a fight or be afraid of anything or anyone. But she lived like she was afraid to upset or offend Tad Beaumont. What did she really think he was capable of?

"Do you want a slice of cherry or pecan?" Lucy asked Matthew.

It took him a second to realize what she was asking. "Definitely pecan," he said.

"Me too." She grinned.

What a delightful child. It made him wonder about his

niece; how she was enjoying preschool, and if she knew her letters and numbers yet. These were things he'd not even given consideration to recently, or hardly ever. Oh, he thought about his niece and nephew. He loved them, but since there wasn't time to spend with them, or because he didn't make the time, he didn't allow himself the luxury of thinking about their day-to-day lives. Because if he did that, it would only serve to make him feel worse.

"Me too," Lucy gave her solid nod of approval.

Matthew suddenly began to look more forward to his trip home in two weeks. Not because he wanted to subject himself to his homegrown roots. Never that. Those were some of the hardest years of his life. Maybe they weren't all bad, but the memories that had stayed in the forefront of his mind weren't the positive ones.

He fervently hoped his brother-in-law wasn't a cheating asshole, and that there had been some kind of gossipy error. It was entirely possible in the small community where he grew up. Chapman was almost an exact mirror to Ministry, with the same kind of narrow thinking and hyper-focus on friends' and neighbors' lives and activities without heed to the consequence of how spreading one's opinions versus hard facts might do harm. Of course, when confronted, the rumor-spreaders *never* meant to hurt anyone.

Matthew could only imagine what the locals were saying about his mother's descent into chronic gambling. He shuddered.

"Everything okay? You look like you're fretting." Emma asked as the clean up from dinner began.

"Fretting? No, not fretting. Just thinking about work."

"Oh? Everything okay with the show?"

"Yes, but the new stylist the network sent is a little out of sorts." This was all true.

"Oh? What's going on?" She asked as they both joined in clearing plates.

"She's, ah, a bit of a fish out of water here. Right now, she's trying to find a place to rent, but not having any luck. So, she's gotten a room at the motel in town."

"That's odd. I know of several rentals around town that are available."

"Well, I think it might be her—appearance that's keeping her from getting something."

"Uh-oh. Tattoos? Purple hair? Piercings?" Emma asked.

"Only one tattoo that I know of and just a small streak of blue in her hair. Two or three earrings, but I can't think of any others offhand." He grinned.

Tess' style didn't cause even an eye twitch in New York, but here in Ministry, she wasn't only a new face in town, she stuck out like a sore thumb.

"Gotcha. I can bring her around to meet a few of the property owners and vouch for her if you think it will help. *Should* I vouch for her?" Emma asked him, eyebrows raised.

"She's a nice girl. I've worked with her in the past and can personally attest that she's not a freak and won't paint the walls black."

"Okay. After the wedding, I'll figure out a time and make a few calls," she said and winked.

Which caused a sudden tightening in the front of his pants. He looked away and focused on the pot rack.

He cut his eyes to her and said out of the side of his mouth. "Thanks."

"What's wrong with you?" She sidled up next to him.

"I can't look at you right now." He continued to study the pot rack.

"What? Why?"

He muttered, "Because my body is behaving like I'm fifteen."

She giggled. "Oh. Sorry."

⊶⊷

"I HOPE I'M not interrupting a private conversation." Her mother had somehow slid behind them without either of them noticing.

"Hey, Mom. Matthew and I were just laughing about how big the kitchen here is." Emma stifled another giggle.

She assumed Matthew's issue had immediately resolved with the approach of her mother.

Maureen looked around as if she'd just noticed the size of her own kitchen. "Oh, I guess it is a good size, isn't it?" She smiled at Matthew. "Young man, I wanted to personally invite you to our wedding Sunday. I do hope you can make it."

He grinned at the older woman. "I'd be honored." Then, he glanced over at Emma. "Would you like to be my date for your mother's wedding?"

Really? Were these two in cahoots?

"Well, of course, she would. Why do you think I asked you in front of her—so she couldn't squirm out of it. Emma has been very resistant to being part of a couple, and since she invited you here with our family, it must mean she likes you. And there's no sense in her coming alone to such a fun event.

"Mom, I'm not ten years old. I think I can get my own date if I choose to." Emma could hear the whiny petulance in her tone, but couldn't help but feel like a child who'd been vexed.

"Emma Jean Laroux, you invited this darling man here for an intimate family dinner, something you haven't done since your college days, so, I'm not giving you the opportunity to slip out of having an escort to my wedding. *Everyone* will be there, you know?"

Everyone, meaning Tad, was the implication. Which was exactly why Emma had avoided asking Matthew to the wedding in the first place. Of course, her mother wouldn't have known that. Or, if she had, Mom would have believed it was because Emma was still pining for Tad in some pathetic, sad way. And, obviously, Mom couldn't be more mistaken about that, but if Emma said as much aloud, it would require some sort of explanation, and there was no way Emma was tackling that conversation here and now. Maybe not ever.

So, of course, she would go as his date. It would resolve some issues, but might cause others. *Win some, lose some.* But Emma couldn't deny the slight thrill at the idea of being on Matthew's arm with him all dressed up. *Oh, my.* She felt her face flush as she had a sudden flashback to their night together.

"Well? Will you go to the wedding as my date?" His expression was expectant and hopeful.

They really did have her in a tough spot. "O-okay."

"And will you be available to escort her to the rehearsal dinner Saturday evening as well?" Mom asked Matthew, her tone really didn't allow for a no.

"It would be my pleasure, ma'am," Matthew bowed toward her mother.

Emma's flashback from the other night was more of a heated memory now. She needed air.

"Are you okay, honey?" her mother asked.

"Me? Yes, I'm fine. I'm just going to step outside for a minute to cool off."

"I'll join you." Matthew followed her to the veranda doors.

"O-oh, that's not necessary. I'll be fine."

But he wasn't having it. He was following so closely behind her, if she stopped suddenly, he'd plaster himself against her backside. The very idea of his parts slamming into her parts only added to her weakened knees. What was wrong with her?

Emma took a big gulp of the night air. The blooms on the vines threading through the pergola overhead gave off a lightly perfumed scent.

"What's wrong?"

"Nothing. I'm just feeling a little—overwhelmed."

"By what, or by whom, I might ask?" He'd moved even closer than the "hot on her heels" close he'd been a minute ago.

"Whom do you think?" She whispered, her breathing less than steady.

"This is my fault? Should I feel ashamed or flattered?" She felt his soft, warm breath on her ear.

Holy moly. This was precisely how they'd ended shucking clothes off on her kitchen floor. And right now would not be the time to get caught by her family bare-assed on her mother's deck with Matthew—

"We have to go. Now." She wasn't kidding around.

"Okay. Where?"

"Anywhere but here." She must have tipped him off with her frantic tone, or could he possibly see the raging within her body through the glazed stare she'd nailed him with? How could he not?

"Oh—Oh. Got it. Lead the way." His eyes darkened with what she recognized as his own brand of what she was experiencing.

The goodbyes were a blur. Emma hugged, kissed, and promised to help with the girls' hair and makeup, then was in her car in about sixty seconds flat and envisioning all the things she had planned for Matthew once she got him home. She wasn't a hoochie mama, was she? Well, she was darn-sure behaving like one now with Matthew.

She continued to be inundated with calls from every single, available guy around town, and some who weren't single or available. Emma had tried to be kind in her refusals of dates, but several had been so insistent that she'd had to be less kind about her rebuffs. No still meant no last time she checked.

But tonight she didn't have any intention of saying no. This was a yes night. *Yes, Yes, Yes,* if she remembered her words from the last time. Good thing she'd bought a Sam's size box of condoms and put a dozen in her glove box just in case. Not that she planned for this, but after last time, Emma realized just how quickly she could and had been overwhelmed by her desire for Matthew and his—charms. And she was nothing if not smart and prepared whenever possible.

She took a quick turn, and decided that his house was closer. Plus, there was a little matter of seeing him naked in his shower that she'd not been able to erase from her brain. Time to test that memory to see if she could create a better ending for her fantasy.

She glanced in her rearview mirror to make sure he was still following. Thankfully, he was.

⤖⫷

"SO, MY PLACE, huh?" He asked when they'd reached the front door.

He'd almost missed it when she'd taken the turn in front of him.

"Your place is closer. Um, could you please hurry?" Her voice was breathy.

He'd been in the process of finding the key on his ring, but her question made him turn around and face her. "Anxious to get inside?" He grinned. He was ready to break down his own door, but hearing her say how badly she wanted him was worth all the frustration in the world.

"Don't toy with me, mister. Open the door—now, please?"

He leaned down to kiss her, holding himself in check and barely touching his lips to hers. Emma wasn't having it. She plastered herself against him, causing his already erect status to spring to life in a very uncomfortable way. Her very lush hips found themselves beneath his hands, and then, with a stealthy movement, Emma launched herself upward, her legs clamping around his waist and she clung like a spider monkey.

"Whoa. Let me get this door opened before we end up on the front lawn." And they would, too.

Writhing and kissing, they staggered, entwined, into his house, barely making it to his sofa before both had stripped off the minimum required garments for access.

"Condom." She breathed.

"Got it." He was already ripping open a wrapper before they'd hit the cushions.

"How did you do that?" she asked between his lips.

"Prepared...just in case," he answered as his mouth made its way down the column of her throat and she moaned loudly.

"Now, please," she begged.

"Definitely." He tried not to grin with intense satisfaction when she shrieked her pleasure, among all kinds of other satisfactions he was experiencing, because that might be gloating.

Aw, hell, who was he kidding, he was all kinds of gloating. Emma Laroux was the hottest woman he'd ever seen, much less been with like this. No, not like this. He'd never been with anyone like this. This—was beyond sexual release. He felt something real with her.

"Oh, my." Her face was flushed.

She stared up at him, her eyes luminous, blonde hair spread out all around the couch cushion. She was flawless. And appeared to be well-satisfied.

"Is that all you have to say?" He teased, kissing the tip of her nose.

"That's all I can say right now."

"I'll take it. And I'll take you to the bedroom where we can do things properly. Without any clothes and such to hinder me the next time."

She breathed a sigh. "Oh, my."

In a single motion, he heaved her over his shoulder, bare-assed but still half-dressed, and headed toward his bedroom.

When they arrived, she tapped him on the shoulder. "Yes ma'am?"

"I've been thinking about that night I saw you in the shower," she said softly.

"You mean the one where I was lying there half-dead?"

She giggled. "Part of you was all the way alive."

"I remember."

"Well, I was thinking we should recreate that situation, minus the throwing up part." She suggested, still hanging upside down.

"Hmmm. Not a bad idea." He popped her on her bare behind and headed toward the bathroom, where a new and far more fun memory was bound to be created.

Chapter Ten

M AUREEN STARED AT her reflection. This was her wedding day. It wasn't the first, but it would definitely be her last. Howard had left her standing at the altar thirty-four years ago, alone and pregnant with her first child. He hadn't known about Maeve then, or nothing would have kept him away. But his parents or, more precisely, his mother had known just how to twist him up and to keep him away from Maureen by using her failing heart to extract promises from him. She'd wanted her only dear boy all to herself and swore it would kill her to see him marry Maureen. And she'd had a believable "spell" for good measure just before he was to get married.

Today, part of her relived both the excitement in preparing to go to her love, and the heartbreak of his not showing up those many years ago. She'd married Justin Laroux, her childhood boyfriend and dearest friend, who'd known Maeve wasn't his child and adored her anyway. He was the most honorable man she'd ever met, and she'd loved him with all her heart until the day he'd died. He'd saved her reputation and brought joy to her life.

Now, Maureen could marry Howard with a clear conscience and a pure heart full of love for him. Her children had given their blessing, which was pretty amazing, considering all five of them had walked in on her and Howard, stark naked in front of a roaring fire at the cabin on Lake Burton. They'd been covered in blankets, but there'd been no denying what had happened only hours before their discovery.

It still affected Maeve the most, but she was getting used to Howard and the idea that he was her biological father.

But this wedding was a good thing for them all. Howard would bind them. The children needed a father figure in their lives, even though they were now all adults. And there was no man better than Howard. He loved that he had a ready-made family and was ready to take them all as his own.

"Mom, you look beautiful." She turned to see Emma behind her in the mirror.

Emma was ethereally lovely in her blush-colored, off-the-shoulder dress. How Maureen'd managed to create such gorgeous children was beyond her. She was in awe of them.

"Thank you, dear. And so do you." Her daughter seemed more relaxed than she had in awhile. That was odd. This was a stressful time of the year for Emma, normally. "You have a look about you." Maureen stood and turned around, then led her daughter to stand in front of her, scrutinizing her face. "Why, you've been intimate with your young man."

Emma's cheeks turned bright red. "*Mom.*"

"It's alright, honey. We're all doing it." Maureen laughed at her daughter's embarrassment. "He seems like a nice young man. And it's unnatural for a healthy woman your age to go without—you know—enjoying the physical company of a handsome, hearty young man. And he looks very hearty, if you know what I mean."

"*Mom!* I don't want to discuss my sex life with you, if you don't mind. No offense, but it makes me uncomfortable." She continued to blush four shades to Sunday.

"Oh, pish. You young 'uns always think we don't know anything about sex, but let me tell you—

"Mom, are you finally having 'the talk' with Emma?" Maeve asked, surprising both.

"Ha. Pretty sure that ship sailed years ago," Jo Jo said behind her.

"Yeah. *She* was the one who gave *me* the talk." Cammie chimed in.

Maeve, Cammie, and JoJo breezed in, equally lovely, each a slight variation of the other. All were exceedingly beautiful in matching dresses.

Maureen laughed at their chatter, which so reminded her of all the years past. The four girls spent their lives bantering with one another, often including Ben. The good-natured poking at one another would likely continue until they were old and gray.

"I was just noticing the color in Emma's cheeks. Doesn't she look pretty this morning, girls?" Maureen couldn't resist.

The others gathered around their sister, giving her their full attention.

Maeve said, "She getting some, y'all."

"I do believe you're right, sister," Jo Jo agreed. "That Matthew is to be congratulated. I wondered if she'd ever be open for business again. Did you notice the way he was looking at her last night?"

"Like she was a big ole piece of cheesecake." Maeve suggested.

"More like he couldn't wait to get her home alone," Jo Jo said.

"She'd better watch out, or all the fiery wenches in town will be after him. Once they see she's gotten herself a man again, it'll be like throwing down a gauntlet and saying, 'Come take him if you can get him, ladies,'" Cammie said.

She would know. Her now-husband, Grey, had been stolen in college by her best friend through a very well-planned drunken seduction that had resulted in pregnancy. It had taken many years for them to find one another again and for Grey to gain Cammie's forgiveness.

⟫⟫⟩✂⟨⟪⟪

EMMA NARROWED HER eyes. "Are y'all finished yet?"

The sisters looked around at one another, then nodded, silently agreeing that they'd said their piece for now.

"I appreciate your snarky comments, and, yes, Matthew and I have, uh, enjoyed each others' company a couple times, but don't read more into it than there is. We are friends. I know that sounds weird, but he's here alone, and we've hit off—"

Someone snorted and muttered, "I'll say."

Emma held up her hand to prevent further snark at her expense. "Anyway, I would appreciate your just backing off and giving me some space to just take this one nice little step at a time, if you don't mind. And, for heaven's sake, leave Matthew the heck alone."

"We like Matthew, and are thrilled he's finally fed the beast," JoJo said, then she turned toward their mother, "Sorry, Mom. You might want to cover your ears."

Mom said, "Oh, please. There's very little that shocks me at my age."

"Fed the beast?" Emma challenged Jo Jo.

They obviously weren't finished with their commentary.

"I mean, you haven't had your itch scratched in a long time, have you?" Jo Jo suggested.

"Uh, could we get on with the wedding business instead of my sex life?" Emma asked the room.

"Sex? Who's having sex?" Ben strolled in the room through the open doorway.

"Everybody here except you, apparently," Cammie said.

"Emma's having sex?" he asked.

Emma would've been the odd girl out unless she now

wasn't.

"Yes, I'm having sex!" Emma nearly shouted.

Too bad the door was opened, because the rest of the groomsmen were right outside and popped their heads in at her loud proclamation.

Junior was the first to bite. "Emma, you doing the horizontal hokey-pokey? I'll have to kill that Matthew, now. Shit. I thought he was a good guy."

"No one is going to kill anyone, except me, if y'all don't be quiet and leave my sister alone. We can harass her, but not you. Get out—all of you guys. We need a minute with Mom. Ben, you can stay if you want," Maeve said.

She was the oldest, so she took the lead in such situations.

Ben went over and kissed his mother on her forehead. "I'll be outside. Love you, Mom, and couldn't be happier for you and Howard. Y'all can do your crying, kissy girl thing now without me."

Ben closed the door behind him and the sisters all moved in together with their mother to do the crying, kissy girl thing.

"You girls are the best daughters a mother could ever hope for. I love you all so much and hope you know how much I appreciate your efforts to accept Howard into the family. I understand how much of a shock all this has been, for you, especially, Maeve."

"I'm happy for you and Howard, Mom. I mean it. Today is a new chapter for our family." Maeve had teared up.

Heck, as Emma looked around the sister circle, they'd all teared up.

"We're all happy for you and Howard, Mom. We're the lucky ones," Cammie said, and they all nodded.

"Tissues?" Emma grabbed the box sitting on the dressing table and passed them around for dabbing any tear smudges.

"It's almost time for the pre-wedding photos. I'll bet Lucy and Samantha are outside chomping at the bit to join the fun," Cammie said.

"They are adorable. I finished their hair and makeup a little while ago," Emma said. "How do you feel about their sparkly Converse high tops?"

Maureen said, "Honey, I don't care if they walk down the aisle barefoot. Those girls can wear their high tops with flowers in their hair if they want."

Maeve rolled her eyes and sighed. "I guess we'll have bigger battles to fight as they get older."

"It's my wedding and we're not going to worry about what anyone else thinks, okay? Those who will gossip, will gossip. Goodness knows they'll have options in their choice of topic with us. We've invited nearly every single top information-spreader in town, so believe that whatever information gets around town will be straight from the horses' mouths."

"You're a brave woman, Mother Laroux," Maeve said, laughing. "Converse high tops will be the least of our worries, I'm guessing. We're serving alcohol in a dry county at one of the biggest social events of the year. Tongues will be wagging, no doubt."

Her mother placed a hand on Emma's shoulder and pulled her aside as they were making their way outside for pictures. "Honey, you know I had to invite Tad and Sadie. Tad makes it known that he expects them to be on pretty much every guest list in town. And I have a feeling he wouldn't miss this one, considering half the town will be here."

"I just assumed he was coming." She gave her mother a bright smile. "It's not what you think with him, you know. I don't have feelings for him—he just acts weird around me sometimes, is all."

The photographer began lining them up before they could speak anymore about it, and the photos would commence for the next hour or so. That was the nice thing about an evening wedding; there was no big rush. They'd made sure to start the process early, so everything was ready and there was plenty of time to prepare and visit. They'd all had so much practice planning other people's weddings that it had all gone very smoothly thus far.

Emma had enjoyed last night's intimate rehearsal dinner sitting at Matthew's side in the private dining room at Chez Philippe, one of the few really nice restaurants in town. She'd been at ease with his occasional easy smiles and gentle caresses on her arm. He'd been affectionate around her family and seemed comfortable. And they'd treated him to a similar harassment of one another. He'd fit in like even Tad hadn't way back.

⊷⊷⊷⊷

MOM HADN'T BEEN specific about how many people she'd invited to the wedding. Emma understood that her mother had been planning and executing weddings in this community, both huge and tiny, for so many years that she could do it with a hand tied behind her back, so Emma had done whatever was asked of her in the way of helping, but had stayed out of the specifics. Mom had employees for that sort of thing. But, wow, there was quite a crowd here—like the entire town. Everyone Emma had known since birth, pretty much.

All these familiar faces, both beloved, and a few not so much, stared with great interest as the Laroux family displayed themselves, hopefully to their best advantage. Emma wanted this day to be as wonderful as possible for Howard and her mom. Because as much as Mom said she didn't care what people in town thought about them, Emma understood how this wedding executed Evangeline House's finest skills. It would be great for business and for Mom's reputation to pull off the wedding of the year—her own. St. Luke's Episcopal Church was decked out with mountains of lovely white lilies and roses. The light, clean smells wafted through the pews, mixing with the beeswax of the hundred-plus candles that lit the sanctuary. The old church hardly needed dressing up, as it was surrounded by handcrafted stained glass windows, each their own work of art. The pews were carved wood, worn smooth by at least a half century of parishioners sliding in and out of them Sunday after Sunday. It was a holy place, whether or not those who frequented it were quite so holy was left up to the Almighty for such judgment.

Emma grew up attending Sunday services here with her family every week. She and her four sisters, often dressed alike, with Ben doing his best to make them shriek in church by pulling a pigtail or sneaking in a pinch here and there. She didn't make it to church quite as often these days, but when she did, mostly on holidays, she felt a peaceful calm overtake her, as she did today. It was right, this wedding. She sensed the blessings it would bring to them all.

Now, if they could get through this day without any catastrophes at the hands of the townsfolk. Because as calm as things were this second, with the strains of the string quartet and the quiet, awed whispers of the guests taking their seats, Emma knew from experience that corralling this many people in the same place with alcohol for several hours at the reception, there was bound to be some sort of ruckus. Often, alcohol wasn't even necessary, but it sure helped speed up the process.

As the music began for the bridesmaids to be escorted up the aisle, Emma's excitement grew. Her escort was her brother, Ben, since they were the only two single adult wedding participants. He wiggled his eyebrows at her in the way that always made her laugh. It ensured her genuinely smiling all the way to the altar to meet Cammie and Jo Jo, who were already standing with their bouquets, gorgeous as always. They were ordered youngest sister to eldest. Maeve would be next, then Rose, Mom's matron of honor, would walk beside her down the aisle. The two women had been together through thick and thin for all the years since even before she'd married their father. Rose had helped raise all the Laroux children, alongside her own, and she'd been Mom's right hand in running Evangeline House with her team of ladies who'd cleaned and assisted during events. The black woman was Mom's best friend in the world. Even during and beyond the Civil Rights movement, they'd had each other's back.

And Mom wouldn't have had anyone else beside her right now. Rosie had fully retired last year, but still popped by, shared coffee, and clucked over anything that seemed out of place at Evangeline House.

Rose was beautiful today in her blush suit, a similar color to the younger bridesmaids, though cut in a more matronly style. She had a twinkle in her eye as she held Mom's arm. Her children were all lined up in one of the closest pews, some with their significant others, and others were still single. But they were family to the Laroux gang as well, and therefore designated as such in the proceedings.

Mom was radiant as she kept constant eye contact with Howard the entire time, sparing a quick, loving glance toward her offspring just before Rose handed her off to her beloved.

"Dearly beloved—" The minister, who resembled Ichabod Crane in his last years, began the ceremony.

Tears welled in Emma's eyes. There couldn't be a more perfect day.

She noticed Matthew, sitting in the pew between two women—two really gorgeous women. One was Sabine O'Connor, which made sense, since Sabine was bound to have been invited, and if he'd been seeing her as his therapist, she was one of the few people he'd likely gotten to know in town. The other one, well, she was a different story altogether. This gal wasn't your typical Ministry resident, in fact, Emma hadn't seen her around. She appeared slick and edgy, with skillful makeup, her hair cut in an asymmetrical style that was longer on one side, perfectly straight and razor sharp at her jawline. It was then Emma noticed the streak of deep color in her dark hair, and the row of earrings. The stylist from New York. She currently had her hand on Matthew's arm as he leaned in close to hear what she was whispering.

➤➤➤◄◄◄

MATTHEW SAT IN the pew and waited while the wedding party took the post-ceremony photos. The ceremony had been romantic and filled with such emotion that he'd wished he'd had been able to film it with his equipment. There were near-perfect moments where life outdid cinematography. This had certainly been one of them, but would have been nice to catch it in cinema quality with all the lighting and angles it deserved.

He watched as Emma crossed her eyes at her young niece, Suzie, making her laugh hysterically. Suzie was the flower girl for today's event, and her bouncing blonde ringlets and large, blue eyes reminded Matthew of a China doll his sister had as child. "Aunt Emma, you're sthoo funny!" Suzie had a lisp that was almost as adorable as she was.

"Okay, last one. Let's get one of all the ladies. Guys, you are done. Go and wait for your dates." The photographer was an energetic, young man who'd managed to snap several hundred photos within the last couple of hours. Matthew could spot a good one, and this guy was definitely talented at coaxing the right shot from subjects. Matthew had worked a little as a photographer's assistant during his college days through his cinematography internship.

"So, you managed to sit between two beauties for the wedding," Grey Harrison, Cammie's husband sat down beside him, grinning.

"It just kind of worked out that way, but I can't complain," Matthew said.

"Sabine is a good friend and awesome therapist. Don't

know the other one."

"I don't know anyone in town, but I know Sabine and Tess. Tess is the new stylist the network sent from New York to work on the set. She just arrived this week, so your mother was kind enough to include her after Cammie explained the situation."

"When did you meet Sabine?" Grey asked, then realized his mistake, after a second, or maybe seeing Matthew's expression.

"Oh, sorry. Not my business. She's our family counselor, but we also consider her a friend." He confided to Matthew, which went a long way in easing the awkwardness of the conversation. "She's been a godsend in helping us sort out all kinds of messy stuff after my late wife died."

"Sorry for your loss, man," Matthew said.

He didn't know what the other man had gone through, but losing his wife and the mother of a child must have been pretty gruesome.

"Yeah. We're all doing really well now. Samantha and I are in a good place, and now we have Cammie." He grinned like the luckiest bastard in the world.

"I'm working with Sabine on a couple things. New Yorkers all have issues and therapists, you know." Now why did he admit that to another guy, especially one he barely knew?

Grey gave a short laugh. "Best way to deal with things and move on, dude," Grey said. "If anyone would have told me I'd be discussing the benefits of counseling with another guy a year ago, I'd have said they were high."

"I guess we have to do whatever works to get through some of the worst stuff." They were obviously both really uncomfortable discussing their shared need for seeking help, but it was good to know Matthew wasn't the only man around here who'd seen Sabine professionally and made progress.

"What are you two up to?" Cammie asked. "Either you're plotting something or having a bonding session. What is it? Football? Cars?"

"Football," both answered, then looked at one another and burst out laughing.

Cammie narrowed her eyes at one another. "I don't buy it. Come on, let's head over to Evangeline House. Hopefully, the natives haven't torn the place down by now." She turned her head as Emma approached. "Great timing. Are you ready to head over to the reception?" she asked her sister.

Emma didn't really meet his eyes. "I'm ready," she said.

What was up?

He gently pulled her back by her elbow and spun her against him as the others walked ahead toward the exit. "Hey, wait a second. I haven't had a chance to tell you how hot you look today," he murmured into her ear.

"Hmm. Wasn't sure you noticed." She felt stiff in his arms.

"What?"

"You seemed, uh, distracted during the ceremony." Her eyes glittered.

He'd never seen this expression on her face except when they'd discussed or been near the mayor.

Tess. She'd asked him a couple questions during the wedding. Of course. "That was Tess, the new stylist. She was asking who everyone was."

"Poor timing, and pretty darn rude, if you ask me."

"I guess. I didn't want to ignore her. She's pretty uncomfortable and likely figured no one was watching her."

"Maybe. I'll admit I whisper at weddings sometimes. She's really stunning."

"Who, Tess?" He considered that a moment. "I guess. But she's most definitely not my type."

"Why?"

"Why isn't she my type?" He had to think a second. "Well, she's kind of edgy in a defensive kind of way. You know, the tattoos and blue hair kind of way. I mean, I don't dislike that kind of thing. I run across it all the time in the industry as the norm rather than the exception, but it's not my preference in a woman's bearing. She's a little—crusty."

Emma laughed. "Crusty? You make it sound like she has an STD."

"No. I don't think she's the promiscuous type, only very hard to get to know, for anyone. She does her job well, is very talented, and has an eye for style, but leaves at the end of the day, doesn't hang out or join the crew for a beer, from what I hear."

"From what you hear? You don't join them either?" Emma eyed him speculatively.

"I'm the boss, so not usually."

"Maybe you should, it might help your crew get to know you and make for good morale."

"We can talk about this later, can't we? You have a reception to attend, and it's my responsibility to get you there."

"Nice dodge of the question, slick."

"You do look hot, you know," he said, crowding her space a little more.

"You're not so bad yourself. I like a man in a tux." She straightened his tie and turned on her heels for him to follow.

⟫⟪

THE BAND WAS cranked up by the time they'd all arrived and the two largest entertaining "ballrooms" were combined into one, with the French doors that lined the lawn opened to the mild evening. Twinkling lights were strung everywhere above what seemed like a hundred tables bearing cream, linen tablecloths, adorned with more lily and rose centerpieces. The flowers had been whisked like magic from the church and served as decor at the reception as well. It was dark now, with the stage for the band set up outdoors and a dance floor in front of the musicians.

It was a perfect setting to celebrate what had thus far

been a perfect wedding. Emma could forgive her date for his distraction during the ceremony. After all, she'd definitely done the same during weddings in the past.

As Emma took inventory of the guests, she couldn't help the tiny fissure of worry that crept in. She'd tried really hard to ignore Tad's intense stare during the wedding as he'd sat beside his loving wife. It was an owning kind of gaze he'd directed toward her. Like a finely woven but invisible net she'd tried mentally to escape from, but couldn't quite break free.

When he'd turned to leave the church, he'd winked at her. No one else had noticed, she was sure, but it made her heart sink. Something about that stare and that wink promised trouble.

Matthew had excused himself briefly to get them a drink, while she made certain everything was as it should be. There was a staff on hand for that, plus the wedding facilitator to make certain things ran smoothly but Emma had been part of this business for so long, and, since it was her mother's big shindig, she felt the need to be sure all was well.

"They're about to introduce the happy couple, so we're all gathering at the family table." Ben had come up beside her. "Where's your date?" he asked.

"He's getting us a drink."

"Good idea. When he gets back, y'all come join us." Ben strode toward the opened doors. Emma was just outside, inhaling the fresh air.

Fingertips grazed her shoulder. "You are radiant this evening, Emma." Her skin seized and she made a monumental effort not to physically recoil.

People would be watching. Anytime the two of them had interaction, folks noticed. Tad smiled his big, fat lizard smile.

"Thank you. I'm waiting for Matthew to bring my drink."

"Matthew again, huh? You two are getting pretty cozy, aren't you?"

"What if we are?" she asked. "Why are you even making a comment about my love life?"

"I told you the other day; I care about you. We have a history." He quirked up the corner of his mouth. "I really don't think he's the guy for you."

"Who, me?" Matthew had approached.

And he stood very close to Emma, having slid an arm around her waist. He was just enough taller than Tad to be intimidating in size. Matthew was lean but so very muscular and fit and gorgeous that almost any guy would find himself backing down given the situation. But this was Tad. Tad believed himself comparable to a god of sorts. True narcissists were like that, she'd discovered.

Tad was as confident as he was predictable. And the crowd, it appeared, had hushed a bit and was watching to see what might transpire. The two men were standing almost toe-to-toe at this point.

True to form, Tad stuck out the mayoral hand, "Matthew, my friend, great to see you. I was just telling Emma how stunning she looked this evening."

Matthew's eyes glittered a warning and sent a chill through Emma. This could mean trouble. "She is stunning, isn't she? Did I hear you tell her I wasn't the right guy for her?"

Tad had the grace to blanch and look slightly embarrassed then at being actually called out on his own words. "I'm only looking out for her best interests, you know? I mean, she might get attached and you'll have to go back to New York, then where does that leave her? So, no, you're not a good bet, are you?"

"Why don't you let Emma, and me, for that matter, decide how this thing between us is going to turn out." Matthew leaned slightly toward Tad and whispered something in his ear.

Whatever Matthew said caused Tad's normally congenial expression to completely lose its composure. His face became an extremely unattractive mottled reddish-purple, which made it impossible to hide his obvious rage. Tad shot Emma a glare of pure disgust and stalked off.

She asked Matthew, "Oh, my God; what did you say to him? I've never seen him react like that."

Matthew's expression was one of pure satisfaction, the total opposite of Tad's. It was a winner's gloat. "I have to apologize, Emma. He pushed me to give him the old, 'So far, so good with Emma, if you know what I mean.'"

She inhaled; shocked that he would gloat to Tad, of all people. "Are you kidding? You bragged about our sleeping together?" She didn't know how to feel.

He appeared sorry then. "Look, I don't know what's with this guy. Why he thinks you're his concern or his property, but the only way to get him to back off is to behave like the bigger asshole. I apologize for that, I do. But I've known guys like him. It's a pissing contest, or more like measuring shoe size, if you know what I mean."

Then, she understood. Of all the things that would shut Tad up, that would. It would also make things infernally worse. For whatever reason that made zero sense, Tad obviously still saw Emma as his property, and as such, wanted to keep her from getting seriously involved with anyone else. The whole idea made her head spin. Now, when she looked back, several things she'd chosen to ignore over the years made more sense when viewing through this new more informed lens.

Before Emma was able to give this anymore thought, the drumroll sounded indicating the newlyweds were entering the party.

"Oh, that's our signal to join my family at the table. We need to hurry." Emma hustled them over where the rest of the Laroux family was assembled.

This was mostly an adult wedding, since it would extend later into the evening, even though it was a Sunday. So, the younger ones in the wedding party were taken upstairs to be looked after by the older ones. This included the youngsters in Rose's family.

"Where were you two?" Cammie asked above the noise of the crowd.

"Matthew had a face-off with Tad a couple minutes ago." Emma had to nearly yell.

It was too loud to carry on a real conversation. And they were cut short as Mom and Howard were introduced as Mr. and Mrs. Howard Jessup. The applause was deafening.

But Cammie's expression seemed confused and worried.

The dancing began, and the wine and cocktails flowed. The food was divine and served in two stations, both out-doors and indoors, buffet-style to prevent too much back and forth traffic cutting across the party. Those who'd chosen to sit indoors where the music wasn't quite as loud, but had a view of the dancing and festivities, were able to obtain food and drinks without coming outside, and the outdoor guests could do the same without going inside.

The Larouxs sat at the head table that presided at the far end of the bricked patio area. Just enough out of the way of any foot traffic but not in the grassy area that sloped toward the water. They were situated within view of both the inside guests and all the tables outside. They weren't right on top of the band either, which was nice, but had a direct view of all the dancers and musicians across the dance floor.

This set up had worked well for many years. It gave guests the opportunity to stop by and offer congratulations during the evening to the happy couple and family. Fortunately, here in the deep South, it was often mild enough to hold weddings using this indoor/outdoor situation.

"So, why doesn't your brother have a date for the wedding?" Matthew asked.

She laughed out loud. "Because he wouldn't want to make anyone mad. If he chooses one girl over another as his wedding date, it will cause a near-riot, and he didn't want a scene at Mom's wedding."

Matthew's expression was comical in its disbelief. "You're kidding, right?"

"I'm deadly serious. Ask him yourself." She gestured toward Ben, who was standing, a highball glass in his hand, inching back, a step at a time every few seconds as if he was being accosted from three or four gorgeous young women who were each trying to gain more and more ground as he retreated and they advanced. The women, ranging in age from what appeared to be late teens to early thirties, were nearly elbowing one another to be nearer to Ben than the other.

Matthew watched for a moment. "Nah. I'm not going anywhere near that. He's on his own there."

"It is a weird phenomenon around here. Nobody really understands it, certainly not his sisters. But one theory is, if you're single, have all your teeth, and have a steady job, and, then, throw in smoking hot in a small town, you're like red meat in a lion's den."

"I get it. I've had a few casseroles dropped off with phone numbers left at my door. I've also been the recipient of a few portfolios for wannabe models and actresses. I guess it's gotten around that I'm in the entertainment industry."

"I'll just bet you have. I'm wondering how much clothing these gals had on in the photos." Emma couldn't help that little bit of jealousy gnawing in the pit of her stomach.

Of course, the women around here wanted to have a go at Matthew. Just like Ben, he had it all going on. Sexy, single, and employed. And his teeth were really nice, too. Worst of all, he'd been seen around town with her. That would make him especially appealing—he was a challenge to take away from Emma. Irresistible.

"Just for the record, I'm not interested. How could I be? I've got the most gorgeous woman in Alabama with me tonight."

They were talking close, so others wouldn't hear their conversation. She imagined it appeared pretty intimate. So what? Let them talk and think what they liked.

"Then dance with me, soldier." She nearly purred in his ear.

"With pleasure." He pulled out her chair and led her through the throng of bodies to the dance floor.

Emma noticed the interested stares. She'd had a couple glasses of wine. And she knew they made a stunning couple. Everybody was famous in a small town. Some more than others, she supposed, and that was alright. With her big personality, it was hard to avoid, and having been Miss Alabama and having held all the other pageant titles around the state, people tended to recognize her and to stare and to whisper and point.

Matthew proved himself an excellent dancer, graceful with rhythm but still so masculine. The band was playing an old classic dance tune and they swayed and fell into perfect steps. He dipped her and then spun her around. It was thrilling. In fact, she hadn't enjoyed dancing so much in years. Not since—

She'd been so focused on the song and Matthew that she hadn't seen Tad and Sadie dancing beside them. In fact, she hadn't even noticed they were the only two couples on the dance floor, and that everyone else had moved to the side, leaving the four dancers to themselves in a sort of dance-off.

Tad was an excellent dancer, and he and Sadie had taken ballroom classes from a friend of hers who owned the dance studio where many of her pageant students trained.

"Well, shit," Matthew muttered. "Does this guy ever give it a rest?"

The band had obviously gotten into the spirit of things and began playing a big-band, fox-trot to test the dancers' skills.

"Do you want to stop?" Emma asked, hopefully.

"Oh, hell no." Matthew grinned. "I learned ballroom during my film training. All that Fred Astaire and Ginger."

Emma recognized a pissing contest when she danced upon one. "Every pageant girl worth her salt knows ballroom."

He spun her around. "Good thing you've got your dancing shoes on." He nodded toward her bridesmaid pumps.

"You bet I do." She nodded and sashayed and shimmied to the music, then circled Matthew, hands on her hips and, glad for the generous slit in her skirt, executed a high kick worthy of a Radio Music City Rockette.

Matthew laughed, obviously enjoying every minute of their performance.

Tad and Sadie were performing a less enthusiastic, but more traditional version of the dance. Their steps were near-perfect in execution, Emma noticed, while she and Matthew were rather—acrobatic in comparison.

The crowd was gathering around the dance floor, and Emma really was becoming uncomfortable with the spectacle since this was her mother's big day. But when she looked up, Mom and Howard were laughing and clapping alongside everyone else, eyes shining, their pride evident.

The beginning strains of a tango began and Matthew pulled her close and gazed deeply into her eyes. His strong hands held her as they spun, dipped, and stepped, gazes hardly leaving one another's. Emma's skin burned, her bones liquid. They moved in perfect unison, one with the music. The crowd and other dancers ceased to exist. The crescendo swelled loudly as Matthew held her close and dipped her low, their hips pressed tightly together.

The wild applause finally broke through the spell Emma

was under. She was still lost in Matthew's magical gaze. She hadn't even realized the music had ended. When Matthew lifted her to a full standing position, she noticed Tad staring at her with such malice that she had to look away. What the heck—

"That was wonderful, my dears. I had no idea you were such fantastic dancers. Emma, I'm so impressed." Her mother and Howard were beside them, congratulating them.

Emma noticed Tad had stalked away a moment ago, leaving Sadie standing alone. "Excuse me a minute," she said.

"Hi, Sadie. Wow, that was really something," she said to the lovely blonde woman.

Sadie had appeared slightly distressed a moment ago, but recovered quickly as Emma approached, and in true Southern belle form, smiled graciously.

"Oh, Emma. That was fantastic. It was just like watching *Dancing With the Stars*; you know that's my favorite program. Y'all were just stunning. Tad went to get us a drink. All that dancing made him thirsty, you know." Then she spoke behind her hand in a dramatic fashion. "And you know he likes to be the best at everything. Y'all just showed him up, I'm afraid." But that didn't seem to bother sweet Sadie.

"Tad's got enough confidence for us all. He'll be fine." Emma laughed it off.

"You've got that right," Sadie said, and Emma's gaze followed Sadie's to the bar where Tad downed a highball glass filled with amber liquid, then proceeded to repeat the process. "Uh-oh," Sadie whispered under her breath. "Maybe I can get him to leave quietly. Tad usually doesn't drink, but when he does, things can get—a little ugly."

"Oh, I'm sorry," Emma said. "Is there anything we can do?" She asked, not knowing how to help poor Sadie.

"No. It might be best to stay out of his way. For some reason, he's been giving you the hairy eyeball all night. Did you get in an argument or something?" Sadie asked.

"No. I can't think of anything he would be mad at me about," Emma said.

Nothing that wasn't stupid or asinine, but she would bite her lip on that part.

"I'll try to keep him at a safe distance from y'all if I can," Sadie said as she kept one eye on Tad as he downed another drink. "See you later."

"What was that about?" Matthew asked.

"Nothing good. She congratulated us on our groovy moves, but she's a little worried about her husband over there slamming straight scotch." Emma nodded to where Tad appeared to be shrugging off Sadie's attempts to pull him away from the bar.

"Does he usually get like that?" Matthew asked.

Emma shook her head. "No. He's normally in total control. I've never seen him drink like that."

They turned and made their way toward the family's table, accepting compliments and comments on their dancing skills along the way. Emma stopped a few times to introduce Matthew to friends or acquaintances.

"Wow, you two. That was crazy, good dancing. Didn't know you had it in you, Emma. All those guys saw how flexible you are—might mean trouble. Phone's gonna be ringing off the wall." Junior threw his two cents into the conversation back at the table.

"Her phone's already ringing off the wall. What are you talking about? Now that they know she's dating again, she's having to beat them off with a stick. But I hate to admit that I agree with Junior on this one. You were one hot momma out there," Maeve said, then nodded toward Matthew. "You weren't so bad yourself, stud."

Emma giggled as Matthew actually blushed at her sister's blatant compliment. "Uh, thanks, I think," he said.

Ben approached and slid into his seat, glancing furtively behind him. "Are they gone?"

"Who?" Emma asked, then understood. "You mean, all of them?"

"Yes; all of them. Don't most people get a date for a wedding?" Ben asked.

"I doubt it. Probably hoping to hookup with you here," Maeve said.

Matthew laughed. "Dude, do you really consider this a problem?"

Ben's expression was anxious and comical. "You have no idea. I can't go to the bathroom without some aggressive female suggesting we find a more private place to get better acquainted. Some want to hookup and some want to get married on the spot. If you weren't dating my sister, I'd beg you to help me out."

"We're going to have to start a herpes rumor, honey. Maybe that'll keep them at bay for a little while." Maeve suggested.

Everyone laughed except Ben. "Don't you dare. That could hurt my business."

"Just trying to help, little brother." She patted his hand.

He scowled, his too-handsome features not quite pulling it off. Emma was enjoying this family time. Everyone's lives had become so busy lately that it was rare to spend time with her siblings just enjoying a wonderful evening. Having such a handsome date was a bonus.

She glanced beside her at Matthew. He was staring at her intently, his gaze smoldering. *Oh, my.* It was a good thing she was sitting down, or her knees would have certainly buckled.

⟫⟫⟫⟨⟨⟨⟨

"OH, DEAR. THIS can't be good." Jo Jo said from the other end of the table.

But it didn't quite register for Emma until she heard Tad's slurring bellow.

"You! You think you're going to come to *my* town and show me up. Who the hell do you think you are? Nobody makes a fool of Tad Beaumont."

Except Tad Beaumont, apparently. Tad swayed, obviously stinking drunk. His tie hung, his shirt was halfway untucked, and his hair stood straight up on one side. He was a mess. And he was clearly out of control.

Sadie tried to step in. "Tad, honey, I know the good people don't want to see you yelling in public." She tried to speak in a loud hissing whisper that he would hear but low enough not to be heard by everyone.

The music stopped. The crowd hushed.

But Tad wasn't to be quieted. He shoved Sadie away, causing her to lose her balance in her high heels and stumble on the flagstone patio. Fortunately, someone caught her before she actually bit the concrete. Matthew stood. Emma stood right beside him.

"You know I used to date Emma Laroux. Isn't she beautiful?" A kind of goofy smile kind of slid into place, transforming his angry visage into a kind of adoring, puppy dog one. Matthew put his arm around her in a proprietary gesture, or maybe a protective one, she wasn't sure.

Emma spoke. "Tad, please go home. You're drunk."

His face hardened. "Yes. I'm drunk. But not too drunk to tell you something, to tell everybody something. I loved you back then. You were perfect—hell, you were Miss Alabama and were destined to be Miss America. But you screwed it all up, didn't you? And him"—he pointed directly at Matthew—"I remember him."

"That's enough." Matthew, quick as lightening came over the table and punched Tad in the jaw.

It put him down on the ground, but it didn't knock him out.

Tad struggled to get up and spat the words at her. "If you'd stayed put that night after I gave you that drink and not gone out wandering around, everything would have been fine. That's why I broke up with you, you know? Because you screwed it all up—"

Before he could say any more, Junior, Ben, and Matthew had him dragged around the side of the house. Emma was standing, open-mouthed, not quite able to process what she'd heard.

Mom and Howard arrived as Tad was being escorted out, not quite on his feet. "Oh, dear. What just happened?" Mom noticed Emma's obviously pale face and distressed expression then. "Heavens, what did that young man say to you, Emma?"

"I—I'm not sure. But something he said or didn't say makes me think I don't know everything about what happened ten years ago between us."

"Come over here and sit." Her mother led her toward the nearest chair.

The crowd was murmuring. The excitement of Mayor Tad getting shit-faced, losing his cool, and professing his lost love for Emma Laroux had been as titillating a bit of scandal that would furnish the gossips enough fodder to last at least a week.

"Oh, Mom, this is your wedding day. I'm so sorry about all this."

"Nonsense. Something was bound to happen. You can't gather this many folks together and booze them up without such goings-on." Her mother dismissed the issue with a wave of her hand.

Howard hovered, obviously concerned. "Can I get someone champagne? Water?" He asked, clearly uncertain of how to handle distressed females.

Emma appreciated his need to help. "Water, if you don't mind, Howard. And, thanks." She gave him a small smile.

He saluted as if he were performing a lifesaving mission on foreign soil. That had been his specialty in a previous life.

"Okay, what happened?" Mom asked.

"Tad started yelling at Matthew for out-dancing him and showing him up in *his* town, like some jealous teenager. Then, he told everyone how much he used to love me and how I screwed it all up." Emma didn't wish to drag up all the confusing past stuff that she'd never really explained to her family.

They'd pressed, but since she'd never really known exactly what had happened that night, she'd given excuses and vague reasons instead of hard facts. Tad had mentioned a drink that night. She had no memory of him giving her a drink that night. But it had been a long time ago.

"Tad always seems so polite and controlled in his actions.

I don't think I've ever seen him behave that way," Mom said.

"Me either. I'm not sure why he's been acting so weird about Matthew either," Emma said.

"Clearly, he feels threatened. Tad does have a pretty huge ego, there's no denying that," her mother said.

"Clearly. But he was so pissed. And so drunk."

"Should I clear everyone out?" Howard asked as he handed Emma the water.

"Emma?" Her mother looked to her.

"Absolutely not. I don't want to give his behavior any more importance than it deserves. And it doesn't deserve any."

Howard grinned proudly. "You're a strong girl, aren't you? Just like your mother."

Matthew, Ben, and Junior returned then.

"What happened?" Emma asked.

"We put him in the back seat. Sadie said she would leave him there to sleep it off if he couldn't make it inside by himself when they get home," Ben said.

"Do you think he would get physically violent with Sadie?" she asked.

Emma hadn't ever known Tad to be violent, but his behavior lately had been odd, and bordering on bizarre.

"We asked her and she said, 'no,'" Ben answered.

"I don't know what's gotten into him lately," Emma said. "He's never behaved like this."

"He's always been a bit of a dick, Emma. You just prefer

to ignore him. And we all know he's been less than support-
ive when you've dated men in the past," Ben said.

"What do you mean?" she asked her brother.

Her thoughts from earlier in the evening, beginning to
resurface.

"Why do you think everyone you've ever dated has mys-
teriously broken it off or things just haven't worked out?" He
asked.

"I guess I haven't looked at it that hard. I really wasn't
that interested in a relationship with any of those guys, so I
didn't worry too much about it."

Ben shook his head. "Because maybe you didn't think
you deserved to be happy or expected things to go wrong?"

She sighed. "Maybe."

Ben took the bossy brother tone with her. "Look, Emma.
As big of a pain as your family has been, we've noticed your
lack of effort when it's come to dating. And I, for one, also
noticed that things, for whatever reason, always conveniently
end after a date or two. I'm putting two and two together. I
believe Tad is behind your not having any long-term dating
relationships."

Emma wasn't sure how to respond or react. "I've never
thought much about it. Things have always ended so conveniently. People's jobs ended, or they were transferred
someplace else. Or their old girlfriends showed up. I'm
seeing the pattern."

⟫⟫⟫⟫⟪⟪⟪⟪

MATTHEW HAD BEEN silent all this time. Tad had mentioned recognizing him to Emma. She hadn't said anything about that yet. There was so much happening right now that she likely hadn't processed that yet. But she would. Of course, he still had to tell her they'd met before. Suddenly, she was vulnerable after Tad's bringing up the past and throwing it in her face. With Ben now forcing her to question Tad's machinations in her life over the last ten years, Emma would need to come to terms with a lot of anger toward Tad.

Discovering Matthew's deception might be more than she was ready to deal with right now. He knew for a fact he wasn't ready to face that music, and with the non-celebratory family reunion looming next weekend, he preferred to slip away without added worry. Maybe his leaving town for a few days was good—cowardly, but best for them to deal with what they each needed to face.

Matthew had no intention of exposing Emma to his mother anytime soon, that was for damn sure; mainly because there was no way of controlling what flew out of Mom's mouth at any given moment.

"Oh, my Lord, y'all, what in the world happened with Sadie and Tad? I couldn't get through the crowd on my scooter. I even tried honking my horn, but nobody paid me any mind." Judith pushed a button, which indeed resulted in an obnoxious Model T aar-u-u-ugah horn sound, cutting short the frustrating train of Matthew's thoughts.

Emma turned toward her and appeared uncertain about how much information to share. "Tad had way too much to drink, Judith. I'm not sure why he was so angry though. He wasn't making a lot of sense."

Judith narrowed her eyes. "He's jealous. You know he's so used to being top dog around here that he hates it when anybody gets attention besides him. He thinks he's some kind of stud or something." Judith batted her lashes at Matthew. "We've got a few studs around here these days, now, don't we?" Judith laughed and fanned herself with her hand like a character straight out of Gone With the Wind. "Sadie can fill me in when Tad's not around tomorrow. I'll let you know if there's anything you need to know." She winked at Matthew, then wheeled her scooter around like a NASCAR driver, causing a few guests to jump quickly out of the way, lest they lose a toe or two. "Toodles, y'all."

Emma shook her head. "I was going to ask how she was feeling, but I guess I got my answer."

"It's a good thing the two of you are friends now. I wouldn't want to be on her list of enemies, that's for sure," Matthew said.

"Tell me about it. One of my more inspired decisions," Emma said.

The rest of the evening proved to be far less mired in drama, thankfully. Matthew's hand was currently resting in a cup of shaved ice after the punch he'd delivered to Tad's deceptively solid jaw.

"Are you ready to head out?" Emma asked.

"Sure. Do you need to help your mother with anything else?"

"She suggested we get going. The cleaning crew will arrive early in the morning to get things back in order. I'll go say my goodbyes if you want to get the car."

Matthew resisted shaking hands with Junior on the way out just in case his hand had a slight fracture. A clean break might be the result should he do so. The family were all gathering their things and saying goodbyes. He was hugged, kissed, and pretty much treated like one of them as he made his way toward the exit to retrieve the car.

Emma sighed once she was inside, closing her eyes. "I don't even know how to feel right now."

"You don't have to put it into words. Sometimes you can't name it," he said, fully understanding what she meant.

She reached over and covered his hand with hers. "Can you drop me at my house? I think I need to be alone with all this tonight." She made a rotating motion around her head, indicating her brain.

"Of course. I had a really great time, up until I punched the mayor."

She smiled. "I'm okay with your punching him. He needed punching a long time ago. Everyone is afraid to piss him off. Afraid he'll get them fired or stopped by the police and given a bogus ticket. But nobody ever says it out loud. Maybe I'm imagining it, but my eyes are beginning to open with regards to him even more than before. I wonder what else he's been responsible for around here."

"Probably whatever he's wanted to be."

Matthew pulled up in front of her house, killed the engine, and came around to open her door.

She'd taken her shoes off at some point and carried them in her hand. "Thank you."

"I'll be walking you to the door, if that's alright."

She laughed. "Of course. I hope you understand why I need a little space tonight."

He turned her toward him when they reached her front door. "I understand. Just like you understood my panic attack. Sometimes we have to work things out. But, Emma, I hope you know how much I like you, and that you can trust me."

"I do trust you, Matthew. And that's saying something for me." She stood on her tiptoes and gently kissed his lips. "Goodnight, Matthew."

Why had he said that? Why had he pushed her to admit her trust for him? For him, the one who was currently withholding truth? What he should have done was encourage her to guard herself against him and maintain her historical belief that men weren't worth the time and effort, because they would eventually let her down. Because, in the end, he was going to hurt her and let her down, wasn't he? It was unavoidable now. Even if he figured out a way to explain why he hadn't told her who he was at the farmhouse on that first day the instant he'd recognized her. But he'd hesitated, then he'd waited until a better opportunity presented itself. Frankly, he'd been terrified to bring it up. There wouldn't ever be a good time to broach the subject of that fateful night ten years ago, because the more he'd gotten to know Emma, the more he understood the reality of what that night had meant to her.

It had been a turning point in her life. She hadn't said as much, but after being around her family, listening and absorbing the things they'd said in bits of conversation with her and about her, it was clear. That night had changed everything for Emma Laroux. In a very extreme and destructive way. It had made her doubt herself as a woman.

Whatever occurred just before he'd whisked her away that night, away from Tad, he now knew after plugging in the timeline from fragments of information, her life had changed course. Like a young river suddenly dammed up and forced to flow in an unexpected direction, she'd been trying to navigate a new course that hadn't ever really gotten back on track. Had Matthew made a mistake in removing her from the situation back then? Or had he gotten there too late?

She seemed haunted in some way. And judging by her reaction to Tad's drunken accusations, there was something she needed to figure out about that night they'd all been present for ten years ago. A mystery that needed solving.

Chapter Eleven

TAD WAS DETERMINED to rid his town of the scourge that was Matthew Pope. First, he would figure out where he'd seen him or met him before. The guy had attended Auburn back around the time he'd been at Alabama. He was certain they'd overlapped someplace in the past? Had Pope been in a fraternity? Tad was fortunate enough in his many contacts and position of power that a background check and an inquiry through certain channels might just yield the information he sought.

If nothing turned up, which he doubted, then he would figure out a way to get Matthew replaced by his network, or, as a last result, pull the plug on the filming of Cammie's show. That would be too bad because the show had put their little town on the map lately. There'd been an increase in tourism in the past couple months, and that was a shot in the arm for everyone. He wouldn't let it be said that Mayor Tad Beaumont didn't have the best interests of Ministry, Alabama as his first priority—just so long as he could get rid of

Matthew Pope in the process.

He was doing the right thing, here, looking out for Emma. She had no business getting so cozy with this guy. He was sleazy, and obviously hiding something. It hadn't gone beyond Tad's notice how the guy nearly wet his pants when Tad said he'd recognized him from someplace. His expression was dead-busted guilty. Too bad Emma hadn't noticed. So now, Tad just needed to get to the bottom of who Matthew really was, or more accurately, who he used to be. Sure, he was a bona fide TV guy now, but Tad never forgot a face or a name. And it was rare that he couldn't put the two together. He'd been called a dog with a bone when he couldn't figure something out. And he would figure this out.

Last night hadn't gone so well with Sadie. It wasn't like him to drink so much and behave badly. So far as his sweet wife was concerned, he was a model husband and father— because he was. No one knew about the time he spent thinking about Emma and wishing things had gone differently between them. His self-control was commendable, he believed. As much as he still admired her, he kept his distance. He was careful to spend his private time with her photos. As much as he would like to touch her again—he refrained.

Seeing her with Matthew Pope's hands all over her body made him want to retch, in fact, his stomach was currently roiling just remembering last night's fiasco. Or, maybe it was the large amounts of scotch he'd consumed. Either way, he would have to make this up to Sadie. Apparently, he'd been a brute and nearly knocked her to the ground. That was unacceptable behavior. Fortunately, his townsfolk were loyal to him and would support him, just as he'd so generously led them these past years as their humble public servant.

Feeling a bit more cheerful after his personal pep-talk, he figured he would need to woo his wife back into a starry-eyed stupor. She wouldn't question him once she understood that he was just human and was bound to make a mistake from time-to-time. That would be his angle, anyway.

He picked up the phone to make a quick call to his police chief. Might as well get the ball rolling on solving the Matthew mystery.

⇢⇛⇥⇤⇚⇠

"HOWARD, WHAT IN the world do you think went on with Mayor Tad last night?" Maureen was buttering her toast after a rousing night of married sex with her handsome, new husband.

Howard set down the coffee pot and carried the two cups over to the table. "Well, darlin,' sounds like you're gonna have to fill me in on some past before I can give my opinion about this."

Maureen smiled softly at Howard and nodded. "Emma dated Tad through high school and through most of their college years. They were a golden couple, if you ever saw one. He was captain of the football team and she was a pageant queen and a cheerleader. But they were nice people, you know. Or, Emma was. I'm not so sure about Tad after what happened in college."

Howard nodded for her to continue.

"Emma won the Miss Alabama pageant her junior year and was preparing for the Miss America pageant when Tad broke up with her and she stepped down from her title. It happened over Iron Bowl weekend one year. Everything was great, so far as we knew, then, poof." Maureen spread her fingers as if things had blown to bits, because they had.

"What happened?"

"That's just it—we never got the whole story from Emma. She said they had a fight and broke up that night, and that she was so upset and distraught and she felt like she wasn't going to be able to focus on finishing school. She said she'd completely lost her enthusiasm for Miss America and knew the first runner-up wanted it more than she did. She... just stepped down." Maureen shook her head, sadly. "After all the hard work and preparation, she just gave it all up. Why? Because Tad Beaumont broke her heart? We all believed she was tougher than that. But she clammed up and refused to discuss it until we finally stopped asking. I mean, you can't force someone to be in the Miss America pageant or to talk about something they don't want to discuss."

"I'm sure y'all felt pretty helpless. Sounds like something pretty awful went down that weekend," Howard said, rubbing his chin.

"It's been a long time now, and for some reason, I think a lot more happened than just a fight and a breakup. After what happened last night, I think it's time to figure this thing out. I haven't seen Emma that upset in years. It's like Tad brought it all back. And this tiger momma isn't going to stand for it."

"Well, darlin', the good news is that you're not alone anymore. You've got support now, and I'll do whatever it takes to help you help Emma find her way back to normal."

"I don't want her back to normal, I want her better than normal. I want whatever happened all those years ago to be purged and healed, because I don't believe the truth has ever come out and been dealt with. And I think Tad was the culprit at the bottom of this."

"Go, tiger momma." Howard's eyes crinkled in the corners, making Maureen's heart spill over with gratitude at how lucky she was to find him again after all these years.

"I'm going to have to pull the others in on this." Making reference to Emma's siblings.

"We'll need to be careful in case Emma is in a fragile state." Howard warned.

"Yes. That's my concern, too."

❯❯❯❮❮❮

EMMA WAS IN a bit of a fragile state, no doubt. Her brain had begun the process of trying to remember—pulling bits and pieces of fragmented still shots from an old movie in which the footage was dark and grainy and had nothing clear to reveal.

She was racking her brain, trying to fill in blanks, realizing more now than ever that something out of her control happened to her that night—something she had only small bits of memory, and only Tad's very sketchy version of an explanation. And a tiny slice of recall of the guy, who'd plucked her out of the situation, brought her to a hotel room for several hours until her roommate had called on her cell looking for her. Emma recalled a deep but unclear voice, that he'd been a large guy, and so very kind that even now, it made her want to cry. But nothing else about him. She'd begged him to get her out of there. He had.

Her vision had been blurry and she remembered a deep fear until he'd put a jacket or blanket or something around her shoulders and she'd felt safe, somehow understanding he wouldn't hurt her. Looking back, she realized how foolish it had been to put herself in the hands of a stranger. Of course, Emma had been so out of it, and obviously drugged, that she had only followed her most basic instincts, and, fortunately for her, the big guy had been her guardian angel.

Her roommate had called very early that morning, concerned, and he'd answered her phone, telling her friend where to come and pick Emma up. He had helped her out to the car, explaining nothing to the girl in case she couldn't be trusted, Emma supposed. But she still couldn't remember what his face looked like because whatever was still in her system had distorted her vision and her memory. She remembered slurring, "Whassur name?" to which he'd either replied, Mark or Mike, she wasn't certain.

Emma had never wanted to know or remember, really. He'd seen her at her lowest—the worst point in her life. She had been so very grateful for his help, but the eventual outcome of that night had changed her life. So, never seeing him again and not having to relive it all was definitely best. She'd been afraid it had been her fault, that she had somehow been irresponsible or that she'd been stupid. And the worst possible thing for her to feel, especially during that part of her life, had been stupid. Because she'd often been treated like she was stupid and hated it.

Blonde jokes, blonde bimbo remarks, and pageant princess comments had all played into the uphill battle of proving that she wasn't just a brainless beauty, and that she'd had worth and intelligence. The more she'd fought against the image, the more pushback Emma had received. So, after that terrible night, when she'd seen Tad, he'd told her she'd been stupid and had acted like a brainless idiot by getting herself into a situation where he'd had to threaten people to keep quiet about what she'd done.

When she'd begged to know what had happened, he'd stared at her as if she was indeed just that stupid. "You mean you don't remember wearing your crown and letting those assholes take pictures of you with barely a stitch on? I never would have thought you of all people were such a whore.

You should have seen yourself—the silly grin on your face. He had his hand on your—"

She'd covered her ears, sobbing uncontrollably after that, begging him to stop talking. "I don't remember any of it, Tad. Don't you believe me? We've been together for five years. Five years. I thought you loved me," she'd cried.

He'd not appeared especially moved by her tears. "I did love you, Emma. And now you've ruined everything. But don't worry. I took care of it. I have the pictures. Those guys will never breathe a word because I threatened them with expulsion from the fraternity. They'd throw their own mothers off a bridge before being excommunicated."

"I told you I don't remember anything. Surely, someone must have put something in my drink or—or something," she wanted to stomp her foot and shriek, but her head hurt too badly.

"It doesn't matter. I can't take the chance that you're behavior brings shame or embarrassment to me. I have a clear plan for my future. That future included you, Emma, but now you've ruined it all. And to top it all off, you went and disappeared before I could get you back to my room safe and sound. Where did you go?" He'd demanded.

"I was confused. I remembered you getting angry and yelling; a friend took me home from the party." That had been only partially true, of course.

The sequence of events had pretty much escaped her. Somehow, she'd gotten away from the hubbub that had gone on upstairs and stumbled upon her gentle protector.

"You'll have to step down from Miss Alabama. If anyone finds out about this, they'll strip you of the crown and you wouldn't be able to participate in the Miss America pageant anyway."

The reality of the horrible unfairness had surrounded Emma then, like a black fog. "But I didn't do anything."

"Yes, you did, Emma, whether you intended to or not. So, now we live with the consequences."

She'd turned on him then. "We?"

His smile was regretful but not quite sad. "You have no idea. Now, I have to start over. Finding the perfect mate who will be a complement for my career moving forward wasn't in the plan. I really wish it had been you. We've had some great times together, haven't we?"

She'd wondered what alien had come down and snatched the Tad Beaumont she'd shared her dreams with, the charming guy who'd professed his undying love for her when she'd given him her precious virginity. The patient, caring boyfriend she'd spent so many hours, days, and nights with over the years. This person couldn't be him.

But he had been. Just as soon as she'd let him down by doing whatever it was she supposedly did, he'd dropped her to avoid any personal embarrassment.

Emma had had lots of time since then to research true narcissism and now understood how slickly a person could be fooled by one. Narcissists, according to what she'd learned, were charming, engaging, and as long as the narcissist's needs and desires were put first, above all else, things could go well in a relationship. Tad had groomed and manipulated her from the beginning to please him. She was pretty, dressed and behaved gracefully, which all served him. She adored him and fell into feeding his ego because he rewarded her with what had seemed like genuine affection when she'd done so. For years.

After high school, they had both been very busy with college classes; Tad was continually swamped as president of his fraternity pledge class, and later the chapter, and Emma in own her sorority and with her preliminary pageants and helping with family events at Evangeline House whenever she could. Their time spent together was attending Greek formals, occasional dinners out together, and snatched time together for sex.

Tad had never been a generous sexual partner. He was far more concerned with hearing that she was satisfied than actually making sure that she was. He was in it for his own personal gratification, without a doubt. But Emma hadn't complained. Complaining to Tad had never gone well. So, she didn't—about anything. Emma preferred peace.

What Emma now understood these many years later was, even though she'd suffered through a confusing and hurtful time losing Tad—the person who she'd believed loved her and wanted to share his life with her—was what a true blessing in disguise it had been getting rid of his narcissistic ass. It had taken a long time to figure it out, but once she'd learned truly what he was, Emma knew she was far better off alone than with him—even if she ended up alone her entire life.

The hard part now was still not knowing the full story. For so many years, she'd been content to turn away from the truth of things just in case she really was somehow to blame. But she'd met Matthew, and after getting a taste of what her future could potentially look like, Emma experienced a surge of strength, of empowerment that she hadn't—ever—had. She needed to take control of what had happened, find out the whole truth of it, no matter how bad it reflected on her. She could handle it now.

Emma hadn't indulged herself in this kind of trip down memory lane in a very long time, and she'd certainly never emerged with an empowered outlook.

The only person with solid information about the night in question that she knew of was Tad. She had been obviously drugged that evening, but by whom? Maybe it was time she and Tad had a real discussion about their past and put things to rest once and for all.

⤜⤜⤜⤛⤛⤛

MATTHEW MADE THE unusual decision to call Sabine Thursday and ask for a last minute appointment. She agreed to squeeze him in at the end of the day, thankfully, or he might have scrapped his plan to head to Chapman after work tomorrow for the weekend.

"I was glad to hear from you, Matthew. What's going on?" Sabine didn't spend a lot of time on niceties; she got right down to business.

"I was thinking about what you'd said—how being back here in Alabama might be the cause of my anxiety. No doubt that's a big part of it. I'm having some real frustration in dealing with my family."

"Is your family nearby?" Sabine asked, her tone neutral.

"About two hours away. My mother and sister live in Chapman, a couple hours Southeast of Ministry, but very similar in size and demographic."

Sabine nodded, knowingly. "I see. Small town where everyone knew everything about you and your family growing up?"

"You got it. My stepdad was a real piece of work. My father left a little money for mine and my sister's education. Somehow Frank, my stepdad, persuaded my mother to dip into it for his personal use. Needless to say, there wasn't anything left when it was time to educate us."

"So, you're angry with your mother as well as your stepfather, obviously. Leaving your stepfather out of things for now, because he was obviously someone who caused you a great deal of negative feelings, let's discuss how you view your mother—what else are you angry with her about?"

"Do you have all day?" His laugh wasn't humorous. "She didn't kick his sorry ass out as soon as she realized what a dick he was. Pardon my language."

Sabine waved his apology away.

"I mean, what kind of parent doesn't step in front of her child when a man raises a hand to him? Frank enjoyed manipulating my mother. And she refused to see what he was. She blamed me later when the money was gone and he finally left town with what little she had. She blamed me because Frank told her I was the reason he was going away."

Sabine sighed. "You know none of this was your fault, right?"

"Yes. But my mother still blames me that she doesn't have a deadbeat husband who stole all our money. I joined the military and nearly died so I could pay for my education because of that asshole."

"You're right, he was an asshole. And judging from what you've said so far, I'd like to hunt him down and kick him in the balls." Sabine looked angry.

Her very un-therapist-like response make him laugh, a real laugh. "It's refreshing that you understand."

"My dad's an asshole, too—my real dad—so, I under-stand. He cheated on my mom and is a very powerful man. I truly understand your feelings of helplessness as a child. I felt very protective of my mother. She was more of a true victim, so I didn't hold the same anger against her that you feel toward your mother, but I get it."

"Frank never hit my sister, but he wasn't nice to her. He made her feel small and insecure. He really did a number on her self-esteem. He didn't have a problem with knocking me around when my mom wasn't at home."

"Sounds like a real prince. Where is Frank now?" Sabine asked.

"I'm not sure, but my mother hopes every day he'll come home to her."

"Was he physically abusive to her?"

"Not that I know of. He pretty much schmoozed her out of her life savings. It's amazing how an intelligent woman could be taken in and believe whatever a man like that told her as opposed to what her children tried to so she wouldn't be without a man in the house."

"Maybe she thought having Frank there stabilized the home or that providing a poor father figure was better than not having one available."

"All I know was that he didn't contribute financially, he was a constant irritant to me and my sister, and kept her at odds with her own children. There wasn't a single benefit to his being in our lives that I can see except for appearances sake."

"What do you mean?"

"She liked having a man by her side, even to our detriment. It was a source of pride for her. She spoke unkindly about women in the community who couldn't keep a man and of single mothers."

"Do you know why that was?"

"I think she hated being alone and didn't want to be pitied."

"That makes sense. What happened to you father?"

Matthew took a deep breath. He hated discussing his father. "He died. But he left us before he died. I was ten."

Sabine's expression was sympathetic. "Help me understand what happened."

"He left because he was dying and wanted to spare us the trauma of watching him suffer through what the cancer would do to his body. But he kept us from spending time with him during the time he had left. My mother never forgave him and blamed us for his decision. She wanted to be with him but had to take care of us."

Sabine closed her eyes as she imagined the scenario. "That had to have been a rough situation for everyone. Did you maintain contact with your father during his decline?" She asked.

"My mom found out where he was just days before he died. He'd checked in to some kind of veteran's hospice facility. He must have been pretty sick when he was diagnosed, because he died about six months later. Dad was the love of Mom's life, and she was inconsolable for a long time, as you might imagine. She never really got over his death, until she met Frank."

"She may have tried to recreate what she'd had with your father when she met Frank and refused to believe it wouldn't work. Or maybe, she would rather go through anything than loneliness again."

"She was a really good mother until Dad left. Then, she just lost it. She's never been the same." He shook his head.

"The little boy you were at ten years old misses his mom," Sabine said softly.

"I miss her," he said, as his eyes filled up. "I miss them both."

Sabine slid over a strategic box of Kleenex on the table between them.

"Thanks. Sorry. I'm not a kid anymore. You'd think I would have outgrown the need for my mommy."

"Are you kidding? I'm still so pissed at my dad I can hardly think about him without wanting to punch him in the face. Hopefully, you don't want to punch your mother in the face," she said.

"No, but I often want to punch the wall when I'm talking with her because I get so frustrated. She's started gambling her paychecks away at the slot machines on the weekends and she's smoking."

"Has she always smoked?" Sabine asked.

"No. It's recent; so is the gambling."

"Has she taken up with new friends?"

"She's mentioned going to the casinos with a female coworker."

"Maybe she's just started going out and learning to enjoy herself instead of sitting at home and brooding?"

"I hadn't thought about that. So, this might be a *positive* thing?" he asked.

Sabine pressed her lips together thoughtfully. "Mmmm. Not sure, but if it's a move toward her becoming more social and less depressed, it could be. Of course, the smoking isn't the healthiest behavior, nor is the gambling if she isn't being responsible with her money and hasn't been paying bills. That's something you should assess when you see her this weekend."

"She's paying bills, but has been calling me and asking for money to cover them."

"Did you ever think she's calling to get your attention more so than being truly needy for money?" Sabine asked.

Damn, the woman was smart. That sounded exactly like something his mother would do. Lisa had told him about the smoking last time they'd spoken, but hadn't really shared a concern about the gambling. So, maybe it wasn't as serious as he thought. In fact, Lisa sounded happy that Mom was getting out more and seemed less mired wallowing in her own woes.

Of course, he and Lisa didn't speak very often and that had been a couple months ago.

"You said your sister, Lisa, lives in the same town as your mother? What kind of relationship do the two of you have?" Sabine asked.

"Occasional. And that's my fault. She has two young kids and I'm the world's worst uncle and brother." He hung his head.

"So, you've been back in the area for awhile and haven't

seen them yet? Did they know you were nearby?"

He shook his head. "Like I said, I'm carrying around a lot of guilt for not wanting to deal with my family. I've been dreading going back there. Lots of baggage I've not wanted to go home and face."

Sabine nodded. "I get it. And no one should blame you, even though they probably will and do. Everyone had their own memory of things and places. Some deal better than others with past events. Some people just never want to go back and feel that way again."

"That's pretty much it. I care about my family, but going home makes me want to throw up."

"The place can't hurt you, even if the memories do. Just remember that. Avoiding things will only make the pain last longer. You will eventually have to go back and deal with this—all of it."

"My head knows this. You're right; I know you are."

"The problem you have to get hold of is letting it control your emotions, which is what causes the physical responses—the panic attacks. The closer to home you get, the more you panic."

"Makes sense."

"So, do you feel any better or less anxious about heading home this weekend?" Sabine asked.

He nodded. "I think so. You've made me think about some things I hadn't. Before I came today, I'd completely avoided even picturing the town, much less my mom's house or memories of my dad, for that matter." He took a deep breath. "I didn't die or have a panic attack. It made me sad but sad is better than angry, or desperately determined to avoid it all at any cost."

"Well, I think you will be fine. I've seen much worse. *I'm* much worse as far as feeling angry with my father. The idea of going back to my home town makes me want to take to the streets, running and screaming." She cleared her throat. "Uh, sorry—your therapy session, not mine."

He laughed. "Now I'm totally curious. I guess we all have some pretty awful stuff, huh?"

"Well, you and I do, that's for sure."

⟩⟩⟩⟨⟨⟨

MATTHEW LEFT SABINE'S office with a lighter step than before, and not such a dread for his weekend ahead. Maybe going back to Chapman didn't have to be a disaster. Having spent time around Emma's nieces and nephews made him miss his own. And he really hoped to get to the bottom of what was going on with Lisa and her husband, Dub. He couldn't shake the feeling Dub was a good guy and that Mom was somehow mistaken about his infidelity. He hoped so for Lisa and the kids' sakes.

He'd tried to call Emma earlier, hoping to catch her between her Pilates and whatever classes she had scheduled today. They hadn't really had much chance to talk this week as both were wretchedly busy and each distracted with their own personal dramas. Matthew really hadn't shared his with her, and because she'd pushed him away the night of her mother's wedding, he figured she was going through some stuff, too, after Tad's big scene in front of half the town. When things got too complicated with women, Matthew tended to avoid the fray. Of course, he'd never really liked anyone as much as he did Emma, but he could feel the beginnings of a fray and how it made him want to run far, far away—not from her, just the messiness of it.

His cell rang just as he pulled up in his driveway. He checked the number and recognized it as a New York exchange but not as one of his contacts. "Hello?"

"Hey, Matthew. It's Tess." That was all, then, silence.

"Hi, Tess. Everything okay?" She'd been on set today and seemed fine.

Tess was a very private girl and did her job, but kept to herself otherwise. So far as he knew, she hadn't had any issues with anyone else on the crew.

"Uh, yeah. Um, I wondered if you wanted to meet for a drink or a bite to eat. I'm kind of going crazy here in this hick town by myself and didn't know if you had plans tonight?"

Oh. Huh. This was unexpected. "No plans. Uh, sure. Are you hungry? I haven't eaten yet."

"Starved. Do you know of someplace casual? I'm still in work clothes."

"I know just the place." He gave her directions to

Marvin's Garden, the soul food place where he and Emma had first gone together.

"I'm on my way. And, Matthew—"

"Yes?"

"Thanks for taking pity on me. I didn't know how hard it would be moving here." Tess sounded profoundly grateful.

"Hey, no problem. I get it. This place isn't an easy adjustment coming from where we did."

They hung up. Maybe he should call Emma and see if she wanted to meet them there. She did promise to help Tess find a more permanent solution to her housing issue as soon as she had time. But somehow that felt awkward.

He would contact her tomorrow and try to set that up. Instead of heading inside like he'd originally intended, Matthew put the car in reverse. Fortunately, he'd managed to get his taillight fixed from the mysterious breakage, so there wouldn't be any more issues with local law enforcement—hopefully. But one never knew what could happen when the mayor of a footloose town had sworn a blood oath as their brand new enemy.

⟫⟫⟫⟫⟪⟪⟪⟪

EMMA AND SADIE had worked on her walk for the upcoming pageant until Sadie could do a seasoned New York runway model proud. Judith had rolled up on her scooter with Jamie in tow to add moral support or comedic relief, albeit a bit on the acidic side. Emma was glad to see Judith here since it had been the scene of her traumatic fall, and the end of her hopes to snag the title in the upcoming Mrs. Alabama pageant. But she'd thus far displayed a grace that surprised Emma.

They'd just finished up when Judith suggested they go out for dinner. "Girls, I can't bear to go home yet. I've been down for so long, I swear I'm gonna just die if I don't get out and see some people for a little while." Judith complained.

"What are we, big J, chopped pigs' feet?" Jamie asked.

Judith was older by about fourteen months and Jamie never let her forget it.

Judith narrowed her eyes at her saucy sister. "I don't care what *kind* of people we see, I just need to get *out* for awhile."

"I like that Marvin's Garden's place. Tad says it's a little tacky, but I've been sneaking fried dill pickles from there ever since I was pregnant with Sarah Jane."

"You bad girl. I love that place. It's one of my favorites," Emma admitted.

Judith frowned. "Well, alright, if y'all insist. But nothing *fried* is going past these lips."

Jamie rolled her eyes and mimicked her sister's words as she followed her out the door.

"Don't think I don't see what you're doing behind my back, sister," Judith threw over her shoulder.

"Who me? I'm just bringing up the rear to help you in case you fall on your ass, honey," Jamie said, her tone pure molasses.

Emma shook her head and laughed at their antics as she locked up, again feeling thankful she'd pushed past the insecurity and embraced these ladies for the fun and genuine people they were—deep, so very deep, down.

"I'll meet you there." She called from behind.

Sadie's melodic voice surprised her by saying, "Y'all go on; I'll ride with Emma." Sadie had hung back from the others. "I hope you don't mind. Those two are gettin' on my last nerve." She giggled.

"Of course not. I'm glad to have the company. They are a handful when they get started on one another, aren't they?" Emma hoped she sounded genuine and sincere.

Because she really did like Sadie. The circumstances were just a little—awkward.

"I hope you don't feel weird or anything. You and I never really get a chance to talk, just the two of us." Emma unlocked the door of her car and Sadie slid in, placing her silver Coach bag on the floor at her feet.

"Nice purse." Emma nodded toward the super-cute, tote-style purse.

Sadie beamed. "Thanks. I just love the outlet mall, don't you? Tad says not to shop there because it's cheap and what will people think, but I've found some of the most *darling* things out there. I just don't tell him because the bags from the outlet look just like the store bags at the regular mall. He wouldn't know an in-season bag compared to last year's model if it hit him square in his Ray-Bans." Sadie giggled at her joke.

Emma couldn't help but let out a giggle of her own at the idea of smacking Tad in the face with her fully loaded Big Louie and breaking his very expensive, mirrored sunglasses.

When they were on the way to the restaurant, Sadie said suddenly, "I'm sorry about Tad acting such a fool at your momma's wedding the other night. I'd like to say I don't know what got into him but I'd be lying." Sadie's normally serene expression appeared troubled in the glow of oncoming headlights.

Emma was completely taken aback by her words. "You mean you knew what he was ranting about?"

"I think so—sorta. He's different at home sometimes. When nobody is there to see him. He gets weird and angry. He locks himself inside his office and won't let me in and tells me not to bother him while he's there. He calls it his 'private time.'" Sadie's face remained serious.

"What happens when you ask him what he's up to?" Emma asked.

"He yells that it's none of my business and that I should give him his privacy—that he works hard and he's earned it. Like my daddy used to speak to my momma when I was a kid."

Emma really didn't have any marital advice to give her but she did wonder what it had to do with Tad's behavior at the wedding the other night. "What makes you think his time alone has something to do with his outburst at Mom's wedding?"

They were nearing the restaurant and Emma really wanted to hear this.

Sadie bit her lip. "He told me to stay out of his office. And he believes that I'm such a trusting little mouse that I wouldn't ever disobey him." Sadie frowned. "But I'm pretty sick and tired of his acting like a first rate asshole, you know?"

Emma nodded encouragingly, feeling really sorry for Sadie.

"Well, when he left for work the other morning, I went in there and saw corner of a picture sticking out from underneath his calendar. It was like he'd meant to pick it up but was in a hurry or something and it was shoved there by mistake. I pulled it out and it was a picture of you, Emma."

"Me? Why would he have a picture of me? Was it a recent one?"

"No. It was from way back when you won Miss Alabama. You were wearing your crown, smiling in your beautiful dress the night of the pageant, obviously. I know y'all dated back then, and I guess it wouldn't be the craziest thing for him to have that picture, but something about him having it out in his office makes me think he has more of them somepiece and this one fell out," Sadie said.

"I'm—sorry?" Emma really didn't know what to say or to think about this information.

"Honey, don't worry about it. There are some hard lessons I've had to learn in life. Unfortunately, one was that my husband isn't the good guy this town thinks he is. Or maybe he doesn't have them fooled like he thinks; I don't know. But I'm not jealous. I don't think he really loves me. I don't think he can—I mean, I honestly believe he's the kind of man who can't truly love anyone but himself. It makes me so sad to say that, but if you've ever known or lived with somebody like that, you'd understand." Sadie's voice was sad, but honest, with a bitter understanding of what Tad Beaumont was.

"I'm sorry, Sadie, especially since you have a daughter together."

"Yeah. That's the really rotten part. He is so sweet to Sarah Jane as long as she makes him proud, but if, heaven forbid, she behaves badly or doesn't shine at school, he treats her like a complete failure, like she's totally let him down." Emma could see the tears in Sadie's eyes. "It's all about him, you know?"

Emma decided then and there, it was time to clue Sadie in. "He's a true narcissist, Sadie. You've got him pegged exactly. Tad did a number on me when we were younger, and it took me some time to understand his personality type. I actually researched narcissism. Tad is the poster boy. Like you said, it's all about him. I know he's your husband, but the things you've said to me are spot on. The fact that you've realized he can't truly love anyone but himself is the hallmark of the personality disorder. It's ingrained in every part of him."

"Can't it be fixed?"

"No. It happened during his development as a very young child and became part of the fiber of who he is. Narcissists believe that everyone else has the problem—not them."

Sadie nodded. "He's *never* wrong."

"We all have some narcissistic qualities or tendencies, but very few are true narcissists. Unfortunately, I'm afraid that Tad is one."

Sadie sighed a big ole sad sigh. "Well, at least I know it isn't me. I've been thinking these things for so long but afraid to do anything to make him mad at me. If it can't be helped or changed, then there's no way I can keep Sarah Jane in that house with him just waiting every day for him to say something that will cut her to the bone or break her heart."

A sudden knock on the windshield scared them both just before they heard a muffled, "You gals gonna sit out here and gab in the car all night? We're hungry." Judith had already gotten out and wheeled herself across the parking lot to where they'd been in serious conversation.

"We'll talk more later." Emma promised, and Sadie nodded.

MATTHEW AND TESS were seated across from one another in

a booth back in the corner enjoying one of God's greatest gifts—fried dill pickles. Matthew's back was to the door and he was caught off guard when Tess said, "Hey, isn't that your wedding date?"

His head whipped around so fast he might need a heating pad for his neck later. "What?"

"You've got it pretty bad, don't you?" Tess laughed and took a slug of her beer.

"Hey, I'm your boss. Show some respect." He admonished without any real heat.

"Then, show some pride, man. Your head nearly came off your neck when you heard she was here. My goodness, look at them. I've never seen so many highlights in one place. And that's saying something in my line of work," she laughed at her own joke.

Emma had entered the restaurant with the blonde twins and Sadie Beaumont. He wondered what in the world the two of them had to talk about after that awkward scene at her mother's wedding. Nothing good, he imagined.

Then, he noticed the one with the broken leg pointing his way and whispering to Emma. Emma's eyes traveled the path of her arm and finger toward where they sat. Her expressive eyebrows shot up in surprise, then back down in confusion, as if she wasn't certain how to react. He lifted a hand in greeting, as did Tess. Emma lifted her hand in a slight wave, then sat down at the table, her back to them.

"Aren't you going to go over and say hi?" Tess asked.

"She obviously thinks we're on a date or something." She rolled her eyes. "You didn't tell me you would get in trouble if we were seen together."

"I'm not in trouble. I can go wherever I want with anyone I choose," he said defensively.

He heard it in his own voice.

"Look, do you really want her steamed with you because you're pulling out your man card and waving it around?"

Matthew felt ashamed. "No. I don't. Excuse me a minute."

"Nope. I'm coming over because I want her to find me a place to live besides that cruddy hotel room I'm in now."

"Oh. Okay, I'll introduce you." He grinned, realizing it was a solid plan.

They rose and walked over to where the four stunning, blonde women were sitting and ordering drinks. He realized how out of place Tess might feel among these four—not because she wasn't just as attractive—but because she was a different kind of pretty.

"Hello, ladies." He bent down to kiss Emma on the cheek before she could avoid him. The look she gave him was a little chilly. "I wanted to introduce you all to Tess. She's our new stylist on the set of Cammie's show. She's just moved here from New York."

The kind Southern women showed their best manners. "Welcome, Tess," Judith said.

"Well, hey there. I hope you're settling in," Jamie said.

"Please let me know if there's anything we can do to help you get acquainted with our fine town," Sadie said.

She appeared a little more disheveled than normal, but spoke the company line with her usual aplomb.

Emma said, "Hi, Tess. I'm sorry we didn't get the chance to meet at my mother's wedding. It was all a bit of a blur," Emma said, graciously.

Tess wasn't the least bit shy or intimidated by these women. "Thanks so much. I appreciate the welcome. I do have one favor—if you can help me. Matthew mentioned that you, Emma, might be able to help me find a good rental while I'm here working in town. I think my, uh, *edgy* appearance has put a few of the local owners off. I guess they're not used to normal people having more than two earrings or color in their hair other than what appears in nature." Tess flashed Emma a great big smile.

Judith spoke up. "Oh, honey, this color doesn't appear in nature, except maybe on a child under the age of five. If anybody tells you it does, they're going straight to hell for lying."

Everyone laughed.

Emma spoke up then. "I told Matthew I would be happy to either take you around or make a few calls to help you break through the glass ceiling of narrow minds around here. By the way, I think you're lovely," Emma said.

Thankfully, Matthew could tell she meant it. "We're eating fried pickles. I wanted Tess to feel a little more at home, and Emma, you did that for me when I got here, so I thought I would pay it forward." He smiled at her.

She smiled back, still obviously not quite ready to forgive him for being seen around town with Tess.

"Oh, I love the fried pickles here—they are my absolute fave," Sadie said.

"Why don't y'all join us?" Judith asked, but it was more like a demand.

Matthew's gaze searched Emma's silently for permission. She nodded almost imperceptibly. Tess wasn't waiting for anyone's permission. She'd hightailed it to their table to gather up the pickles and beers while he pulled over a couple extra chairs.

"Now, this is what I call a party." Judith beamed.

⟫⟫⟪⟪

EMMA WAS ENJOYING herself, even though she'd started off feeling stiff and uncomfortable walking in on Matthew and Tess, sitting together so comfortably. She'd never expected to experience this kind of insecurity again when it came to a man. She'd never cared enough since Tad. Even then, it had been frustration over other women trying to get him to betray her. He hadn't while they'd dated, so far as she knew, but she'd hated feeling always on guard. Just seeing Matthew laughing with another woman brought back a sliver of that uncertainty, and even now, it felt awful.

But, as she sat at the table alongside the others, Matthew

had slowly, without being too obvious, scooted closer and closer until she was warmed by his radiant heat right next to her, not quite touching, but nearly so.

Tess was a lively spirit and was regaling them with tales of living as a single woman in New York City. Even Jamie and Judith were laughing with Tess as if they'd known her their entire lives. Emma understood how unusual that was. Normally, an outsider had to work for years to break through the established circles here before she was even nominally accepted, especially by someone like Judith Dozier-Fremont. But stranger things had happened, and Tess really seemed like a genuinely nice person, besides having been out in public with Matthew when they'd walked in.

Maybe Emma could forgive her that so long as Matthew wasn't interested.

She suddenly felt Matthew's warm breath near her ear as he whispered, "I've missed you, Emma."

She involuntarily shuddered as heat and a chill went through her at his words and from his nearness. Instead of answering right away, imperceptibly to the others, she leaned back into his body and felt a growl in response as he moved in closer with his chair until their bodies were touching—his chest to her back and he slipped an arm around the back of her chair. She doubted anyone noticed except the two of them.

Until she looked up and saw Tad standing in the doorway of the restaurant, eyes locked, not on his own wife, whose back was to him, but on Emma and her now-cozy situation with Matthew. For a moment, his expression appeared murderous, then, just as quickly, he worked it into a more pleasant one, straightened his shoulders, and made his way toward their table.

"Well, I wondered what was keeping you." He addressed Sadie with a playful smile, but his annoyance was barely below the surface of both his words and expression.

Sadie must have noticed, too, as she seemed a little too brightly brittle. Maybe only Emma noticed that because of their earlier conversation in the car.

"Oh, hey, honey. We decided to come grab a bite after we finished up with pageant practice. I texted you where I was."

"I saw it earlier, and I knew y'all were having your girls' night, but had no idea you'd met up with these two." He gestured toward Matthew and Emma.

"Oh, that was all a coincidence. Matthew was with Tess having dinner when we arrived." Jamie piped up and supplied the details.

Tad frowned in momentary confusion, but since Matthew was cozied up with Emma, he obviously dismissed that. Matthew had pulled Emma even closer to him once Tad had slithered up to their table. "Sarah Jane's tucked in and Gerta's there, so I thought I would come join you." Tad's phony smile made Emma want to retch.

"Here, take my seat. I've had a long day and I'm going to pay my check and head out." Emma nearly toppled her chair as she simultaneously disengaged from Matthew and stood abruptly.

Matthew stood as well, obviously understanding her need to get the hell out of there and away from Tad. "I'm going to take off, too." Then, he glanced over at Tess, who seemed to be having a blast. "Are you going to stay awhile?"

She looked around at the other women. "Are you leaving or staying?"

Judith and Jamie shared a silent communication. "It's time we head home, too. But this was so much fun. Let's plan to do it again soon. Tess, give us your number and we'll shoot you a text next time we go out," Judith said. "Oh, and don't worry about finding a place to live. We've got you covered. I guarantee that nobody will give you a hard time around town from this moment forward—and if they do, you'll let me know, won't you, dear?"

Tess beamed. "I can't tell you how much I appreciate that."

"Well, I guess we won't have to go house-hunting will we?" Emma asked.

"We can still get together though. I'd like that," Tess said.

Emma smiled at Tess. "So would I." Tess was an infectious personality. One couldn't help but like her.

Sadie appeared relieved the party was breaking up. "Sorry, hon, it looks like you caught us at the tail end of things tonight."

Tad's mouth tightened, then he smiled. "Well, at least I can give my best girl a ride home."

Sadie, God bless her, never faltered. "I am a lucky girl." The waitress brought the checks, which they'd pre-arranged to have split up to avoid confusion. Sadie took hers and headed toward the bar to pay it away from the rest, Tad in tow, because the too-smart Sadie gave him no choice.

As they moved chairs back to their original positions, Matthew said privately to Emma, "Can I follow you home?"

She wanted to say no, that she needed some time to figure things out. But he stood there, staring at her, his blue gaze so direct and sexy. He said he'd missed her. She'd missed him, too. Maybe they could hang out for a bit and talk. Sure. They could talk.

"We could—talk."

His grin was expressive. "Yeah. We could. It's totally up to you. I'd like to spend time with you. I know we've both had a long day, but talking's good."

"Okay. See you in a little while."

She'd been a little shaken when Tad had come into the restaurant, eyeballing her like that, but he didn't have the kind of power over her he believed. Maybe she'd allowed it more than she'd realized in the past, but Emma was prepared for a fight now. Tad wouldn't intimidate her into breaking things—whatever "things" were at this point with Matthew.

Chapter Twelve

$$\infty$$

AFTER WHAT HAD happened at the wedding, Maureen had been doing some homework via her husband and Ben. She really hadn't known where to begin, but as a typical meddling mother, she'd had to start someplace. Since Emma pretty much refused to discuss what had happened with Tad in the past, or her decision to step down from her pageant title all those years ago, Maureen mined what resources she could. She began with Ben. Ben knew most of the girls who had attended college with Emma, mainly because they'd wanted to know *him*, even though he'd been a few years younger.

Ben's position as an attorney, and as, well, *Ben*, allowed him to gain entry into places others were denied. Ben had agreed to go on this fact-finding mission after what had gone down at the wedding. There were too many unanswered questions they felt led to Tad as the cause of Emma's life not being what it might.

So, Ben started with the women who he believed were

close enough to his sister and might have known what happened. He was reporting back to Maureen tonight.

Ben's face was grim as he spoke. "Her roommate at the time, Marianne, says she picked Emma up that night in her underwear with a blanket around her from a hotel. Says she recognized the guy as a member of the Auburn Football team but didn't know his name." The night in question was the "Iron Bowl" ten years ago on Thanksgiving weekend when the University of Alabama historically played Auburn University in a grudge match of epic proportions for the year's bragging rights.

"Did Marianne explain why Emma was at a hotel in her underwear with an Auburn football player?" Maureen was truly shocked.

She realized they'd been in college and young people did crazy things, but she also knew that Emma had been devoted to Tad in those days.

"Apparently Emma was completely out of it. The guy wouldn't tell Marianne anything except to watch her carefully and to get her home safely—oh, and not to tell anyone where she'd been because he wasn't sure who'd drugged her." Ben's eyes darkened when he ground out these words.

"Drugged her? Oh, my." Her poor baby. Maureen put her hand to her chest.

Howard had been listening intently, quietly until now. "Sounds like our Emma found herself in a heap of trouble that night."

"We need to discuss this with Emma. There's no getting around it. She's got to come clean so we can help her. Whatever she's been keeping from us has caused a lot of damage to her life. It's time her family shared this burden. Someone did something to her and never paid for it," Ben said.

"I just hope she won't get too upset that we went behind her back to find out about it," Maureen said, knowing it was far too much to hope.

"Honey, anytime you go digging up old dirt, you'd better plan for messy situation. I can get any kind of background checks done quietly through unofficial channels if you need them," Howard said.

Ben narrowed his eyes at Howard. "Are you ever going to tell us what kind of secret service you did for the government?" he asked.

Howard shook his head. "The less you know the better, son. Suffice it to say, I can get stuff done that most civilians cannot."

Ben shook his head. "Well, I won't question it unless I have to use it in a court case. If I obtain illegal evidence on someone it wouldn't be admissible."

"Don't worry about it, son." Howard reassured Ben again.

"Honey, Howard gets stuff done. Let's not ask how, okay?" Maureen suggested.

"I'm an attorney; I have to ask." Ben turned toward her.

"Anyway, we need to have an intervention with Emma. Even if she doesn't want us to find something out, she needs to know we know something bad went down that night besides Tad breaking up with her and her struggling to cope, and that we are here to support her if she wants to bring it to light."

"We want to know because we want to help, but I doubt she's going to willingly share it with us. You know how private she's always been," Maureen said.

"At least she'll know she doesn't have to guard some awful secret anymore if she doesn't want to. It gives her the option. After living with a burden for a long time, it's often a relief to let it go." Howard said and smiled at her.

Maureen had lived with an awful secret for so many years that had burdened her heart in the worst way. At least Justin, her late husband, had known the truth and she'd not had to hide it from him. And now, they all knew. There was a huge relief in that.

"You're right about that, honey," she said as she smiled at Howard.

"Well, we'll get her over at some point this weekend to have a talk, when she's not running around like a mad woman," Ben said.

"Do you think we should look into Matthew's past as well? Since she's showing so much interest in him—and him in her?" Maureen hated that she was so distrustful, but she felt like she had to ask.

Ben frowned. "I don't like the idea of digging into Matthew's past, Mom. He hasn't given us a reason to doubt him."

Maureen tended to agree. "But think of how disappointed Emma would be if he turned out to have some awful secret or worse. You know she already has such issues trusting men. I know that's why she hasn't gotten close to anyone since Tad," she said.

"I'm now of the belief she hasn't gotten close to anyone because Tad made sure she didn't," Ben said.

"That's a pretty big accusation, son. Care to elaborate?" Howard asked.

"It's a constructed hunch, but every time Emma has had even a mild dating interest in anyone since they broke up, it seems that the guy has conveniently been removed from the situation."

"How so?" asked Howard.

"Well, that nice boy who worked for the timber company got a company promotion and moved to Dallas right after he and Emma started seeing one another," Maureen said.

"And there was Joe from Atlanta, whose family had moved here a few years earlier. He came home after finishing his graduate degree at Vanderbilt to visit and he and Emma hit it off. They were inseparable during a couple weeks at Christmas that year until Joe was suddenly arrested for possession of cocaine and the family moved back to Atlanta, saying they never wanted to set foot in this town again. The charges were dropped due to a clerical error after that," Ben said.

"I don't think she ever heard from poor Joe again," Maureen said.

"It does sound like some fishy business for sure." Howard scratched his chin.

"I'm not sure any of it is provable except by talking with the guys and, even then, they might not know exactly how their circumstances came about."

"Maybe they were warned to stay away from Emma and didn't listen before the bad circumstances befell them?" Howard surmised.

Ben made a note on his phone. "I'll look into it. Maybe I can find out where they are and speak with them."

"What's your goal here, son?" Howard asked.

"I think what we all want is for Emma to understand that she has been played and that she is free to go after anything she wants. She may not even know how she's been manipulated. If we could show that Tad has been pulling her strings all this time, she could get some satisfaction out of taking him down. And we could figure out a way to expose him for breaking the law in the process. And who knows what he might have done around the time they broke up? I'm getting a bad feeling about all the things from back then now that I realize what's been happening up 'til now," Ben said.

Maureen saw a larger picture now. "Yes, I see where

you're going with this. Emma needs to know all the facts so she can decide how much she's comfortable sharing and if she wants to proceed with taking Tad down in a big or small way for the wrongs he's done to her."

They agreed to call Emma over to Evangeline House Saturday when everyone would be available, at which point the intervention could commence.

⁕⁕⁕

THEY TALKED. SEX, of course had been on the table as well Emma knew, but it hadn't been what the end of their evening was about. When Matthew came inside just a minute behind her from the restaurant, he sat on her sofa, ready for her to make whatever move she decided upon to set the tone.

She watched him, his long, muscled legs stretched out onto the ottoman from the big, oversized chair where he sat. His jaw had more like a ten o' clock shadow, which did things to her down in her woman places. But she decided they should talk about whatever needed saying. She wasn't one to over share, but he really hadn't shared much about himself with her at all, and maybe it was time.

"How about a beer?" she asked.

"I had a couple with dinner. Water's fine."

His good sense still surprised her. "I assume you're planning to drive home tonight," she said with good humor.

"I don't take anything for granted. I'm happy when

things work out in my favor though."

"Water it is."

She brought brought out two tall glasses of ice water, set them on the coffee table, then sat down on the couch, tucking her feet under her. Emma had already kicked her shoes off the minute they'd come inside the door. Wearing heels all day might seem glamorous, but it was hell on her feet.

"So, here we are, all ready to talk," he said.

"Yep. Let the talking begin."

"Any topic you want to start with?" He asked.

"You."

He frowned. "Me? I'm not that interesting."

"Oh, I think there are fathomless depths I know nothing about yet." And she really was interested in finding out what made him tick.

"Hmm. Well, let's see; There's my sister, Lisa, who's a couple years younger. She's married to Dub, who my mom believes is having an affair. She has two cute kids, a boy and a girl. My mom is living and my dad is dead. My stepdad took all the money and left her, so now she's started to gamble. Tomorrow, I'm headed to my hometown where I haven't been in a really long time because the idea of going back makes my skin crawl."

She stared at him, eyes wide, not knowing what to say or how to respond to such a literal info dump.

He shrugged. "You asked."

"Uh, yes, I did. I just didn't expect so much information at once. Wow. So, your stepdad ran off with the money? How long ago?" She didn't know where to begin, so why not the there?

"When I was in high school. It was a relief for me. My mother didn't think so."

"How long were they married?"

"Too long. From the time I was about eleven or so until I was almost eighteen. He was a nasty bastard to my sister and me, but my mom thought he hung the moon."

"She didn't know how he treated y'all?" Emma couldn't believe a mother would condone poor treatment of her own children by anyone.

"She knew, but pretended not to. To her credit, I don't think she realized how bad it was for us because he hid his true nature in front of her. It was a real talent that he had, being two different people in the same household."

"I'm so sorry you had to grow up like that. What happened to your dad?"

"Cancer. He left to die, literally. He found out he was sick and took off to check himself into a VA facility to spare us watching it happen. But we just thought he'd run out on us. Mom found him a few weeks before he passed."

Emma's face crumbled. "How awful."

She thought about her own family, her parents, and how close they'd all been her whole life, and couldn't imagine poor Matthew with his little sister going through such horrible things at the hands of their own parents.

"Are you close with your sister?" she asked.

"In some ways. We aren't in constant contact, but she keeps me posted about what's happening with Mom and the kids. It's my fault that we don't talk more. I've avoided going back because of all the bad memories."

"And yet Lisa stayed to be with your mom?" Emma asked.

"She met Dub in high school. He was her way out of the house and away from all the emotional mess that was my mom. He works offshore in the Gulf of Mexico on a rig, fourteen days on and fourteen off, so she stayed in town to be near his family and because my mother has a way about her that is incredibly passive-aggressive and guilt-inducing."

"Sounds—difficult."

"She's difficult, not a deep-down bad person, just really good at making you feel like you somehow owe her to make up for the consequences of her own bad choices."

"A victim." Emma knew this kind of personality and had dealt with a few over the years, which had made her determined not to behave like one.

"Exactly. Always the victim and never able to take any responsibly for her own poor judgment."

"Sounds a little harsh, but I haven't lived with the situation," Emma said.

"It is harsh, and I try really hard not to be angry with her, but she works so hard to gain sympathy when she really just needs to stand up and stop wallowing in the fact that the asshole left and realize she's better off."

"Sounds like she really loved him."

He ran a hand through his hair. "I hated that bastard so much, I never really thought about the fact that she could have felt true love for him. I guess if she really loved him and has been suffering from a broken heart instead of a blow to her pride that would make all the difference. I really believed she just didn't want to be alone or wanted to hang onto him so people wouldn't talk about her having had two husbands run off on her."

Emma stood and came over and sat on the arm of his chair, and gently placed an arm around his shoulders. "Sounds like you have a great opportunity to show your mom some compassion this weekend. Obviously, you care a great deal about your family. Mine are crazy, but they would do anything to protect me, and I know they love me."

He sighed. "I guess you're right. I have been pretty harsh with her because of my feelings toward Frank."

"It doesn't mean you have to change your opinion of Frank. He did what he did. Too bad I can't hunt him down and punch him in the face." Emma really wanted to.

"You look fierce right now, and I really appreciate it, but Frank isn't worth your spending your time or emotions on. He'll get his one day, unless I find him in the meantime to guarantee it."

"You're right. Karma is a bitch, and it will bite him on

the butt eventually."

She slid down beside him into the chair. "Nice talk. So, where is home?"

Instead of answering her question, he leaned over and kissed her.

⟫⟪

WHAT ELSE WAS he supposed to do? He'd spilled his guts to her and it had felt so good and right, because this woman had a heart three times the size of his. But was he really ready to tell her everything? Because if he did, would she ever want to speak to him again? He couldn't handle the answer if it was no. Not yet.

"That's enough gut-spilling tonight," he said. "It's been a long day. See? I am capable of just talking." He disentangled himself from her very soft and undeniably sexy body before he changed his mind about all his good intentions of going home and letting them both get a good night's sleep.

"So, I guess I won't see you until after the weekend?"

"Guess not, but I'll give you a call if I get some time."

"I'll answer if I see your name on the caller ID."

He kissed her lightly once more and could see the light strain in her expression. "Hey, is there something wrong?"

"No. Just tired," she smiled sleepily.

"You look more than tired to me," he said

"Tonight was our night to talk about you. Next time, we'll talk about me, okay?"

He frowned. That meant something was wrong. "Are you sure it's nothing I can help with?" They were walking toward her front door now.

"It's nothing that hasn't been around a lot longer than you. And it's certainly nothing that won't still be around when you get back after the weekend. And it has nothing to do with you; so, no, you can't help with this. We can talk later. I'm fine." She smiled at him and shut the door behind him as she ushered him out.

Matthew got into his car, concerned about what she'd said, or didn't say, really, and wondered if her current concerns were about what had occurred with Tad at the wedding and were tied to their shared past. But if he went back, he would most definitely be forced to come clean about knowing who she was about five minutes after their first interaction on the set. He would tell her when he got back after the weekend. He would.

Hopefully, whatever it was that was on her mind wasn't something to be alleviated by any admission he might make. In fact, what he had to say was sure to make things more complicated. There wouldn't be any way for him to drop that bomb then leave town in good conscience. It was his conscience that he'd been wrestling with for so long now and would continue to do so until he got back and came clean with Emma. But, for now, he had to focus on his family and hopefully, make some sort of headway toward a more peaceful relationship with his mother.

This had all been weighing on him for a long while. It was time to release some of this pent-up frustration from holding in his emotions and not communicating properly with those he cared about. It had become easier to avoid rather than confront these conversations because he hated the drama.

Hopefully, tomorrow's workday would go smoothly, considering they'd planned a series of holiday baking items to shoot. Cammie was an expert baker, and she and the food stylist had pre-prepared most of what she was to demonstrate. Much of what they would do tomorrow involved Cammie's discussing family holiday traditions and the usual Friday routine of answering questions sent in by viewers from the previous week. They'd gotten great feedback from social media regarding this weekly segment.

Hopefully, he could get out of town before dark, but now that the time had changed, he doubted that would be possible.

He went to bed with his thoughts running through all the possible scenarios he might face upon arriving home tomorrow. Funny that he should even think of Chapman, Alabama as home, because he hadn't in a really long time.

⟫⟫⟫⟪⟪⟪

EMMA HAD TWO pageant students who were participating in the Miss Alabama Teen pageant this weekend. Emma wasn't required to attend as a coach, as coaches weren't allowed backstage during the pageant practices or the actual pageant. But she did want to be there to support her students and share in the culmination of all the hard work, time, and effort they'd put in together. Driving to Montgomery took about an hour and forty-five minutes, so she wouldn't stay overnight Saturday after the pageant.

Today would be a slower day since those two girls were headed out of town, as they'd recently been taking up a great deal of her time in preparing for this weekend. She still had three students scheduled for private lessons and one group class after school ended, but this morning, she was free to attend her Pilates class and run some errands.

The bell sounded at the front door of the diner as she entered, and Emma experienced an overwhelming sense of déjà vu when she saw Matthew sitting at the exact same booth where she'd run into him here that first time. He looked up and a smile spread across his extremely handsome face upon seeing her. The warmth in his blue eyes made her knees want to buckle. Something happened then; she experienced belonging, and it all clicked into place in that instant. She loved Matthew Pope. She guessed that was what it must be, because nothing she'd ever experienced had ever threatened to take her legs out from under her.

"Hi there. Are you alright?" He appeared concerned now.

"Um, yeah. I'm okay."

"You look like you might need to sit down. Care to join

me?"

"Sure." She hardly recognized the sound of her own voice, it was so faint.

"You're pale. What's wrong?" His concern was obvious now.

"Just need my donuts. I haven't eaten this morning yet," she said, hoping not to reveal the stunning truth that had her sitting across from him, lying through her teeth, and wondering how in the world this had happened without her realizing it.

Sure, they'd been having a very fun and enjoyable—whatever they had been having? But, *love?* She'd been so far removed from such a possibility and hadn't even dared hope for such a miracle in her life that it seemed inconceivable how this had snuck up on her and taken her by such surprise. Should she tell him how she felt? No, this was too new. He was leaving to confront his family and had his own troubles. What if he wasn't emotionally invested? Sure, she knew he liked her, but what if he *liked* her and nothing more? How would she know without making herself so vulnerable that he could crush her heart with a mere word or response?

"Emma? You seem upset by something more than low blood sugar." His voice was soft, concerned.

Thelma shuffled up at that moment, and placed two donuts on a plate and a big glass of fresh-squeezed orange juice on the table in front of Emma. "Honey, you don't look so good. Eat your breakfast."

"Thanks, Thelma," she answered.

She raised her gaze to Matthew. "I'm okay." But she wanted to know how he felt about her, about them, and if he just saw what was happening between them as a temporary thing.

So, she mentally and emotionally suited up, deciding she had to know. "I've realized something, Matthew."

"Oh? What's that?" he asked, separating the two halves of his English muffin, or what she deemed as cardboard.

"That I really like you."

He looked up at her and grinned broadly, then picked up a knife. "I really like you, too."

"It's occurred to me that I haven't felt this way about anyone in a really long time, and it scares me just a little— well, a lot."

He stilled from spreading fruit on his English muffin. "If you're wondering if I feel the same way, Emma; I do. I don't want to push you into something you're not ready for, but I'm pretty crazy about you, in case you haven't noticed." He put down the bread and grabbed her hands between his and looked into her eyes. "I've never met anyone like you— you're gorgeous, sexy, smart, and you're one of the most compassionate women I've ever known. I keep wondering why you let me come around."

She let out a small, sad laugh. "I was so worried I wouldn't ever meet anyone and that I would end up alone."

"You? Alone? If you ended up alone it would only be because you didn't let anyone near you." He was serious, she realized.

"I didn't know if you thought of me as a fling. I was afraid to tell you how I felt," she admitted.

"We are not a fling. We are as much as you want us to be," he said, very serious.

Her heart soared. They were in a relationship—together. "Okay. I know you've got work and you'll be gone over the weekend, and I've got a pageant to attend. But I needed to know one way or another where this was going."

"When we both get back after the weekend, we're going to spend some real, quality time together." He leaned forward and whispered in her ear, "Not just talking." His eyes held such promise and her heart lurched.

"Sounds heavenly." And it did.

As busy as they both were right now, just having an evening to themselves to explore each other and spend the time getting to know everything about the other would cement their bond and strengthen this tenuous new relationship. In Emma's heart, she felt their connection, and had from the beginning. Something had clicked into place this morning though. He hadn't told her he loved her, but they really hadn't been in a good setting to speak intimately. And she could wait. Her revelation had come as a bolt of lightning; maybe his hadn't come yet. But based on what he'd said, she had high hopes that it would. They just needed a little more time together.

〰〰〰

MATTHEW'S DAY HAD gone as smoothly as could be expected, he supposed. Cammie made his work look good most days. She was great at what she did and such a natural that when problems cropped up, they usually arose from technical issues with equipment or some other source of human error.

He'd managed to get out of town before the worst of the jam up at the red light at the center of Ministry, which was typically caused when some of the locals, celebrating the end of their workday, stopped to talk and visit in the middle of the town's only regulated intersection. Things often went awry for those who were actually trying to make their way home instead of hanging out and making plans for later or gossiping about the day's events.

Matthew's impatience for such nonsense stemmed from his lack of real integration thus far into Ministry besides his budding relationship with Emma and her family. Back when he was a young man in Chapman, he had friends there and could better relate to wanting to connect with others at the end of the day. But he'd never really been a relaxed personality as a teen and young adult due to Frank's presence in their home. After he'd left for Auburn, he worried about his mother and sister. He envied those who'd felt a deep sense of comfort and belonging throughout their lives.

He subscribed to satellite radio, so his choices of music and other programs were endless. He stumbled onto an old country station playing the George Strait song, "Amarillo by Morning" that unexpectedly brought him straight back in time to a memory of him and his dad sitting inside the garage while his dad worked on refinishing an old dresser for his mom.

"Matt, the key to getting the stain to take is making sure you sand it just enough. If you sand it too much, you'll lose the grain."

He'd held his little square of sandpaper and worked beside his father diligently, hoping to do a good job.

His dad had patted him on the head and smiled at him, pride shining for his son's hard work. "You keep working like that and you'll grow up to be a fine man someday."

Matthew hadn't thought about his dad or even allowed himself those memories in decades. He'd kept such a tight lid on his emotions where Dad was concerned because the burning he experienced in his chest made him feel exposed and vulnerable. Here he was, driving toward Chapman in the dark, back to all those emotional land mines that lay all around there, just waiting for him to make a tiny misstep and blow his carefully constructed nonchalant facade all to hell.

And everyone there would call him Matt. Just like Dad had. And Frank.

Emma was the one person who came to mind as he started downward toward sadness. She would understand, she would give him a hand up and out of the sludge as she always seemed to do, even without trying to, or realizing the positive effect she'd had on his life since they'd met. She was sunshine when his world became clouded and overcast. And whether or not she was ready for it, he'd fallen crazy in love with her. But he'd wanted to wait until he returned from this weekend and resolved some of this mess with his family before moving forward toward a future with Emma.

Matthew hoped to be less encumbered by the anger and frustration with his mother and the worry and pain of his past. Hopefully, this trip home would help. Sabine's shining new perspective on his mother's actions made him realize that he really needed to take his own anger toward Frank out of things and listen to her.

And, he hoped and prayed Dub and Lisa would be alright. Of course, that wasn't his responsibility, as Sabine had also pointed out, but he wanted to be there for Lisa and the kids if things blew up.

So, instead of declaring his undying love for Emma and then blowing out of town, he would clean up his personal life as much as possible, then go for it. His heart expanded with hope and excitement at the thought of filling his world with her everyday and suddenly all the sadness evaporated. He would be able to solve any problems knowing she was by his side. He was leaving the lonely and sad Matthew behind, finally for a future of promise.

Chapter Thirteen

S ADIE BEAUMONT HAD noticed changes in her husband, Tad's, behavior. Oh, he'd been a decent husband early on, especially in public, but never an especially good man. She'd seen through his affable, good guy act, because when it came right down to it, he was out for number one—always. His comfort came first; his needs came first; his reputation in the community was the most important thing, above all else. Tad Beaumont had an incessant need to be loved and adored by everyone.

But she saw his dark side more and more lately. He used to try and hide it because he was afraid she would tell someone he wasn't perfect, so it behooved him to treat her like a princess and with great kindness. But no longer. He'd become darker recently, to the point of verbal and mental abuse to both her and Sarah Jane. Sadie wasn't quite certain what to do or how she could get out of this situation.

"Don't ever think about leaving me or our marriage, Sadie. I would never allow it—I'm not kidding." His eyes had become dark and threatening then and she'd shivered, understanding her position.

She'd loved him; not so much anymore, now that he'd begun to reveal his true self to her. But she had been completely besotted in the beginning. The disappointment in finding out one's husband wasn't as advertised was a confusing thing that hit in waves over time. But Tad had no idea how she felt. In fact, he had no idea her IQ was about fifty points higher than he believed it to be. So, Sadie supposed she'd deceived him in some ways, too.

Today, she'd made a horrifying discovery and was on her way to take steps to protect both her daughter and herself from the fallout that would inevitably come once she turned over this information. She would confront her husband, but not until all was in place to ensure her safety and Sarah Jane's future.

She wasn't jealous. Her husband's sickness had nothing to do with her. He had the problem. Sadie had come to recognize this as a bigger issue than she wanted to handle alone, so she'd sought help awhile ago from the town's newest therapist, Sabine O'Connor. Her realization had come in waves as things had gone from bad to worse in her marriage.

Sabine had saved her from feeling as if her life had ended. Sadie'd managed to sneak away to discuss all this with the counselor outside of her office in Ministry so Tad didn't find out. They'd met in the next town at the office of a friend of Sabine's. It was the only way to keep their sessions on the down-low. The very last thing Sadie needed was Tad knowing she'd sought counseling.

But today's discovery was the very last straw. Today, things would change for good for Sadie and Sarah Jane, but mostly for Tad. It might take a little while for him to realize it, but she wanted to be protected from his anger when he did.

She arrived at Ben Laroux's office and parked in the back, in the employee lot off the street where no one passing by could see. She recognized his car, relieved he was there. Ben's office was a little too close to the courthouse and municipal buildings for her comfort, but there wasn't anything she could do about that. Tad was likely either at his own office or wandering around another of Ministry's buildings sticking his nose in where he likely wasn't welcome. Of course, no one would do anything other than pretend that he was. The men would shake his hand and slap him on the back and the women at the desks would flirt with him. It was like stepping back to the sixties around here when administrative assistants were all women and called secretaries. Wretched Southern small town politics.

Sadie was pleasantly surprised to see a male administrative assistant when she entered Ben's office. Maybe not everyone in Ministry was stuck in decades past.

Sadie approached the desk of the young professional who was typing at a rate that would have fried her fingers. "Hi there, I'm Sadie Beaumont and I don't have an appointment, but I really need to see Ben. Is he available?" she asked.

The bespectacled man raised his eyes from his keyboard, focused, and smiled. "Let me check."

He clicked a button on his headset. "Mr. Laroux, Ms. Beaumont is here asking to see you—she says it's important."

He listened. "Yes, sir."

"Ms. Beaumont, Mr. Laroux is finishing up some paper-work, but has asked me to seat you in a conference room in the back. Will that be alright? I'm Chase, by the way. So nice to meet you." Chase held out a hand.

Sadie took it. "Thank you, Chase, that would be lovely." She paused just for a second. "Chase, could you do me a small favor? Please don't tell anyone you saw me here."

Chase made a show of crossing his heart with his fingers. "I'll take it to my grave, Ms. Beaumont. You have my word. Plus, you'll have attorney-client privilege. We are the souls of discretion around here. Otherwise, I wouldn't have a job." Then, he leaned forward and whispered, "And I really like my job and want to keep it."

Relief flooded through Sadie as Chase showed her back to a very comfortable conference room with wood floors and a beautiful, huge mahogany table with at least sixteen chairs surrounding it. There were richly framed oil paintings along the wood-paneled walls.

"This is lovely," she said.

"I know. Looks more like we ought to have Christmas

dinner here instead of a miserable old meeting, doesn't it?" Chase laughed. "Can I get you coffee? Water?"

"No thank you; I'm fine."

"Well, have a seat and get comfy. Mr. Laroux will be here momentarily."

Sadie lowered herself onto the surprisingly comfortable upholstered chair and tried to relax. At least she didn't feel like a sitting duck out in the waiting area where anyone might walk in and recognize her.

She still clutched a zippered sleeve of information that was tantamount to her visit. She'd chosen Ben because he was good at what he did. His reputation was spotless and character beyond reproach. And he was Emma Laroux's brother, so he would have even more motivation to make certain this information was handled appropriately.

The door opened and Ben walked inside. He was a really handsome guy. She'd gone out with him a few times in high school, but they really hadn't hit it off. He just wasn't her type.

"Hello, Sadie. This is a nice surprise." He kissed her cheek.

"Hey there, Ben. I'm so sorry to barge in here like this, but I have something very important that I know you'll want to see."

"Oh. Okay." He looked at her closely for a second. "Sadie, is everything alright?"

Tears filled her eyes. Darn it, she wasn't going to cry; she wasn't.

So, she took a deep breath and gathered up her wits. "This is very hard for me, Ben, and it's going to come as a big surprise, but Tad is a really bad person. He's not just a bad person; he's done some super bad things. And I needed to bring this information to someone I can trust."

Ben's gaze was solid and unwavering. "You can trust me, Sadie. What's going on?"

She pulled out the folder, unzipping it carefully. "Tad left his safe unlocked. I don't think he meant to, just didn't turn the knob enough to make sure it was locked and I just pulled open the door. He's been locking himself away inside his office lately almost every night and snarling at me if I ask him about it or what he's up to."

"So you got curious."

She gave a weak smile. "I knew he was up to something. He's always been a little secretive—so then, after I found the photos, I kept snooping. That's when I found his journal. Believe me, I wish I hadn't."

⟫⟫⟫⟨⟨⟨

BEN HAD BEEN surprised at learning Sadie was in his office asking to see him, and he also knew she wouldn't have just stopped by for an innocent chat. As he scanned the photos they'd spread out on the conference table, Ben tried to control the bile that rose up in his throat. Emma's image smiled back at him in some, away from him in others. But some—well, those made him want to kill Tad Beaumont. Emma appeared drunk or drugged in one grouping. Her Miss Alabama crown askew on her head as if holding on for dear life.

"I'm sorry you have to see these. I knew he had some kind of hang-up on Emma. I thought it was because they used to date, but I had no idea he had this kind of sick attachment." She slid the journal toward Ben. "This might explain a lot of what has happened over the past several years."

Ben began to read handwritten notes in Tad's near-illegible scrawl. "*Emma Jean Laroux is so hot. Today's the day I ask her out. Today's the day she becomes the lucky girl that all the girls wish they could be. I have big plans for the two of us.*"

"He obviously started writing in this journal back in high school when he met her," Sadie said, without emotion.

"Sadie, I'm so sorry. Are you alright?" Ben wondered how she could discuss this kind of betrayal as if it were someone else besides her husband and father of her child.

"I knew something was wrong, Ben. This has been going on quite awhile; I've even been in counseling because of his awful behavior. This just proves everything I've been suspecting—that he's really reprehensible or very sick—or both. Either way, it's not something I want to live with or hang around and hope it gets better, even if he turns over a new leaf. I'm out."

He could tell Sadie meant it, and that she was pretty

much over Tad Beaumont already. He looked at the hundred or so-plus pages and asked, "You've read all of it?"

"No. I just found this today, but I read parts of it that you'll want to see. Parts that Emma needs to see. It won't be easy, but she has to know if she doesn't already."

"What are you going to do now? Divorce Tad?"

"Yes. But I'm worried about his reaction. That's partly why I came to you. I need to protect my daughter and myself. I know Tad will try and destroy my character and do everything in his power to take Sarah Jane from me. He warned me that he would never let me leave him."

Ben nodded. "Where is Sarah Jane now?" he asked.

"I kept her out of school. She's with my parents. I'm headed there after I leave here. Should I try and get a restraining order?"

Ben thought for second and shook his head. "I don't think it would work. Tad wouldn't allow the order to go through. He pretty much has all the officials and judges under his thumb. Unless we could file it very quickly and very quietly with a judge who wasn't susceptible to his corruption. Would your counselor give a recommendation?"

"I think she would be thrilled to. She's pretty new here and has strong feelings about how Tad's treated both Sarah Jane and myself."

"Has she spoken with Sarah Jane?"

Sadie shook her head. "No. I didn't want to take the chance that Sarah Jane might accidentally say something to

Tad about seeing her, so I've kept my sessions with Dr. O'Connor a secret, even to the point of seeing her over in Cheyneville to stay out of sight of the gossips in town."

Smart girl. Ben had to give it to her; Sadie had done a fantastic job of maneuvering this mess thus far. But he was nearly chomping at the bit to find out what else Tad had written in that journal. He took a deep breath for patience with himself. He had to make certain Sadie was safe and well represented here as well.

"Okay, Sadie. Are you officially hiring me as your attorney to represent you and your interests?" he asked.

"That's why I'm here. Well, I'm here for that and to make sure you protect Emma from my husband, too."

"Alright, now that we've gotten that out of the way, I need a sworn statement of what Tad has done to make you fear for your safety. Anything you've felt threatened by or any reasons you feel like he would be unfit to be near Sarah Jane when this all comes out. Chase will record the information while I ask questions, okay?"

She sighed. "A-Alright. He seems like a nice young man."

He buzzed the intercom for Chase, who moved so quickly that Ben often wondered if he listened outside the door.

The more responses he heard, the deeper his understanding was of how manipulated and mentally abused Sadie and Sarah Jane had been. And the strategy of how to handle Tad Beaumont was beginning to form. He would need to get with his mother and Emma, just as they'd already planned this weekend; well, like he and his mother had planned. Dealing with a first class cretin like Beaumont was going to require circumventing traditional procedure, because a person who didn't follow the rules wouldn't be taken down by doing so.

When they were finished with the deposition, Ben said calmly to Sadie, "I want you to go straight to your parents' house and pick up Sarah Jane. Don't call anyone to let them know what's happening. Then, I want you to head directly to Evangeline House. I will let my mother know you're coming."

"I don't want to impose," Sadie said.

"You won't be imposing. We will bring Emma there so we can all discuss this. Sarah Jane can hang with the nieces, so she's entertained and not concerned by what's happening."

"Sarah Jane loves Lucy."

"We need to make sure you're surrounded by people in case Tad reacts badly to this."

"What are you planning?" Sadie whispered.

"I'm going to make Tad a proposal he'll be hard-pressed to turn down."

"I like the sound of that," Sadie said.

"I'm working out the details, but I don't want you to be alone in the meantime. Evangeline House has at least eight empty rooms, and is built like a fortress. You'll be safe there."

"You're sure Ms. Maureen won't mind?"

Ben nodded. "I'm certain. I'll call your parents and fill them in while you're on your way. They'll have Sarah Jane ready when you get there."

Sadie's phone began buzzing then.

She jumped, and then looked down at who the caller was. "It's Tad. What should I do?"

"Let it go to voicemail."

"Will he miss this?" Ben indicated the journal.

"Probably not until this evening. But he'll know something's up when I don't come home and make dinner." Sadie's hands flew up to cover her mouth as if something had just occurred to her. "He can find us with my phone locator," Her voice held an edge of panic.

Ben had suspected as much. "After you get to my Mom's house, power it down. Better yet, leave it at your parents' house and have them follow you to Evangeline House. Howard, my mom's husband, will be there. He is a retired operative in a branch of secret government ops. He's pretty badass, so you and Sarah Jane will be in good hands."

"Wow. Okay. I guess we can talk about everything when I get back with Sarah Jane. Are you coming over to Evangeline House soon?" she asked, biting her lip.

"Yes. I've got to get busy filing the order of protection on your behalf. If we can get this done without Tad knowing it's coming until after the fact, it will be really helpful. I believe I have enough proof of his being a threat to pull it off. I know a judge who doesn't play by Tad's rules and it drives him nuts because this judge has him figured out."

"So, I should go get my daughter now?"

"Let's get the paperwork signed, then I'll walk you to your car."

"Thanks."

"I'll wait to hear that you are at Evangeline House before letting this go through. That way, Tad can't interfere with your getting Sarah Jane to safety."

"What do you think he would try to do?"

Ben frowned. "I don't know. But even a simple traffic stop is something he might try, and something he has the tools to pull off."

Sadie's hand went to her heart and he heard her sharp intake of breath. "I hadn't thought of that."

He really wanted to reassure her but didn't feel comfortable giving her a false sense of security. Ben believed Tad was more than capable of using any tool at his corrupt disposal to accomplish his goals. "I doubt he would do that, but you never know what kind of lengths he would go to if pushed or threatened with exposure."

After she'd signed the paperwork, he walked her to her car outside. Fortunately, she'd had the forethought to park behind the office which wasn't visible to anyone passing by. There were large trees and shrubs surrounding the old home that Ben had converted for office space, then paved the fenced backyard for parking. He'd left the surrounding green space, which did a lot for privacy, making his office feel very discreet. For an attorney, that could be a very good thing when clients visited.

Chapter Fourteen

⁘

MATTHEW'S ARRIVAL LAST night had been heralded by his mother's Cocker Spaniel, Daniel, peeing excitedly on his leg.

Mom was a mess. Her house was a mess. And he had wanted nothing more than to get right back into his car and hightail it back to Ministry.

"I can't believe you're here, Matt." She'd wrapped him in a big hug.

He'd felt relieved to see her, but her hair smelled like cigarettes, along with everything else around them. The once-tidy home where he'd grown up was now strewn with newspapers, used food containers, and ashtrays overflowing with cigarette butts. Things were dusty and had a shabby, unkept appearance that he'd never remembered as a kid. Even when Frank had been at his worst, Mom had worked tirelessly to keep a nice home.

"I've ordered pizza for us. Pepperoni, your favorite, honey."

He tried not to grimace as she led him toward the kitchen. She'd pulled out paper plates, presumably because all the dishes were dirty and stacked up in the sink.

She saw the direction of his gaze. "Now, don't judge. The dishwasher is broken and I've been too busy to spend time washing dishes."

Or anything else for that matter, apparently. The small kitchen was cluttered and stacked with more magazines, junk mail, and various clutter besides the pots, pans, and dishes. He controlled the urge to shudder.

It was about eight o' clock, so he figured Lisa was putting her kids to bed over at her place. "Is Lisa at home?" he asked, picking up a cold piece of thin pizza from the delivery chain in town, noticing the whitened and congealed grease sitting on top the almost brown circles of pepperoni. It took everything he had to push it toward his mouth.

"Lisa said you should stop over in a bit after you eat and get settled," she said, reaching for a cigarette and her bright pink Bic lighter.

"Mom, cigarette smoke really bothers me indoors. Do you open a window or a door when you smoke?"

She waved her hand as if his words were a mosquito to swat away. "What's the point if I'm sucking it directly into my lungs anyway?"

"So, you're trying to kill yourself and it's quicker to not ventilate?" He was appalled.

She laughed and wheezed at the same time. It was a horrible sound that made him shudder.

"Since when did you become such a whiner?"

"Watching you become like this makes me sick to my stomach, truth be told. Mom, you used to take care of our home and keep things clean. You'd never have smoked in a million years. I'm looking around and I can't believe it."

His mother's hair looked like a small animal had taken up residence and was nesting there, and her shirt was stained and wrinkled. She took a long drag on her cigarette and looked around, then nailed him with a glare. "You don't have an opinion here." Her voice was raspy and bitter.

The air was still, as the smoke hung in waves, and the sharp silence created a tension that squeezed Matthew's heart and his lungs. She was right. He'd sent her money to appease his guilt, but he'd not allowed any emotional investment in several years. He'd cut her off.

"You're right, Mom. I left and I pretended I didn't care. I don't blame you for being angry with me," he said.

She didn't respond to his statement. "If you think being a woman alone in a town like this is easy, think again. They judge you and they laugh at you because you're not good enough."

"Who laughs at you, Mom?" he asked.

She pointed to nothing and no one in particular. "All of them. All the old gossiping biddies out there."

"Mom, how long has it been since you've left the house?" He ventured. An awful thought came to him.

"What do you care? You're doing your big shot thing out in the world. I'm just your stupid, sad old mother who can't find the courage to go out in public and face people."

"So, you're not gambling at the casinos?" Relief and dread flooded in at the same time.

"I haven't been anywhere in ages." She stubbed out her cigarette and put her face in her hands and sobbed.

He felt like the Grinch whose heart melted and grew a few sizes in his chest. An overwhelming sadness and empathy overcame him then. He moved toward his mother, who now seemed frail, and he took her gently into his arms as she wept. She continued to cry as if her world had ended. And he guessed it had, maybe a long time ago. Probably, when his dad left them to go and die alone.

Tears rolled down his cheeks, and he wondered how this kind of sadness could hole up in hearts and stay for such a long, long time without being released.

Then, he thought of Lisa, and how she must have taken on their mother's burden alone, not wanting to worry him after his physical injuries and PTSD. She'd managed this as well as she could, he guessed.

She'd quieted, so he asked, "Is Dub having an affair or were you just trying to get me to come home?"

She hiccupped. "I'm a terrible person. I figured you'd come back if you thought Lisa needed you."

"So, Dub isn't having an affair?" he asked again, carefully.

She shook her head, but didn't lift it off his chest. He should have been angry, but he wanted to laugh with relief. *Thank God.*

So, his mother was an unemployed agoraphobic and a chain smoker, but she wasn't a gambling addict, and his sister's marriage was still intact. Somehow, that was better.

He began to laugh. And laugh. Daniel the Cocker Spaniel got excited and ran over to see what the fuss was about. "Oh, no you don't." He gave Daniel a stern look and the dog responded by wagging his nub of a tail.

His mother's head popped up and she looked at him as if he'd lost his ever-loving mind. "Are you alright, dear?"

"Mom, thank you for manipulating me to come home." He grabbed her and kissed her cheek.

She looked puzzled. Certainly, his response wasn't what she'd been expecting. "Uh, you're welcome. You mean you're not mad at me anymore?"

He stopped laughing. "No. I was worried you had a gambling problem and that you were wasting your hard-earned money. But what I realize is that you're sad and scared and lonely. Those are things we can help you with. But the smoking needs to stop because it's going to kill you."

"I can stop smoking—well, I'm willing to try. But I don't know how to get things back on track. It's all such a mess. I don't even think I have any friends left." She shook her head, then looked down at her hands twisting in her lap.

"I'll bet you've got more going for you than you think.

And you've got two kids who love you and believe in you."
He smiled at her.

"That's what Lisa always says."

"We'll take it slow. Do you feel up to taking a shower?"

She looked at her stained clothing. "Yes. I do need to
bathe. And Lisa dropped off a bag of clean clothes yesterday,
so I'll put on some clean pajamas."

"I'll run by her house while you're showering, then I'll
stop by the grocery store on the way back. I'm assuming you
don't have fresh vegetables and fruit in the house?" he asked
in a kind tone.

"Lisa tried and tried, but I kept letting them go bad, so
she gave up. So, no, I don't have any."

He walked over to the refrigerator and looked inside, appalled at what he saw. So, he shut it and turned back to her.
"No worries. I'll pick up some things at the store and we'll
have some nice, healthy meals for the next couple of days."

"I eat pretty well because Lisa drops off dinner and her
leftovers to me most days."

That was a relief to know she wasn't eating pizza every
day. "I'll get to work helping you get things cleaned up when
I get back."

She looked around as if she was looking at the mess with
new eyes. "I'm not sure how it got so bad."

"Mom, we're going to get you back on track, okay?"

"Do you really think I can do better?" she asked.

"I do." He hugged her again.

"Oh, and honey, Lisa is happier than a pig wallowing around in a mud hole. And you ought to see your niece and nephew. They're just the sweetest things." A light came back into her eyes as she spoke about her grandchildren.

It gave him a renewed hope that this would all work out. "I can't wait to see them all."

⤜⤛⤛⤛⤛

"SO, WHAT DID you think about Mom?" Lisa asked him. His little sister, who no longer wore pigtails nor sported continuously scraped knees. Lisa was a grown woman now, and she was beautiful. Matthew could see the resemblance to their mother in her dark hair with its auburn highlights.

"Why didn't you tell me, Lisa? I thought she was losing her paychecks at the casinos in Biloxi."

"She couldn't bear for you to know. And I didn't quite know how to tell you that she'd slipped so low. I've been trying to get her to take better care of herself and her house, but she just kept getting more and more hopeless. I was glad that she even bothered to call you and ask for money. It meant that she was still trying to reach out. If she'd stopped trying to contact you, I wouldn't have had a choice but to not honor her wishes. But I held out hope that she would come out of it eventually. I've been dropping off food and gathering her dirty clothes and washing them, but she wouldn't let me clean the house."

"We had a pretty good talk. She's agreed to try and stop

smoking."

Lisa's mouth dropped in pure shock. "You're kidding. Well, I guess the prodigal son's return made all the difference. I don't mean to sound bitter, but do you know how many times I've tried to discuss her quitting?"

Matthew understood how that might have gone. "I can only imagine. She was pretty angry until we both broke down," he admitted.

Lisa frowned, then came over and put her arms around him. "I'm sorry it came to that. But don't you think it was about time the two of you broke down the wall, big brother?"

He gave her a hard squeeze, then pulled back. "Yeah, it was. And it's time I came back here and faced you, too. I'm sorry I left you to handle things with Mom. That was really shitty of me."

She smiled at him. "Um. Yes, it was, on the one hand, but I didn't blame you, you know? I remember you stepping in front of me when Frank was ready to rip a strip off somebody for something, and taking the blame for things I'd done so he didn't come after me."

He'd pretty much forgotten. "I hadn't even thought of that. Frank was a mean bastard. There was no way I'd have let him lay a hand on you."

"Well, you took enough abuse for both of us; don't think I don't remember. And I don't blame you for hating Mom for looking the other way."

"I didn't hate her, exactly, I just wanted her to find the guts to leave him so we could be happy again. And I have to admit; Frank was brilliant when it came to the sneak attack while mom was gone to the store or not looking."

"I'm a mother now; she knew. If someone were hurting my children, I would know—and I wouldn't hesitate to kill them," Lisa said with a calm finality that convinced Matthew without a doubt.

"Speaking of your children, when do I get to see them?" he asked, suddenly having an intense urge to protect and love them as his own.

Lisa smiled. "Jordan is five now, and loves soccer and Star Wars Legos and action figures. Claire is three-and-a-half; don't ever forget the half, by the way. She adores anything Hello Kitty and wants a real kitty of her very own to love and squeeze and play dollies with."

His eyebrows went up at the thought of a real cat being forced into a pinafore. "That better be one docile cat or she'll be hacked to ribbons."

Lisa giggled. "Exactly. Kitty better sharpen his claws if he means to take on Claire for tea party time. Oh, and she loves Star Wars Legos, too. So, there's some contention there with big brother."

"So, she's to be a star ship commander as well?" He laughed at the idea of his curly-haired little niece commanding from the bridge.

"She wins more than half the time. Jordan is already intimidated by her interminable will. Lucky for him, he gets to go to school and have friends outside his own starship."

"So, I guess they're already asleep?"

She nodded. "They begged to stay up to see you, but meanie that I am, said no."

"Is everything alright with you and Dub? Mom lured me home by telling me she thought he was having an affair."

Laughter burst forth from Lisa before she covered her mouth to quiet it. "Oh, my. Is that how she finally got you back here. That was really creative of her, I must say."

"She admitted tonight that it was a ploy. Said the two of you were happy as pigs in the mud."

Lisa grimaced. "Icky analogy, but we're fine. He's crazy about the kids and still crazy about me. I miss him so much while he's away, but offshore work pays good money and it's solid, dependable employment since his degree is in petroleum engineering."

Matthew let out another sigh of relief he didn't realize he'd been holding in. "I'm so glad to hear it. I didn't know if there was some truth to what she was saying. You can never tell with Mom."

"Well, you can put that worry to rest, brother. We're fine. He comes in next weekend. I know he wishes he were here to see you."

"Please give him my best." He stretched and yawned, just now realizing how tired he was. "Well, I promised to stop by the grocery store on my way back to Mom's house."

"Better hurry or the sidewalks will roll up on you." She checked her watch. "The Buy-Low closes in twenty-five minutes."

"Gotta run. I'll see you and the kids tomorrow."

"We're planning on it. We'll come over to Mom's house. Now that you're here, maybe we can work together and make progress with her."

"So, what are her finances like?"

Lisa sighed. "I really don't know. I know she still gets Dad's pension pay and Social Security. Frank couldn't get his hands on that. But I swear I don't know. Hopefully, she'll share that info with you."

"Okay. I'll see you tomorrow."

"I've missed you."

"You, too. I'm glad to be home." And for the first time ever, it was true.

※»»««※

SADIE'S PARENTS WERE worried sick by the time she arrived to pick up Sarah Jane. Ben had said he would call them and she should focus on driving and her next moves.

"Honey, do you want us to follow you?" Her mother hovered as she snapped a napping Sarah Jane into her booster.

"I knew that boy was no good from the minute we set eyes on him. But you loved him, so we went along," her father muttered.

After quietly shutting the car door, she turned to her parents. "Momma and Daddy, this is the hardest thing I've ever had to do. I'm worried and scared. Tad is a little bit crazy, and I need to protect me and Sarah Jane right now by heading straight over to Evangeline House. I can't explain everything right this minute, but I need you to not say anything to anyone, can you do that?" They both nodded.

"You know y'all are the most important people in the world to us. We wouldn't do anything to put you at risk," her mother said.

"Can we follow you to Evangeline House?" her dad asked.

"Yes. In fact, I'd appreciate it."

"How about we let your momma ride with you?"

"Okay, thanks."

Her mother climbed inside her car, and Sadie'd never felt so loved as she did right then. This was awful, but it would all be okay. One way or another, she would make it through with the help of family and good friends. People could say what they liked about small towns, but right now, she was very happy she lived in one, surrounded by those she loved and trusted with her life—even though she understood Tad was just as close and might mean her harm in just a few hours.

They made their way through town toward Evangeline House, and Sadie breathed a huge sigh of relief when she pulled into the drive. Sarah Jane woke up then and asked,

"Mommy, why are we here?"

"Honey, we're going to go inside and have a talk about some things. I don't want you to worry, okay?"

"Grandmomma's here, too, honey. Remember Miz Maureen? We're at her house. She has the prettiest house. Did you know they have weddings here?"

They sounded rather like they were trying to convince her to take medicine. "O-okay. But are we going back home later?" Sarah Jane wasn't a fool. She could tell something was up.

"Let's go inside now, honey, and we'll talk about everything," Sadie just wanted to get inside the house. Inside meant safety from Tad.

⤜⤜✦⤛⤛

BEN GOT WORD that Sadie and Sarah Jane had arrived at Evangeline House. He also knew that Tad was at city hall, which was right across from the courthouse. Ben called Judge Boudreaux's cell phone. "Boudreaux." The judge's Cajun accent came through the phone with authority.

"Judge, I'm sorry to bother you. This is Ben Laroux calling with a matter of vital importance and urgency—and sensitivity."

"What are you trying to sneak around and do, son?"

Ben understood that the judge minced no words and he appreciated it. "I need an order of protection for the mayor's wife—against the mayor."

Ben heard a soft whistle on the other end of the line. "Boy, do you have any idea what kind of shake-up this will cause in this town?"

"Yes, sir. She's made her deposition and signed the papers. He has no idea he's to be served, and she's in a secured location." Ben took a breath. "And, sir, the mayor has broken more than a few laws against our citizens for which his wife has provided inarguable proof."

A low rumble of laughter came from the judge. "I'm coming to your office with Elizabeth, the county clerk. I won't even tell her what's going on until it's done. Then it'll be indisputable, even by our corrupt mayor."

"Thank you, Your Honor. Most of all, Sadie Beaumont thanks you."

"No, thank you. I've been trying to figure out how to bring this clown down since the day I was elected. You've just handed him to me on a plate. I'm in your debt."

"I hope all goes as planned. He's a slippery one."

"Tell me about it. Most folks around here think he's the second coming. Or, maybe they're afraid he'll have his police department plant drugs on them if they don't behave that way. Either way, I'm happy to do my part to cause some real trouble for the puffed up pissant."

The judge wasted no time dragging the unsuspecting clerk over, who was clearly giddy over causing Mayor Tad some embarrassment as well, once she realized what was happening. The judge instructed her to remember her oath as a fellow elected public official and not leak a word to anyone regarding this filing. Ben felt confident by the gleam in the woman's eye that she only meant to celebrate the downfall of the mayor and wouldn't do anything to jeopardize that.

Elizabeth Jones, Clerk of Court, shook Ben's hand and nodded. "My lips are sealed, of course. I was elected to serve this county with the utmost professionalism, and I take my job very seriously. Sadly, there are others around here that do not." She sniffed, her posture rigid and unyielding.

"Thank you, Mrs. Jones," Ben said.

Mrs. Jones nodded, her job done here.

Ben would only be able to breathe again once he was at Evangeline House with his eyes on Sadie Beaumont when this all went down. So, he thanked the judge again, assured this would be filed with the court immediately.

Ben grabbed his briefcase and his cell phone and headed out to his car, and straight home to Evangeline House, calling Emma on the way.

She answered on the first ring. "Hey, brother, what's up?"

"What time can you get away?"

"Well, hello to you, too. What's going on that's got you all het up?" she asked.

"Emma, Sadie came by my office and filed an order of protection against Tad. She's headed to Evangeline House now where I assured her she would be safe."

"Oh. Oh, my. Okay, but what does it have to do with me?"

"She found a journal he's been keeping since the two of you met. Emma, honey, you need to see what's inside. I don't want to discuss this over the phone. I haven't read it yet, but Sadie says he's committed criminal acts against you that she's not sure you even know about."

He heard Emma's intake of breath. "My last client just canceled. I'll be right over. But I've got to leave for a pageant first thing in the morning."

"Just come over to Mom's as soon as you can. And don't say a word about what's happening with Sadie. No one knows—not even Tad. I just filed the papers and who knows what he'll do when he finds out."

"Tell Sadie to hang tight. I'll be there soon." Emma sounded truly worried about the other woman.

"I didn't know the two of you were such good friends." Ben was surprised at Emma's empathetic response to Sadie's situation. Not that she wasn't an empathetic person, just that he expected Emma to be a bit more cynical toward Sadie.

"We've recently come to friendly terms and I don't envy her living with that asshole for all these years."

He hung up the phone satisfied that Emma was on her way.

❧❧❧

EMMA'S HEART RACED, her hands shook, and a sudden

weakness overtook her limbs. *Oh, boy.* What had Tad revealed in his journal? She wasn't surprised that he'd documented his nefarious actions. Whatever they'd been over the years, he was likely to be proud of them, even if he'd been unable to boast about them to others. At least he could write them down and savor them over and over. Sounded like him.

She'd just set the alarm and was locking the front door of her studio when she heard approaching footsteps. She looked up to see Tad towering over her. *Damn.* Emma'd had years of practice training her facial expressions. This was the moment of truth, knowing what she did. He was hovering over her and she was sandwiched between him and the front door. Unfortunately, the small covered entrance shadowed the two of them to passers-by.

"You're in my space; can you step back an give me some breathing room, please?" She took the position of strength, because bullies fed on weakness, she well understood. When he didn't step away, she very loudly barked. "Back off!"

He did, but then laughed, a low rumble from deep in his throat. "You're such a tiger, aren't you?"

"I'm on my way out and I've had a long week, Tad. What do you want?"

"But still no manners. Isn't that what you're supposed to be teaching our young women in the community?"

"I teach them to find their dignity, strength, and pride from within—things I wish I'd known more about several years ago."

He clutched his heart dramatically. "Oh, ouch. That was a direct hit." He grinned. "I like your spirit, Emma. I always have. Too bad my sweet Sadie doesn't have much of that. Makes for a boring life."

"I think Sadie has more going for her than you're giving her credit for." *Way more, asshole.*

He waved away her words. "I'm not here to discuss my marriage, but I am here to prove my point that Matthew *Pope* isn't the man you thought he was."

Something in his tone made Emma take notice. She wasn't going to like this.

"Did you know he went to Auburn? At the same time we were at the University of Alabama?" Tad's tone was smug.

She had braced herself for something bad. Her eyes widened. Why hadn't Matthew told her this? "So what? Why does that matter?" She challenged Tad.

"I'll bet you're wondering why he didn't tell you? Let me fill you in. Because he was a hayseed kid who played football back then—looked completely different. He even had a different name. Matthew Blanchard, I believe it was." Tad peered expectantly over his Ray-Ban's at her. "No? Still no little jingly bells going off?"

Something about his being a football player at Auburn was totally making her stomach flip. Then, Tad pulled out an old photo. It was a faded, but pretty clear individual helmetless, black and white of a football player. He looked vaguely familiar—handsome with serious eyes. She turned it over. *Matt Blanchard*. No.

"Putting it together yet?" He continued to watch the comprehension dawn on her face. "Yeah, I thought you might. I did some digging because I remember seeing him in the fraternity house the night you let those guys put their hands all over you."

"You're wrong."

But Tad wasn't wrong.

It was him. Matthew Pope was Matt Blanchard, the football player who took her to his hotel room that night. And he hadn't told her; all this time they'd spent together, he'd allowed her to trust him and he'd lied to her. He'd known how mistrustful of men she was and likely how that had come about. *But he hadn't said a word.*

"No. You're in denial about what he is. Did you even remember him? What he did? So, what do you think of your Prince Charming now? Just goes to show, you can't trust anyone, can you?"

She tried to push past Tad, but he caught her by the arms and pulled her against him, turned her around and shoved her back against the door. She could feel the front of him pressed against her, his hot breath on her mouth. He had an erection. Emma thought she might throw up. Instead, she instinctively brought her knee up as hard as she could, with possibly super-human strength, leaving him writhing in agony on the brick path leading to her studio.

Resisting the urge to kick him in the perfect teeth, she ran to her car, peeled out of the parking lot, and headed straight to her mother's house. Taking a couple deep breaths, she tried to tamp down this awful sense of free-falling.

She could hardly process what Tad had told her. Matthew, the Matthew she'd just discovered she loved had lied to her about who he was. What did he know about that night? He'd witnessed her worst nightmare and hadn't said a word? Who could do that to another person?

She pulled into the drive at Evangeline House and fervently wished she could avoid everyone, run upstairs to her childhood bedroom, and throw the covers over her head. Her heart was broken.

But of course, that wasn't to be. "Emma, thank God." As soon as she opened the front door, Ben grabbed her in a hug. She collapsed into him and sobbed.

"Emma?" He pulled back and looked at her. "What's happened?"

She looked around then and noticed Sadie, her parents, Mom, and Howard all just beyond the foyer in the main sitting area, their expressions grim and concerned. "Can we talk in the other room?"

"Of course." He turned to the group. "Excuse us."

They went into the kitchen where he made her a cup of hot tea. "Now, tell me what's happened."

She did her best not to cry as she filled him in on Tad's visit to her studio, then pulled out the crumpled photo from her pocket where she'd shoved it at some point on her between then and now. He frowned as he looked at it. "I did a background check on Matthew, but haven't had the chance to read it yet."

"Why did you do that? Did you suspect him of something?" She asked.

"No. But with everything that's happened, I went ahead with it. I wasn't even sure I would pull it up unless I felt the need. I didn't know about any of what happened that night, Emma. Why didn't you tell us?"

Emma shook her head. "Because I was ashamed, and I really didn't know what happened that night. I was so out of it. I-I thought that maybe I was somehow responsible."

His expression was thunderous. "How could you be responsible? You were so obviously taken advantage of in some way." He paused a second to unclench his fists. "Sadie says that Tad admits he's responsible for what happened."

Something clicked with Emma. "The night of the wedding he said something about giving me a drink before I wandered off and ruined everything."

"Let's go have a look at what's written in the journal."

They stood and she said, "I'm-I'm in love with Matthew, Ben. After all this time. I haven't been involved with anyone, and haven't even allowed myself to really like anyone." Tears rolled down her cheeks.

"Maybe he was waiting to find the right time to tell you about the past."

She gave him an incredulous look that said he had the brains of a rock or maybe a turd. "Really. Don't you think it was pretty pertinent information? 'Oh, by the way, I've been meaning to tell you now that we're dating seriously and having sex that I met you ten years ago when you'd been drugged and we spent the night together in a hotel room when you were Miss Alabama.'"

Ben cringed. "Hopefully, it will be a better explanation than that."

"Nothing he could say will make me trust him or make this okay." She shook her head sadly.

"Let's just see if we can piece this together, okay?"

They reentered the room with the others. Sadie came over and hugged her. Somehow, they'd developed a kinship over one really nasty bastard.

❊

SATURDAY MORNING DAWNED cooler than it had been, but it was perfect weather for working with the windows open with his mom to get things moving in the right direction. "Honey, do you want me to turn the game on later?" Mom asked, as she leaned up from petting Daniel.

He frowned at the dog. He'd been so distracted by his thoughts that he hadn't realized Auburn was playing LSU at noon today. "That would be great. Thanks."

"I know how much you love your team."

He looked over at her. She seemed tired, but in a better

frame of mind, certainly more than she'd been last night when he'd arrived. He'd pulled out all the nasty remains in her refrigerator when he'd gotten back from the grocery story after a quick run-through at the Buy-Low just as they were locking up for the evening.

He'd stocked up on eggs, cheese, fresh lettuce, tomatoes, carrots, milk, orange juice and any other staples he'd been able to grab within the fifteen minutes he had. Lisa was there now, getting things like toilet paper, soap, and other items he'd noticed Mom was low on.

Lisa had stopped by this morning with the two adorable munchkins to say hello on their way to the store. His heart had nearly come out of his chest when he'd gotten such an enthusiastic hello from them. Jordan and Claire weren't a bit shy meeting their uncle who they hadn't seen since Claire was a newborn. Both threw themselves into his arms as if they'd known and remembered him their whole lives.

"Hey, guys. Wow; look at you two." He hugged both, getting a whiff of baby shampoo from Claire's shiny curls and noticed a scrape on Jordan's elbow when he'd removed his jacket that was undoubtedly the result of some carefree childish excursion, bringing him back to his own childhood with Lisa.

It warmed him to see these two looking so happy and peaceful, something he and Lisa likely were at some early time in childhood, but that he couldn't quite remember. It relaxed him, too, and he experienced a sensation of healing and well-being just knowing Lisa was content with her family, because he was well on his way to happy, too—

finally.

After managing to separate them from Daniel, Lisa took off, kids in tow, for the grocery.

Now, if they could work through the issues with Mom, maybe they could all find some closure.

"Mom, you take the lead on throwing away the things you're comfortable getting rid of, okay?" He'd pulled out several large, black trash bags and placed them out in the living room. He'd already thrown out the actual trash, as in the food containers, empty or opened cans and cigarette butts. And he'd tinkered around with the dishwasher and realized the breaker had flipped, probably during a storm, and needed no further repair. Now that the dishes were clean and the trash was cleared, things were looking much better. The place really needed dusting, vacuuming, mopping and deep cleaning top to bottom after a few months of neglect. But they would take it a step at time.

She looked around, taking in the changes. Her clothes were clean, and he noticed she'd made an effort with her hair this morning. "There are some things around that I really don't need, I guess. Let's face it, I won't read all these newspapers and I can throw out the advertisements I've gotten in the mail. I guess that's as good a place as any to start."

"Okay. If you want to work on that, I'll mow the grass and do a little yard work, okay?" He noticed a doggy door through the utility room that opened out to the fenced backyard. Ah, Daniel was able to go outside at will. Matthew wondered how the carpet had been spared his urination issues. Or, maybe Daniel treated him special.

Mom had a twinkle in her eye when she asked, "Are you sure you remember how to do that? I mean, do big time TV producers know how to mow grass and use a weed eater?"

He laughed. "Touché, Mom. How about you do your thing in here and I'll go muddle around and try to remember how to start the lawnmower outside?"

"Deal."

As Matthew made his way around the corner of the garden shed, he dialed Emma's number again. He'd tried to call her last night, but his call had gone straight to her voice mail. The same thing happened again now. He knew she was headed to a pageant a couple hours away today, but thought she would have at least called him back, especially after their last conversation.

Frowning, he dropped his phone in his pocket; he would try her again later. Now, he had a mower to deal with. Then, he noticed Daniel the spaniel eyeballing him from two feet away. "No, Daniel, go back inside."

The spaniel sighed as he lay down, stared at Matthew, and refused to move.

Matthew got the message. *You're an asshole and I'm going to either pee on you or keep an eye on you at all times.* Or something like that.

At least the kids liked him.

Chapter Fifteen

$\mathscr{E}$MMA TURNED HER phone off last night, and only turned it on again briefly to check on her pageant contestant. She couldn't bear the thought of hearing it ring and knowing Matthew was calling. He didn't know she knew about his past—their past. He still believed that when he came back here tomorrow night, they would pick up where they'd left off. No matter what he had to say, she couldn't ever look at him the same way again.

Emma wondered if she could ever look at anything the same way or trust her judgment after what she seen written in Tad's own handwriting last night. Emma couldn't bear to even think of what a fool she'd been. Yes, she'd been young and naive, but could she have been that wrong about the person she'd given her innocence and heart to? She'd believed in Tad Beaumont, and even though she'd found out the kind of person he was later, this—this was so much worse than what she'd even imagined.

A knock at the door pulled her out of her miserable

thoughts. "Yes?"

"Honey, it's Mom. Tad's been served papers this morn-ing. I just wanted to let you know."

She shook off her own self-judgment and tried to focus on what Sadie must be going through right now. Sadie and Sarah Jane were the ones whose futures were currently most affected by Tad's actions moving forward.

"Okay, Mom. I'll be out in a minute."

"Are you alright, honey?" Mom asked from just beyond the door.

"I'm okay."

"Take your time."

Emma had already showered and dressed. She'd been sitting on her bed wondering what the next step could possibly be in her life. It was all such a mess. Right now, she could do her best to divert her own worries and think about someone else.

Just as she descended the staircase, a loud banging on the front door left her with no doubt who was trying to beat his way inside.

"Ben. What should we do?" She'd made it to the bottom of the stairs just as Ben was heading toward the front door.

"No. Not yet." He turned and called to Howard, who'd just appeared from the kitchen as well. "Howard, he's here."

Howard picked up what looked like a walkie-talkie. "Close in." He waited a beat, as the loud banging stopped, followed by a thud.

The walkie-talkie came to life. "We've got him."

Howard opened the front door. "Well, hello there, Mr. Beaumont. Thanks for dropping by. I want to make certain you're aware that your wife, Sadie, is here at Evangeline House."

Tad was being held tight between two very large and extremely capable-looking men in dark sunglasses who made Tad, squirming ineffectively in his loafers and golf shirt, look quite ridiculous. "Of course. I know she's here. I've come to talk some sense into her."

Howard frowned. "So that means you're aware that you're breaking the terms of the order of protection filed by Sadie Beaumont against you?"

"What—of course, I'm aware. Nobody's going to arrest me. Who are these assholes and whom do you think you are, accosting me in *my* town? I'm warning you—"

"Ben, did you get that?" Howard looked behind him.

Ben had recorded the whole incident. "Tad, these men are private security hired to protect Sadie just in case you decided to make a bad decision. Howard, here, has extremely high US government security clearance that you really can't compete with as a mayor in a tiny town in Alabama.

Tad's entire body tightened and his expression became truly enraged. "You've got nothing on me."

Ben pulled out the journal and a few of the photos of Emma, the damning ones. "In your own words, written in your own hand, you son of a bitch."

"You took my personal property without my consent or a warrant. It will never be admissible," Tad yelled.

"I didn't take it, Tad. Sadie took community property from the home you share. She has every right to do with this as she chooses. By the way, you really shouldn't have been so careless as to leave your safe open."

"That bitch!" Tad screamed, obviously referring to Sadie.

Emma thought the top of Tad's head was going to blow off like in the cartoons. He hadn't seen her yet. She was off to the side and out of his line of vision. But he was about to see her.

She stepped out. "Hi, Tad." She wavered between feeling a bit sorry for him and the urge to beat him to death with her bare fists.

"Emma. Tell them. Tell them this is all a mistake."

"I read the journal," she said with no emotion.

His facial expression registered comprehension of that, but there wasn't any kind of regret attached to the comprehension. On the other hand, she saw anger flare in his eyes. "So, you know, then. You know how badly you screwed everything up for me—for us back then."

She now wanted to beat him with something much more substantial than her fists. Had she misunderstood?

"Me? I screwed up? In you own words, you wrote that you drugged me because you'd met an incredibly sexy woman who was willing to spice things up by having a three-way sexual escapade with us, but I was such a boring stick-in-the mud that you knew I'd never go for it." She got very close to his face and nearly spat. "You *drugged* me. But you see no fault in that? Somehow, in my confusion, I stumbled out of the room in my underwear, still wearing my Miss Alabama crown from the game. I wound up in some frat guys' room where they groped me and took photos. She ran over to the table and grabbed a handful of disgusting pictures, holding them up.

"I told you to stay put while I went to get your surprise. But you snuck away from me. How dare you leave and let others guys touch you like that, let them *touch* you? It ruined you. You didn't deserve that crown or me anymore. But I fixed it for you to save you shame and embarrassment. Don't you see how much I still cared about you even though we couldn't be together anymore?"

They all stood, mouths open and speechless at his crazy rant.

"You drugged me and caused the whole thing, you asshole. Don't you see that none of it would have happened if you hadn't done that? I wouldn't have been photographed like that and no one would have taken advantage of me in any way. And Matthew wouldn't have taken me out of there to try and protect me."

"Do you really think that's what *Matt* did? Try and protect you? Are you kidding? *I've* been trying to protect you from him. He's a predator. He has an arrest record as a sex offender. It's public record if you don't believe me."

Emma's legs buckled then, and Howard and her mother were there to assist. Sadie had been listening, and she came out swinging. "You're the predator, Tad Beaumont. And you'll never, ever be a husband to me or a father to Sarah Jane again, do you hear me?"

"Sadie, you'll regret this. Get hold of yourself and don't think to embarrass me."

"Tad, you've already broken the terms of the protection order, which will likely land you probation at the very least and a lengthy trial. Embarrassment is the least of your worries," Ben said.

Sadie came over and put her arm around Emma, who was still dazed by Tad's final zinger.

"Tad, I think it's time you and I strike an agreement." Ben suggested.

"Why would I do that?" Tad challenged.

"Because your reputation seems to be all that really matters to you. And saving face is the one thing you might be able to do if you go along with our terms," Ben said. "So, let's go in to the study and see what we can come up with."

It must have dawned on Tad that the position he now found himself in was at direct odds with what he wanted most out of life, so he, along with his new babysitters, preceded Ben toward the study down the hall.

Everyone in the room let out a sigh of relief. Except Emma.

"What do you think he meant about Matthew having a

record as a sex offender?" she asked, her voice a single thread.

Howard looked grim. "I guess it could mean just about anything, if he's telling the truth. Sounds like a truth you'd want to hear directly from Matthew, if you really care about this young man."

Emma was shaking. "I'm so afraid. He lied about meeting me the way he did when I didn't recognize him, and I find out that he could be a sex offender. Could he have done something to me when I was drugged that I don't remember?"

"Oh, darling. I'm sure that isn't true. He seems like such a nice guy."

Howard cleared his throat, looking grim. "It's often the nice ones who fool young women, Maureen; I'm sorry to have to say that."

⫸≪

BY THE TIME Matthew was ready to leave Chapman Sunday afternoon, much had changed in his personal life where it pertained to his family. They'd managed to get Mom outside to sit on her patio and sip on a glass of sweet tea. Lisa and the kids planted some pansies in the flowerbed.

"It's not that I'm afraid of going out, it's just that I've gotten out of the habit. I wanted to sleep more and do less. I didn't want to see people, and it just all got to be too much," she admitted.

"Mom, will you see a counselor? Your insurance plan and

Medicare will cover the visits. And, please don't feel strange about seeking treatment. I've been seeing a therapist," Matthew admitted to both his mother and sister.

His mother's eyes widened in surprise and maybe just a little pride. "Well, son, if you can admit you've got problems that need working on, then so can I." She looked over at Lisa. "Honey, will you help me find someone?"

Lisa grinned. "Of course, Mom. Do you think you'll be able to go out to see someone?"

She nodded. "I really think I've been depressed more than truly afraid to go out. I just haven't had the motivation to leave the house. But with you both here and knowing Matthew doesn't blame me, well, knowing he isn't so angry with me anymore, makes me want to be here for you kids. I'm your mom and I know I matter to you."

"Mom, you really do. We love you very much," he said the words that had been so terribly hard to utter for such a long time.

"I know, son. You were always both such great kids, even when I was pretending not to notice. I love you both so much. Thank you, both, for helping get me out from under this funk I've been in for so long. I'll do my best to be your mother instead of such a burden from now on."

"Mom, we'll always be here to take care of you," Lisa said and he nodded in agreement.

Matthew looked at his watch and stood. "It's time for me to take off. I'd like to get back to Ministry before dark, if possible."

"Tell the young lady who's making you so happy that we said, 'Hello and thank you.'"

That took him aback for a second, then he smiled. "Her name is Emma, and I can't wait for you to meet her."

⟶⟩⟩⟩⟨⟨⟨⟵

TAD HAD BROKEN many laws and he'd broken trust with people he had vowed to love and protect, but the worst thing about all of this coming out, was he truly didn't seem to feel or try to show any humility of remorse. It was the least satisfying takedown Ben could have ever imagined—on the one hand. Then, there was the other hand. Tad would be cut off from what he most desired—the people of ministry's constant, though often phony, public overt adoration and ass-kissing.

Ben and Judge Boudreaux had discussed it. Most of Tad's wrongdoing wouldn't stick unless Sadie and/or Emma pressed charges. There were a few items that the city could pursue against him, but the judge agreed their immediate world was far better off without Tad Beaumont anywhere nearby.

Ben had put forth a rather specific deal to Tad. Ben would hang on to the journal outlining his crimes—and there were many—if Tad agreed to leave Ministry permanently, file for a divorce from Sadie, giving her full custody of Sarah Jane, with visitation privileges at Sadie's discretion in conjunction with her weekly sessions with Sabine. They would do what was best for the child, and would take Sarah Jane's wishes into consideration. Tad would be required to see a counselor wherever he landed, if he wanted to be considered eligible for supervised visitation with his daughter. He would not contest any of this. He would provide monetary restitution for the pain and suffering they'd endured in his household.

Tad had been a husband obsessed with another woman their entire marriage and he'd treated Sadie like a trained dog, only being kind when she performed to his expectations; otherwise, he was verbally abusive and downright hateful and demeaning. Yes, he'd bought her expensive clothes and they'd lived in a nice house, but those were things to improve and maintain his image.

Now, Sadie would continue to live within her accustomed standards—and Tad would pay for it without the benefit of living within the same state. Ben's contract with Tad included a gag order that he never discuss Sadie or Sarah Jane, or the town of Ministry, for that matter. Tad had a business and political science degree, plus, he had piles of money and a deep trust fund. He could work or not, and set himself up at a country club on a golf course in South Carolina or the south of France, for that matter, and live out his life quite nicely. The attorneys could handle everything—so long as he never came around again.

The only thing that would remain of Tad Beaumont in

Ministry, Alabama would be questions and rumors. He could tell his immediate family that he'd done some really crummy things and that he was going away to outrun damage to his family's reputation and to keep from facing criminal charges. They would buy that, knowing him as they did, and likely they would appreciate his good decision to spare them any embarrassment.

But none of this could undo the damage from one man's selfishness, or his need to shine and be number one at the expense of hurting good people. Then again, if Tad was truly broken, who was to blame, Ben wondered? What did one do with such bone-crushing anger left behind within the victims? If arrested, Tad might have figured a way to serve the lightest sentence, bribed or blackmailed his way out of things, with Sadie and Sarah Jane worse off than now. Tad was like a cat, who almost always landed on their feet.

"Is he gone?" Sadie asked.

"He's gone. The only things he'll take from the house are his personal effects and car. Howard is over there now with his two security people to make sure of it. I've drawn up a property settlement, if you want to have a look. It basically states that he will not impede your access to his trust for living and household expenses for you and Sarah Jane. I've checked into his finances, and they are very sound. Sarah Jane has her own trust fund, set up by Tad's late father for when she turns twenty-one."

She waved her hand as if none of that mattered. "I really

don't want to talk particulars right now, if you don't mind. Thanks for everything you've done. I just want him gone. I've called Sabine over to help me talk with Sarah Jane. She'll be here in a few minutes."

"Sabine, the therapist?" Ben tensed.

"Yes, do you know her?" Sadie asked.

"We've been introduced," he said.

He'd seen her at his mother's wedding, but she'd seem to always be in a different place. The woman had had the most peculiar reaction to meeting him.

Emma entered the room and Ben asked. "Have you been binge-watching those commercials about the abused animals and sick children again?" She looked like hell.

Sadie giggled, breaking the doomsday feel. "Y'all will say anything around here to get a laugh, won't you?"

Emma almost cracked a smile. "Don't tread on puppies and babies to try and make me feel better."

"What time do you expect Matthew home tonight?" Ben asked Emma.

"I'm not sure. I turned my phone off yesterday after I called Debbie's family to let them know something came up and I wasn't able to come to the pageant."

"Do you know how she did?" He asked.

Emma smiled. "First runner-up. I sent her a message late last night to congratulate her."

"Did Matthew try to call?" Ben asked.

She nodded sadly. "Three times. But I didn't listen to the

messages—I couldn't. We made plans to discuss a future together when he came back. I can't even imagine what to say to him now."

"You might as well rip off the band-aid, Emma. It isn't going to get any easier," Sadie said. "And I know what I'm talking about." Sadie had confronted Tad with great dignity just before Howard and company had escorted him out. "I just knew if I waited, I wouldn't have the nerve or maybe the opportunity to ever speak to him again. And I really needed for him to know how I felt about how he'd treated me and Sarah Jane."

Emma nodded, admiration in her eyes for Sadie's courage. "You're right. I really care about him, whether I should or not. I was ready to go all in and tell him that I love him. I need to know how badly off the mark I was about him."

"You'll never know the whole truth until you hear it directly from him," Ben said.

The doorbell rang then, interrupting their conversation.

"That must be Sabine. Ben, would you answer it while I go upstairs and get Sarah Jane?" Sarah Jane had been playing dolls and video games in the playroom with Lucy, Maeve's daughter.

Ben suddenly felt out of his depth, but of course, he couldn't refuse. "Sure. You can talk in the study."

As he walked toward the front door, his stomach felt unsettled, an unusual sensation for Ben, who rarely got rattled by much of anything, especially one lone female. The doorbell chimed again, making him jump. He took a breath, then opened it.

The raven-haired woman stood, her features calm and serene, and utterly breathtaking—until their eyes met. Then, her expression changed abruptly, as irritation and distaste shot through her features. It was a subtle change, and gone in an instant, replaced again by a cool, polite air.

"Sabine?"

"Mr. Laroux. So nice to see you again." She held out her hand to shake.

He took it, and held it, maybe just a bit too long.

She pulled back and narrowed her eyes at him. "Where's Sadie?"

"She's gone upstairs to get Sarah Jane. Y'all can talk in private down the hall in the study," he said as he led her inside.

For the first time ever, he hoped his butt looked good in his jeans. Then he nearly laughed out loud thinking what his sisters' reaction would be to that.

When they came through the family room, Ben introduced Sabine to Emma. "Sabine, have you met my sister, Emma?"

Emma offered her hand to Sabine. "My sister, Cammie, says such nice things about you."

"They're one of my favorite families here in Ministry. Grey, Cammie, and Samantha have become good friends."

"You've done a lot to help their family. They really appreciate it. Samantha has made such fantastic progress," Ben said.

Sabine stiffened. "I can't discuss my patient's progress. It's a slippery line when patients become friends."

You moron. She might as well have said to him. He was an attorney. He knew about discretion with clients. Everyone here knew Samantha was her patient and that she'd come a long way because of the time and hard work through therapy with Sabine. "Yes. I'm an attorney, so I'm aware."

What did this prickly woman have against him? Women loved him. Like, all women.

"Here we are." Sadie had arrived with Sarah Jane.

They greeted Sabine warmly.

"Great." He led them into the large study, that was actually more a library, with rows of bookshelves all around. There were two love seats covered with heavy damask fabric, facing each other with an antique coffee table between. On one end was a heavy mahogany desk where his mother oversaw the business of Evangeline House. This was where she met with clients and potential clients.

"Thanks, Ben," Sadie said.

"We can bring in hot tea, if you like," he said.

"That would be nice; thanks," Sabine said, but didn't sound especially grateful.

He nodded and shut the door, still baffled by her attitude toward him.

MATTHEW DROVE DIRECTLY to Emma's house since he'd been unable to reach her the past two days. He'd gotten a weird vibe that he was now unable to shake. He discounted the possibility that she might have found out his secret. But, what if—

He rang the doorbell. Emma, dressed in sweats, with no makeup and dark circles under her eyes opened the door and faced him, her face clearly told him something was very wrong.

"Emma, what's wrong?"

She opened the door to allow him inside, but didn't speak.

"Emma?" He asked again. This wasn't good.

"Have a seat." Her voice was dull, without its usual energy or spark.

"Please tell me what's going on," he encouraged.

"How about you tell me what you've been hiding. Or, do you even know where to start?"

"I-I'm not sure what you mean." He hated this, because she was right.

He had more than one confession to make, and while he was coming clean, he'd better do a complete job of it.

"Emma, I haven't been honest with you."

She laughed. It was a not-funny kind of laugh that made him physically uncomfortable.

"How about I help with a conversation-starter? You didn't tell me that we'd met ten years ago."

Here it was, and he'd been waiting for it. "I wanted to. I recognized you the day we met. I couldn't believe it."

"I'll bet you couldn't."

"I tried to call you after that night. I left a message for you to call me back."

She shook her head. "I never got a message. It doesn't matter. I didn't know who you were. I wouldn't have recognized you on the street if we'd passed."

"Emma, I wanted to tell you. I kept thinking a better time would present itself; then, we really hit it off and things moved quickly between us. I didn't know how to bring it up. I kept getting deeper and deeper and couldn't find a way to backtrack to that night. I was planning to tell you after this weekend so we could move forward."

She sat silently for a minute, then said, "Sadie found a journal that Tad's been keeping. He drugged me that night. I never really knew what had happened or how I ended up with you. I was so out of it that I don't even know what happened between us." Her eyebrows went up questioningly.

For a split-second, he missed her meaning. "Wait. You think I took advantage of you that night. How could you even suggest such a thing? You know me better than that." Matthew was horrified.

"I thought I did. Really, I wouldn't have considered anything other than that you'd rescued me from an awful situation, but then, Tad, of all people, revealed to me that you have a past none of us knew about. I wouldn't have believed him but my brother did a background check. Sexual predator? Of all the things I might have discovered, nothing could have sickened me more, Matthew." She put her hands over her face.

Comprehension and anger dawned on Matthew then. "Is that what you think of me? Emma, look at me. I never laid a hand on you that night, nor would I have taken advantage of any woman in such a position."

Her head came up. "But you were convicted as a sexual predator; what was I supposed to think? You haven't been honest with me."

He shook his head. This was a true deal-breaker, if there had ever been a deal. "The fact that you believe I could somehow have misused you proves you and I can't be together."

"What was I supposed to think? You've been lying since we met—again."

"I'm not going to dignify that by telling you what happened. Since your family is so good at digging up dirt, why don't you figure out what happened on my eighteenth birthday? By the way, I was taken off that list within a couple months."

He stood. "Emma, I'm more sorry than you know that I didn't tell you about how we met. What was done to you by someone you trusted makes me want to rip down things with my bare hands. I tried to protect you the only way I knew how back then without scaring you to death. I didn't tell you because I didn't want you to turn away from me without giving me a chance. It's obvious you haven't given anyone a chance since then and I didn't want to spook you. But the fact that you have so little faith in my character to think that I might have done something terrible to you, based on what Tad told you or some report that didn't tell the whole story, wounds my heart beyond repair."

He walked slowly toward the door, his feet nearly as heavy as his heart.

Emma was crying. It was more a keening, sobbing kind of sound and he likely wouldn't get it out of his head for a long time, if ever. "Goodbye, Emma."

"Matthew, wait." He could hear the pain in her raw throat.

But he didn't. He couldn't, because if he faltered on the way out now, he'd give in. If he did that, this pain would scar over and never really heal, only fester.

⤖⟞⟞⟞⟞⟞⟞

EMMA DIDN'T WANT to know, but she needed to find out what Matthew's ghosts entailed. So, she Googled. Now that she had his name he used back then, apparently his adopted name, she could pull up court records. They were there, and they made her want to cry—for him.

On his eighteenth birthday, he and his steady girlfriend, Betsy, had gone out to the lake and made love, not for the first time, but for the first time with him as an eighteen-year-old. Betsy was sixteen, about to turn seventeen. They were only a grade apart in school.

He was a senior and she, a junior. But Betsy's parents found out about their sexual relationship that night and her father used all his small town political pull to have Matthew tried and convicted as a sexual predator. Fortunately, after his conviction, the ruling was overturned and the case thrown out as cooler heads prevailed. The court decided that if it used its time and resources to prosecute every teen couple to the full extent of the law, it set a bad precedent for angry parents who couldn't control their hormonal children.

The damage to Matt Blanchard was that the whole messy incident and damage to his good name in the records couldn't be completely erased. What had been done was done.

Emma's head throbbed after reading the files. The un-shed tears now rolled down her cheeks. How could she have even considered such awful things about him? He was a good man. And he'd been treated poorly by her and by so many others.

"Hey, honey. You okay?"

"Oh, Mom. I've done Matthew such a disservice. He is the victim here." She turned the laptop toward her mother.

Mom read silently as she held Emma's hand. As she finished reading, she said, "This has been a confusing time for everyone, Emma. When you're wrong, you just have to say you've made a terrible mistake and own it. I know Matthew really cares for you. I have a feeling you two aren't done yet."

Emma shook her head. "I don't know. He sounded pretty sure when he left the other night." It had been two days since he'd walked out the door and, so far, she hadn't heard a word. Cammie said he'd been at work. Emma had gone through the motions at her studio and jumping every time the bell jingled on the front door.

Somehow, she had to make this right.

>>>><<<<

HIS FAMILY VISIT had gone so well and that momentum seemed to have carried him with such exhilaration that he'd hardly remembered the ride back to Ministry. After a couple days' work, he'd shut off the thinking and now was trying to only focus on getting through his days. He knew that he'd screwed things up with Emma by not telling her immediately who he was, but the very idea that she could believe something so disgusting about him made him want to hide under a rock and not come out.

He'd just arrived home from the set, wanting only to shower, eat, and try and sleep. Then the doorbell rang, he cursed.

Ready to growl at whoever invaded his privacy, he opened the heavy door. Emma's brother, Ben stood outside, his expression grim.

"Ben." He nodded by way of greeting.

"Hello, Matthew."

SUSAN SANDS

"What can I do for you?" Matthew asked.

"I wanted to apologize for my part in this."

"For getting partial information to confirm Tad's suspicions about me so that Emma believed me capable of doing something unspeakable?"

"Yeah. I guess that's part of it. I ran a background check on you when we were gathering all the info about Tad. The only reason I did it was because I knew Emma couldn't take it if you weren't who or what you said. She's been let down too much in her personal life because of Tad, and I didn't want anything else to keep her from being happy. The background inquiry was more to confirm that you were a good and honest person rather than disprove it. Unfortunately, because of Tad's bad intentions to scare Emma, it worked against us all."

"I appreciate your trying to protect your sister. I love my sister and probably would have done the same thing. And I would have wanted to protect Emma as well. But you can't go throwing words like 'sexual predator' around in this day and age, man. It can mean anything. I had sex with my girlfriend on my eighteenth birthday. We'd been in a relationship, as young and immature as it was, for a year. It wasn't until that particular day that anyone had a problem with it. I fought tooth and nail to regain my good name so that I could get a job. That kind of thing follows a person around."

"I'm an attorney, man. I, of all people know that. The

document only had a short paragraph, mostly in pure legal jargon regarding the indictment, conviction, and the subsequent overturn. I hadn't read it yet when Emma got hold of it. All she saw was that you'd been convicted. She was beside herself with grief and believed that yet again, she'd trusted her instincts and was wrong."

Matthew ran a hand through his hair. "I still can't believe she thought I would have hurt her in any way. It's not who I am."

"She knows that and she knew that before, but after Tad cornered her and intimidated her alone at her studio and then having what he said reinforced in black and white, it was pretty damning in her eyes."

"Wait, what do you mean, he intimidated her?"

Ben's eye grew dark. "Emma said he came to her studio as she was leaving and physically cornered her and got personal with her."

"What did he do?" Matthew saw red.

"Not much before she racked him with her knee. He'll be lucky if he recovers full use of his testicles."

"Good. I hope she put that bastard down. I wish I knew where he was so I could have a shot at him."

"Best that you don't. Believe me, we put him in his place. He won't be able to hurt Emma or anyone else in this town again unless he wants to spend many years in prison. We made sure of it."

"That's a relief. Thanks."

"So, what about you and Emma. Are you going to forgive her and put you both out of your misery? You know she's crazy about you, don't you?"

Matthew didn't know what to say.

"She didn't want to believe what she thought was right in front of her. It was a perfect storm of misinformation and emotional manipulation. Not many of us could have stood up against that. Plus, you lied to her the entire time you've been in town. You really can't blame her." Ben said.

Ben was right. This was, in large part, his fault. "Thanks for coming over, man. Sounds like Emma and I need to talk."

"The sooner the better." Ben slapped Matthew on the shoulder and turned to go, leaving Matthew with that crazy hope again.

Chapter Sixteen

∞

T HE WEEKEND HAD come around again, and she hadn't
any commitments on her calendar. The whole idea that
things had gone so wrong with Matthew was just beyond
sad. The fact that Tad had been the ultimate player in
bringing it all about made her angry beyond belief. He'd had
the last laugh after all. Wherever he'd gone, he could bask in
the satisfaction that he'd screwed up things for her once and
for all.

Her family had tried to get her out of the house, but in
the end they'd given up. Her plan was to turn her television
on, not shower, order takeout and binge-watch old, sad
movies until she couldn't cry anymore. There was no time
like the present to get started. She'd stocked up on Big Al's
favorite squeaky toys so at least she had company during her
weekend-long cry-fest. Hopefully, he'd not need therapy
after the weekend. So far, he was happily chewing and
squeaking away, occasionally casting her a sympathetic
glance.

"Thanks, buddy."

It wasn't often she allowed herself to give into such a pity party, but Emma was predicting one for the record books. She had stocked her freezer with an obscene amount of Ben and Jerry's Chunky Monkey and bought three new boxes of Kleenex with the lotion built right in, so her nose wouldn't show obvious signs of wear and tear.

She'd pulled down all her window shades in the front of the house; well, just in case.

As Emma settled in with her first pint of Ben and Jerry's, the infernal doorbell rang. The words that streamed from her lips were neither kid-friendly, nor adult-friendly, and she'd likely only used a couple of them one or twice in her life. She paused Scarlet O'Hara on the screen just as she was hanging on to Ashley's lapels, begging him to leave her milksop of a sister. Emma decided to be very still and quiet, and since there weren't any other lights on in the house, maybe the intruder to her peace would go away. Of course; she'd meant to close the garage door, but hadn't gotten around to it. *Dammit!*

Big Al, who saved her life from possible intruders on regular basis, sounded the alarm in his deep, scary bark—just in case.

The bell rang again, followed by an insistent knock— more like a banging.

Then, she heard a muffled, "Emma, I know you're in there. I spoke with your mother."

Al whined excitedly, obviously satisfied she wasn't about to be home invaded and personally assaulted. So much for his being an excellent judge of character.

It was Matthew. She wanted to see him less than anyone right now. She was purging him. It was what she'd done with the others when things hadn't worked out.

He rang and banged on the door again. "Emma, open up. I'm not going away."

Apparently he wasn't going away. She bit her lip. Who was she kidding? Ben and Jerry's wasn't going to solve the Matthew Pope, or whatever he called himself, problem.

She disentangled from her blanket cocoon and regretfully set down the container of perfection on the coffee table. "Fine. I'm coming."

She unbolted the door and opened it. The sunlight hit her eyes full force and she blinked like a possum whose hidey-hole had been unexpectedly exposed. She didn't say anything as her eyes adjusted to him. She'd forgotten how heartbreakingly gorgeous he was. She drank in his wavy dark hair and beautiful, sculpted jaw. The scent of him reached her nostrils, and it was all she could do not to inhale deeply, and obviously.

"Hey, there." He grinned, obviously happy to see her.

Then, she remembered how she must look. *Ack.* She hadn't shaved her legs since Thursday morning. Had she even brushed her teeth today?

"I wasn't expecting anyone. In fact, I was expecting *no*

one at all."

"Can I come in anyway?" he asked, then not waiting for her permission, stepped inside, giving Big Al a moment of his attention.

Al, content with the greeting, left them to their issues and went back to his job of liberating the squeak function from the hairy/feathery faux fowl next to the sofa.

She frowned. "I don't think so. I'm having a party."

He looked beyond her at her paused television screen and the pint of ice cream on the coffee table. "Party for one?"

"Yes. My favorite kind."

"I like *Gone With the Wind* and I love ice cream. If I promise not to take all the covers, would you mind a little company?"

"Why?" she asked.

Emma thought they were done. Finished. Why was he here? "Why are you here?"

"Because I spoke with Ben. Because I was wrong. And because you are the best thing that's ever happened to me and, if you'll allow me to, I'll spend the rest of our lives proving it to you every day."

She blinked again, but this time it wasn't from the sunlight; it was from pure shock and dawning comprehension. "You want to be with me? After everything that's happened?"

"Only if you'll try to forgive me for lying to you all this time. I should have come clean the day we met on the set." He ran a hand over her tangled hair.

"Hang on one sec." She held a hand up, turned, and ran toward her bedroom.

A few minutes later, she returned. She'd run a brush through her hair, brushed her teeth and put on deodorant. But Emma would never reveal that to Matthew. "Now, where were we?"

"I was groveling and telling you how much I love you and want to marry you." He'd dropped to one knee and produced a ring box.

He was smiling, his expression joyful and filled with such hope that her knees nearly buckled right with his.

"Oh-ooooh." She opened her mouth and closed it again, unable to communicate her thoughts. The ring was the most gorgeous thing she'd ever seen. "I c-cant. Not until I apologize to you and know that you forgive me. I'm not sure I forgive myself. How could I have thought that you would do anything to hurt me—or anyone for that matter? You're good and kind, Matthew, and I misjudged you in the worst way." A tear rolled down her cheek for the wrong she'd dealt him.

He took her left hand and slid the ring on her ring finger. "You had no other way to protect yourself. Look, I understand why you might have questioned my character; you were set up and manipulated to do that. But we know each other, and we both understand how strong Tad's motivation was to keep us apart. Everything else just played right in."

"Don't ever speak of him to me again. He is not relevant to us anymore. I love you, Matthew Pope, or Matt, or whatever your name is. I don't care whether you're from Alabama or New York City. I love *you*—the man you were ten years ago who protected me, and the man you are standing here now. Yes, I will marry you."

"You can call me Matt." He kissed her then, the kind of kiss that made her very glad she'd brushed her teeth. "And being here, in the South isn't a punishment. It's where I grew up and where I belong. My family is here—you are here. I'm not sure what my future with the network looks like, but for now, everything I care about is right here in Alabama."

She sighed. "I like the sound of all that, Matt."

"So, I have one question," he said.

"What?"

"You gonna just let that Ben and Jerry's go to waste?"

"Ice cream? Really? There's a pretty high fat and sugar content in that container, you know."

"I don't care. In fact, Next time we're in the diner, I'm ordering a donut."

She grinned. "I would never deprive you of your healthy and tasteless breakfast just so you could prove something."

"Are you kidding? I love doughnuts. I'm just not feeling quite so rigid about things anymore."

She snuggled close. "You feel pretty rigid to me."

He growled and scooped her up in his arms.

"But our ice cream will melt."

"Stick it in the freezer for dessert."

Epilogue

"**H**OW'S SARAH JANE?" Ben asked Sadie.

"It's been a confusing few months, but with Sabine's help, I think she's been able to talk through a lot of her feelings about her father. She was mostly worried about disappointing him or angering him all the time. She's a much more carefree child these days." Sadie said.

"What about visitation?" he asked.

"So far, Tad hasn't answered Sabine's e-mails or voice messages about seeing Sarah Jane for Christmas. Sarah Jane hasn't shown any real interest in seeing him, or we would have hunted him down and tried harder. I think eventually maybe they'll see one another. It might just be too soon. He had been very harsh with her leading up to his leaving town, so I think she was very intimidated by him."

"Please let me know if I can do anything more to help," Ben said.

"Thanks so much. I can't tell you how much I appreciate everything you did to help me get free of him." Sadie replied.

Ben wondered at his friendship with Sadie. She was completely uninterested in him and it was such a relief. They could chat like brother and sister without any friction.

But when Sabine O'Connor entered the room, it was as if the ground shook beneath his feet. She seemed as unaffected by him as Sadie. Actually, she was adversely affected it seemed—as if his mere presence made her want to empty her stomach contents. It was confounding.

"Hey brother." He turned to see the bride, looking especially lovely with her groom at her side.

"Well, aren't you two a sight?" He grinned at them, so relieved they'd decided to tie the knot almost immediately. Of course, Emma discovering that she was carrying a Mini-Matthew likely helped with the timing of things.

"Hey, y'all." Cammie, Grey, and Samantha approached and appeared just as happy, and just as glowing with the news of their own upcoming bundle of joy. Nothing like all the good stuff happening at once.

One at a time, the others in the family gathered around—Mom and Howard, Maeve, Lucy, and Junior, then Jo Jo and Beau and their two little ones. Rosie and her girls were there in the mix as well. His family meant everything to him.

"Has everyone met my mother, Lillian, and my sister, Lisa, and her children?" Matthew brought his family into the circle as well. They were pretty much complete now.

"Oh, hi, Sabine, so glad you could make it," Emma said from behind him.

And the ground shook.

The End

Book Club Reader Guide

1. At the beginning of the story, Emma seemed irritable around Tad, but unaware of his role in causing her failed relationships in the last ten years. Do you think deep-down she knew his part in it, or do you think she was truly unaware? Why?

2. For the most part Emma was a strong, independent, and seemingly happy person. Do you believe one can truly be happy with such unresolved issues?

3. Life often throws us things we can't control. Do you make the best of these situations and live every day to the fullest, or find the root of issues to work toward real happiness? What do the characters in the book do?

4. Do you correlate Matthew's insistence on strictly controlling his diet and routine in his inability to control his daily environment as a child? Why or why not?

5. Do you think Matthew's panic attacks were a result of his PTSD or being in Alabama against his will, or both? Why?

6. Emma's dog, Big Al, is her steadfast and loyal companion. Have you ever depended on, or do you depend heavily on an animal for much-need support?

7. Emma's overly large family constantly nudges her to tell them her secrets regarding the past. They won't accept that she prefers to keep things private, to the point of official background checks and staging a full-blown behind-her-back intervention. Do you think her family oversteps their boundaries? Or are they just trying to help?

8. Small towns. Love 'em or hate 'em? Why?

9. Did you read *Again, Alabama* and get to know the Laroux family before you read this story? If you did, did knowing the family history help you appreciate *Love, Alabama*? If not, do you think this book stood alone without already knowing the family history?

10. Which secondary characters would you like to know more about? Why?

More by Susan Sands

Again, Alabama

Cammie Laroux is back in Alabama—again.

Dragged back to her small town to help her mother recover from surgery while rescuing the family event planning business should be a cinch. Even for a disgraced television chef, right? Wrong.

Among the many secrets Cammie's family's been hiding is the fact that their historic home is falling down. Oh, and the man hired to restore the house, Grey Harrison, is the same high school and college love of her life who thrashed her heart and dreams ten years ago. Yeah, that guy.

Grey, a widower with a young daughter, has never stopped loving Cammie, and when they are face to face once again, the chemistry is off the charts. Cammie may be in full-blown denial, but letting go is no longer in Grey's vocabulary, even when winning Cammie's forgiveness and renovating their love may seem like an impossible build even for a master architect and carpenter.

As Cammie finds herself forgetting all the reasons she can't trust Grey or love again, he finds himself remembering all the reasons he wants her to stay with him in Alabama… forever.

Available at your favorite retail store and online everywhere.

About the Author

Susan Sands grew up in a real life Southern Footloose town, complete with her senior class hosting the first ever prom in the history of their tiny public school. Is it any wonder she writes Southern small town stories full of porch swings, fun and romance?

Susan lives in suburban Atlanta surrounded by her husband, three young adult kiddos and lots of material for her next book.

Visit her website at SusanSands.com

Thank you for reading

Love, Alabama

If you enjoyed this book, you can find more from all our great authors at TulePublishing.com, or from your favorite online retailer.

TULE
PUBLISHING

CPSIA information can be obtained
at www.ICGtesting.com
Printed in the USA
LVOW12s1723180418
573963LV00003B/680/P